P9-DDB-407

the shade of the moon

OTHER BOOKS IN THIS SERIES

life as we knew it
the dead & the gone
this world we live in

SUSAN BETH PFEFFER

the shade
of the moon

HARCOURT
Houghton Mifflin Harcourt
Boston · New York

Copyright © 2013 by Susan Beth Pfeffer
All rights reserved. For information about permission to
reproduce selections from this book, write to Permissions,
Houghton Mifflin Harcourt Publishing Company,
215 Park Avenue South, New York, New York 10003.
Harcourt is an imprint of Houghton Mifflin Harcourt
Publishing Company.
www.hmhbooks.com
Text set in Spectrum MT STD

Library of Congress Cataloging-in-Publication Data
Pfeffer, Susan Beth, 1948-
The shade of the moon / Susan Beth Pfeffer.
pages cm
Sequel to: Life as we knew it.
Summary: "Jon Evans is one of the lucky ones—
until he realizes that escaping his safe haven may be the only way to truly survive."
—Provided by publisher.
ISBN 978-0-547-81337-0
[1. Natural disasters—Fiction. 2. Interpersonal relations—Fiction. 3. Social classes—Fiction. 4. Family life—
Tennessee—Fiction. 5. Tennessee—Fiction. 6. Science fiction.] I. Title.
PZ7.P44855Sh 2013
[Fic]—dc23
2012046800

Manufactured in the United States of America
DOC 10 9 8 7 6 5 4 3 2 1
4500425141

For Miranda and Alex

Their families and their friends

Part One

Chapter 1

"No. Jon. No."

Jon Evans sat upright in his bed. It was Gabe, he told himself. Gabe must have had a bad dream. He listened for Carrie, Gabe's nanny, to calm the little boy. He waited to hear Lisa run down the hallway to soothe her son.

But Carrie was quiet. Lisa was quiet. The house was quiet.

It wasn't Gabe he'd heard. It was Julie.

How long had he known her? A month, six weeks. But he'd been haunted by her for two and a half years.

Jon knew better than to believe in ghosts. Billions of people had died in the past few years. There'd be no room for the living if all the dead were ghosts. And if there were ghosts, there were others Jon would prefer to be haunted by. His father, who died of exhaustion and hunger on the way to Sexton, Tennessee. Jon would welcome his ghost.

But it was Julie's voice he heard in his sleep. Julie who cried out to him in panic, in anger, her accusations too real, her death too unforgivable.

If the moon's orbit hadn't been pushed closer to the earth, Jon would never have met Julie. He'd be a senior in high school, living with Mom back in Pennsylvania. His parents had been divorced long before, but Dad and Lisa and Gabe would be in Springfield, close enough for the occasional visit.

But the moon's orbit had changed, and the world as everyone had known it had changed in horrific ways. Billions had died from tsunamis, famine, and epidemics.

Dad was one of those billions. His death came a hundred miles before Jon and his family had reached Sexton. They were all half-starved by then, and had neither the strength nor the tools to bury him.

Julie hadn't died like that. Julie died because of what Jon had done. Of the billions of dead, only Julie was his own. Only she would haunt him.

Jon got out of bed and walked to the window. It had rained all day, and the wind was from the south. The volcanic ash, which ordinarily covered the sky, had thinned as it sometimes did when rain and wind cooperated. Jon could see the pale outline of the moon, ominous and engorged, dominating the night.

Tomorrow, Jon hoped, the air would be clear enough to see the sun. And one day, the sun might appear on its own, not dependent on rain and the direction of the wind. He would wake up, the world would wake up, and the sun would be warm and glowing. Nothing would be so bad anymore.

But the billions would still be dead. Dad would still be dead. And Julie would still haunt his dreams.

Thursday, April 30

Jon didn't know what time it was when he woke up, but it didn't matter. It was still nighttime, hours to go before he ordinarily awoke.

Sometimes when he woke up in the middle of the night,

he'd go downstairs, knock on Val's door, and tell her to get up and make him something to eat. He might not even be hungry. It was more the comforting sensation of knowing there was food; there was always enough food. Even after two years of living in Sexton, Jon still needed the reassurance. And Val, a grub just like Carrie, would know better than to complain. Without her job as a domestic, there'd be no food for her.

But this time, Jon went downstairs to the kitchen by himself. Maybe a glass of goat's milk would be enough, he thought. He still hadn't developed a taste for it, but it was better than nothing.

To his surprise, he saw Lisa sitting at the kitchen table. She looked up and smiled. "Couldn't sleep either?" she whispered.

Jon nodded. "I thought I'd get a glass of milk," he said. "Is there enough?"

"Quiet," Lisa said. "Val's sleeping." She got up, found him a glass, and poured him some milk. "There's enough for our breakfast," she said. "Val can pick some up at the market tomorrow."

Jon sat down and drank the milk. "You okay?" he asked.

Lisa nodded. "I'm glad we have this chance to talk," she said so softly Jon almost couldn't hear her. "It's the evaluation."

"Do you have a date yet?" Jon asked. Everyone in Sexton got evaluated regularly. Those who weren't pulling their own weight were made to leave the enclave. The rest were allowed to stay for another three years.

"Not yet," she replied. "Jon, I'm not supposed to know this, so keep this to yourself, but Gregory Hughes is in charge of my evaluation."

"Tyler's father?" Jon asked, and Lisa nodded. "But that's good, right?" he said. "Tyler's my friend. That's got to help."

"I think so, too," Lisa said. "It's like what your father used to say. It never hurts to be friends with the boss. Not that Tyler's your boss. Of course he isn't. It's just, well, don't pick any fights with him. Just go along with whatever he says, at least until the evaluation is over. Promise me, Jon."

"No problem," he said. "I don't fight with him anyway. I promise."

"Thank you." Lisa sighed. "I know I must sound crazy, but I don't know what I'll do if I fail the evaluation."

"You won't fail," Jon said. "Go to bed, Lisa. You need your sleep."

"So do you," she said. "Leave it for Val to clean up. She's the only one who gets enough sleep around here."

Friday, May 1

Sexton University, where Jon's high school was located, had been built to withstand tornadoes. No one had worried about earthquakes, but it turned out the buildings could withstand them also. A good thing too, since in the two years Jon had been in Sexton, there were no tornadoes but a dozen or more quakes.

At the first rumble they all knew what to do. The students and teachers in the various grades left their classrooms and sat on the hallway floor. They were supposed to cover their heads with their arms, but no one bothered. Even the teachers looked relaxed.

But the new girl, Sarah, was clearly upset. This was her first day at school, and from the looks of it, this was her first earthquake. At least her first one in Sexton. Jon didn't know what the earthquake situation was where she used to live.

He inched over to her. "It's okay," he said. "We get them all the time. It'll be over in a minute."

"All the time?" she asked.

"Well, not all the time," he said. "My little brother, Gabe, doesn't like them either."

"How old is he?" Sarah asked.

"Three," Jon said.

"Great," she said. "I have the maturity of a three-year-old."

Jon laughed. "He's a very mature three-year-old," he said.

"Rise and shine," Mr. Chandler, their chemistry teacher, said. "Earthquake over."

"Class period is over, too," Tyler pointed out.

"All right," Mr. Chandler said. "Go to lunch. I'll see you all tomorrow."

Ordinarily Jon ate lunch with Tyler, Zachary, Ryan, and Luke. He'd had lunch with them ever since he'd made the soccer team, two years ago. But Sarah looked like she could use the company, so Jon walked to the cafeteria with her.

"Hey, Jon," Luke called, but Jon shook him off and sat across from Sarah.

"I know your brother's name," she said. "But not yours."

"Jon Evans," he replied. "And you're . . ."

"Sarah Goldman," she said. "That was my first earthquake. And my last, I hope."

"Don't count on it," Jon said. "We're near the New Madrid fault line. The geologists think the tremors are a good thing, letting pressure off. You'll get used to them."

"I don't want to," Sarah said. She took a bite of her lunch, then put her fork down. "I don't want to get used to this lunch either. The vegetables are fresh. Why are they cooked so badly?"

"The woman in charge of the cafeteria was a tax lawyer," Jon said. "Her brother's on the town board. That's how she got the job."

"They should make her brother eat this crap," Sarah said. "Make the punishment fit the crime."

"We hang people here," Jon said. "We don't poison them."

Sarah laughed. "I must sound horrible," she said. "I'm sorry. This is all so new to me. Let me start over. Hi, Jon. Are you from Sexton?"

"From Pennsylvania originally," he said. "Where are you from?"

"Connecticut originally," she said. "Then we were relocated to North Carolina. Is your family in agriculture? Is that why you were settled here?"

"No," Jon said. "We're slips." She was going to find out anyway, he figured. She might as well hear it from him.

"What's a slip?" she asked.

"We slipped in," Jon said. "We had passes for an enclave, so they had to let us in. We ended up here because it was the only enclave we knew about."

"I don't think we had any slips in our enclave," Sarah said. "The whole town was a medical complex, much smaller than Sexton. My father's a cardiologist. He was transferred to the White Birch clinic. That's why we moved here."

"My mother lives in White Birch," Jon said. "With Miranda and Alex. My sister and her husband. Mom teaches high school there. I have an older brother too, but he doesn't live around here." It startled him to share so much about his family. In a matter of minutes, Sarah had learned more about him than any of his friends had in over two years.

"Do you live with your father?" Sarah asked.

Jon shook his head. "Dad's dead," he replied. "Lisa, my stepmother, and Gabe and I used the passes."

"My mother's dead," Sarah said. "She died a couple of months ago. Then Daddy got transferred. It's been hard on him. The clinic is terribly understaffed. There was a nurse there, but now it's just Daddy and me. I do my afterschools there."

"I play soccer for my afterschools," Jon said.

"That's your afterschool?" she asked. "Playing soccer?"

For a moment Jon was irritated. All the students did afterschools — four hours of work each afternoon — and he knew soccer seemed more like play than work to the kids who held what they thought of as real jobs. It didn't help that the Sexton team played all its games on the road, so no one at home ever saw them.

But work was work, and Jon didn't need to hear from some new kid who thought she knew it all that what he did wasn't necessary. All the clavers knew someday the White Birch grubs would try something, and when they did, the clavers would be outnumbered. That's why the enclave was so heavily guarded. That's why on Saturday afternoons all the students spent their afterschools in judo and rifle practice.

The idea was to hold off that someday for as long as possible. Civilization depended on it. The grubs outnumbered the clavers throughout America, but they had no idea how to grow crops in a cold and sunless world. They had no idea how to treat illnesses with limited amounts of medicine. They had no idea how to run a government, a school system, a city, an army.

Jon knew how lucky he was to be a slip, and how lucky it was that Lisa had found a job in administration right away. Alex had sacrificed his three passes so that Lisa and Gabe and Jon could live in a safer environment, one with food and shelter and electricity. The kind of life Alex had taken for granted when he was seventeen.

Jon had had two years of intensive study of botany, chemistry, and physics. There was no point studying history when history no longer mattered. Instead he was taught civics, government, leadership. He played soccer, not for the love of the game but because he was an athlete and he represented the strength and the power of the enclave system.

"We train five days a week," Jon said. "On Sundays we travel all around the state, for hours sometimes, to play. Coach says if we lose, it reflects badly on Sexton, on all the enclaves. It would make us seem weak, inferior. Winning shows the grubs who's boss."

"Grubs?" Sarah said.

"Yeah, grubs," Jon said. "You must have had grubs in North Carolina."

"You mean laborers," she said.

"Is that what you called them?" he asked. "They're grubs here. White Birch, all the towns around here are grubtowns."

Sarah frowned. "That sounds so ugly."

"It's just a word," Jon replied. "You don't mind being called a claver. Why should they mind being called grubs?"

"I guess you're right," she said. "I mean, I do understand about the difference between us and them. Why we get to live in enclaves, in nicer houses, get better food, better everything."

"It's always been like that," Jon said. "The rich always live better. Here, at least, people are rich because they have special skills. The botanists are rich, not some millionaire's kid. And the grubs know how lucky they are to have jobs. Our domestics are grateful to be working in Sexton. I bet yours feel exactly the same."

"I haven't asked them," Sarah said. "Maybe I will."

"No," Jon said. "Don't. It's better not to bring that stuff up."

"If you don't ask, then how can you know how they feel?" Sarah said. "Maybe you think they feel lucky because you don't want to admit just how unlucky they are."

"I'm not saying I know all the answers," Jon replied, "but I trust the people in charge do. Have you seen the greenhouses? There are miles of them now and more going up every month. They weren't here three years ago, and now they're growing food for people all over the state. Including the kids at White Birch High."

"Yes," Sarah said. "But theirs is probably better cooked."

"Couldn't be worse," Jon said. "They're not saddled with a tax-lawyer chef."

Sarah laughed. Jon liked the sound of it, just as he liked how she looked: sandy hair, green eyes. "Lunch tomorrow?" he asked.

"I can't," she said. "I won't be in school tomorrow. I'm going into White Birch with Daddy, to help him set up the clinic. We're opening on Sunday."

"Monday, then?" Jon persisted.

"Will the food be this bad?" she asked.

Jon nodded. "Maybe worse."

"How can I resist?" she said. "Lunch on Monday, with you."

Sunday, May 3

Jon got home to find Lisa putting Gabe to bed. He didn't disturb her. Sunday was the only day Lisa had with Gabe. Like everyone else in the area, she worked Mondays through Saturdays. Everyone but him. Jon worked on Sundays, also.

Usually after a match Jon was in a good mood. Winning always felt good, and the bus ride back to Sexton was spent in celebration.

But not today. Of course Sexton had won. It was never a contest. The grubtown team was filled with guys who worked six days a week in factories or greenhouses. They had no time for practice. On Sundays maybe, in preparation for the match against Sexton, they played a little and drank a lot.

The Sexton team spent two hours daily on workouts and two more on soccer drills. They went to high school or college, and if they got drunk, they did it after the match was over.

The first half of the match had gone as always. Sexton led 3–1, keeping things close enough that the other squad and the grubs who came to see the match felt like they had a real chance. The clavers wouldn't last. They were sissies and wimps. Grubs did real work. They just needed time and a little luck and the victory would be theirs.

During halftime the Sexton team went back to their bus, drank juice, and sucked oxygen while listening to Coach yell at them. Everything was fine. Everything was exactly as it should be, exactly as it always was.

But this time instead of winning 10–1, they won 8–2. And that was enough to put Coach in a rage.

He started the bus ride by screaming at Mike Daley, the college student who was the team's top goalie. He should never have allowed that second goal.

It didn't matter to Coach that the score was 7–1, with only ten minutes to play. Coach would have liked shutouts every game, except he'd been instructed to let the other team score at least once. Let them have their moment.

So Coach let the other team score, but one point was enough. Two was a show of weakness, and Daley had no business letting it happen.

Then it was Jon's turn.

"You could have scored two more points!" Coach shouted. "Don't give away chances like that, Evans!"

Actually, Jon had had three chances but had chosen to pass rather than go for the score. He'd never done that before. He was the team's striker, and it had always seemed right to him that Sexton beat their opponents by as big a margin as possible.

But not today. Today it seemed like rubbing their noses in it, and he couldn't see the point.

"You're a friggin' slip!" Coach screamed. "A pansy-ass grub lover. Were they your brothers, Evans? Or were they your boyfriends?"

A few of Jon's teammates snickered. Jon would have snickered too if he weren't the one being reamed.

"Sorry, Coach," he muttered.

"Sorry isn't good enough," Coach said. "You're off the team, Evans, if you keep playing like this. Out of Sexton, if I have my way."

"I'm sorry, Coach," he said again, this time in a stronger voice. "It won't happen again. I'll show those grubs who's boss."

Coach grinned. "That's the spirit, Evans," he said. "Sure, you're a slip, but that doesn't mean you aren't a claver. And a damn good one at that."

But sitting in the living room hours later, Jon still had a bad taste in his mouth. And it wasn't from the bottle of potka they'd shared on the bus ride home.

Jon looked up as Lisa walked into the room. "Are you hungry?" she asked. "There's some leftover chicken in the fridge."

"Maybe later," Jon said. "We ate on the bus."

"All right," Lisa said. "If you don't want it, Val and Carrie can have it for lunch tomorrow. How many goals did you score?"

"Four," Jon replied. "We won eight to two."

"That close?" Lisa said. "I bet Coach was angry."

Jon laughed.

"Laura called," Lisa said.

"Didn't she know I was out?" Jon asked. It was hard for Mom to make a phone call. None of the apartments had phone service, and no one was allowed to use the phones where they worked. There were a handful of pay phones in White Birch, and it took hours on Sunday to get to the front of the line.

"She tried last night," Laura said, "but there were five people ahead of her when the curfew siren went off. She said Matt's going to be there next Sunday."

Matt lived in Coolidge, a couple of hundred miles away, working as a bike courier. He traveled all around the area, transporting letters and small packages for clavers. Sexton wasn't on his route, but when he could, he swapped with another courier. Jon had seen him last in November, but he knew Matt had spent a weeknight with Mom, Miranda, and Alex in February.

There had been a time when Jon felt closer to Matt than to anyone else in the world. When the bad times had come, he and Matt had spent endless hours chopping down trees so there'd be firewood. The work they'd done had kept the family alive, and it had provided Jon with the opportunity to get to know his big brother. They worked and they talked, and Jon had felt grownup and respected.

But then Matt married Syl, and everything changed. And now Matt lived hundreds of miles away, and Jon was lucky to see him twice a year.

"You must be due a Sunday off," Lisa said. "I can't remember the last time you had one."

Jon counted back. Ten Sundays, he thought. There were twelve men on the squad, and only eight went to each game, so no one was supposed to travel to more than eight games in a row. But Jon was the team's best scorer, and Coach tended to forget the eight-game rule. Besides, slips were supposed to do a little more than anyone else.

"I really want to see Matt," Jon said.

"Of course," Lisa said. "And it's wonderful for Laura to have all her children with her. I'm sure you can get next Sunday off."

Jon wasn't nearly as sure, not the way Coach had been screaming at him. But he'd have to try. It could be another six months before Matt was in White Birch on a Sunday, and it was never safe to predict six months ahead.

Monday, May 4

Most of the grubs who commuted to work in Sexton were taken by bus to the factories or the greenhouses and then picked up at the end of the workday for the ride back to White Birch. The only grubs permitted to walk in Sexton were the domestics, who did the shopping while the clavers were at work.

Clavers never walked. Even though most of the volcanic activity, caused by the change in the moon's gravitational pull, had stopped nearly two years ago, the air quality was still bad, and it wasn't a good idea to spend too much time outdoors. Buses ran regularly for clavers, with stops every few blocks.

Jon would have preferred to bike to school. It would take less time, and he'd enjoy the exercise and the privacy. But even though it wasn't forbidden to bike, it wasn't encouraged either. All the buildings in Sexton—the homes, the schools, the offices—had air purification systems, but there was no way to purify the outdoor air. So, like everyone else, Jon rode the bus.

Sarah got on the bus right as he did. Ryan and Luke were already on, but he sat next to her instead.

"How was the soccer match?" she asked him. "Did you save civilization?"

"I did my part," Jon said. "You can sleep safely tonight."

Sarah tilted her head toward the window. "With all the guards here, I don't have to worry. Unless they get ideas of their own."

"You must have had guards in your other enclave," Jon said.

"Yes," Sarah said. "But not as many. At least not as many on the streets. I don't know. Everything seems darker here."

"Everything is darker here," Jon said. "The farther west you go, the darker the sky."

"That's not what I mean and you know it," she said.

Jon glanced back at Ryan and Luke. He caught Luke's eye. Luke pointed to the empty seat by his side. Jon shook his head.

"Is it really that different?" he asked.

"I don't know," Sarah said. "I didn't want to leave. I guess I'm just homesick."

By the time his family had left Pennsylvania, all Jon had wanted was to get away. But he supposed if you had food and water and electricity, you'd want to stay put.

He looked up and saw Ryan standing by him. "Come on, Evans," he said. "We miss you."

"It's okay," Sarah said. "Go. I'll see you at lunch?"

Jon nodded and followed Ryan back to the empty seat. "What's this about?" he asked.

"Tyler will tell you," Ryan said.

Jon looked at Luke, but he didn't say anything. They sat in silence until the bus stopped at school. Tyler and Zachary were already there.

"He was sitting with her on the bus," Ryan said to them. "They were going to have lunch again."

"What of it?" Jon asked. "Sarah's new here. She hasn't made any friends yet."

"She isn't going to make any friends," Tyler declared. "Keep away from her, Evans."

"Why?" Jon asked.

Zachary looked like he was about to punch Jon. Tyler put his arm on Zachary's shoulder.

"Look, Evans, you're a slip," Tyler said. "An outsider. But Luke and I are cousins. Zach and Ryan have been my friends since kindergarten. The four of us were in Cub Scouts together, Pop Warner, all of it. You're a good soccer player, and you're okay. We like you. But you're not one of us. You don't belong."

"Fine," Jon said. "I don't belong."

"It's my grandfather!" Zachary yelled. "You stupid slip."

"What the hell are you talking about?" Jon said.

"Zach's grandfather was a doctor," Luke said.

"A great man," Zachary said. "A great doctor. He was a doctor in Sexton for over fifty years."

"It was crazy when the government turned Sexton into an enclave," Luke said. "People trying to keep their homes, their families. We're the lucky ones. Our parents all were selected, so we got to stay."

"They said Granddad would have to leave," Zachary said. "Fifty years didn't count for anything."

"But my father stepped in," Tyler said. "Dad owned half of Sexton. He had powerful friends. So they had to listen. They worked out a compromise. Zach's granddad got appointed as the White Birch Clinic doctor, and they let him stay in Sexton."

"That's the job Sarah's father has," Jon said.

Luke nodded. "There were some problems at the clinic," he said.

Zachary took a swipe at Luke, but Tyler got between them.

"There weren't any problems!" Zachary screamed. "It was lies. All lies."

"Grubs lie," Ryan said. "The women lie worst of all. They'll say anything to hurt a claver."

"Only good thing was they shut those bitches up," Zachary said. "Sent them to the mines. Hope they're dead."

"I bet they are," Ryan said. "No one lasts long in the mines."

"I don't get it," Jon said. "What does any of this have to do with Sarah?"

"Sarah's father is a doctor," Tyler said. "He must have done something real bad, because he got kicked out of his enclave. Only he has powerful friends, even more powerful than Dad. So they fired Zach's grandfather and gave his job to Sarah's father."

"Not just the job," Zachary said. "They gave Granddad's home, the furniture, the grubs—all of it—to Sarah's father. Everything. They wouldn't even let Granddad stay here with us. They won't let him live in my aunt's enclave either. He had to move to the grubtown near her. My grandfather, living with those pigs."

"Sarah and her father shouldn't be allowed in Sexton," Ryan said. "They were thrown out of one enclave; they shouldn't be allowed in another."

"But it's not like they knew your granddad," Jon said to Zachary. "They're not responsible for what happened."

"That's what I mean about you not understanding," Tyler said. "It's the slip in you, Evans. Zach's grandfather is a great man. People around here know that. No one believes what those grub bitches said. He could have kept his job, his house, except they needed a place to put Sarah's father."

"But it's still not Sarah's fault," Jon said.

"Jon, drop it," Luke said. "It doesn't matter if it's Sarah's fault. She doesn't belong here. No one wants her here."

"You're either with her or you're with us," Tyler said. "Take your pick, Evans."

Jon looked around the schoolyard. Sarah had already gone inside.

He owed her nothing, he told himself. He owed Lisa everything. He'd made her a promise, and he had no choice but to keep it.

"I pick you," he said. "Sorry, Zach. I didn't understand."

"No one expected you to," Tyler said, slapping Jon on the back. "You're a slip, Evans, but you have possibilities."

Tuesday, May 5

Cowboy Gabe had time to shoot only one more bandit while riding his gallant steed, Jon, before going to bed, when the doorbell rang.

Lisa looked up from her paperwork. "Who could that be?" she asked.

"Come on, cowboy," Jon said. "Let's find out."

Gabe slid up so that he was resting on Jon's shoulders as Jon rose and walked to the door. Sarah was standing there.

Gabe stuck his finger out and pointed it at Sarah. "Bang, bang!" he yelled. "I shot you."

Sarah promptly collapsed on the front step. Gabe looked down at her. "I didn't really shoot you," he said, a worried expression on his face.

Sarah got up laughing. "I'm glad to hear it," she replied.

"Jon, aren't you going to introduce us?" Lisa asked, walking over to the front hallway.

"Oh yeah," Jon said. "Lisa, this is Sarah. She's new at school. Sarah, this is Lisa. Lisa Evans. My stepmother."

Lisa smiled and extended her hand for Sarah to shake. "It's nice to meet you, Sarah," she said. "Jon's friends don't come over nearly enough."

"She didn't come to see me," Jon said. "She wanted to meet Cowboy Gabe."

"It's time for Cowboy Gabe to go to bed," Lisa said. "Jon, let him down."

"No!" Gabe screamed, but Lisa and Jon ignored him. Jon set him on his feet, and Lisa took hold of his hand. Gabe struggled, but Lisa held on and managed to get him upstairs.

"Gabe's nanny has a headache," Jon said. "Lisa always says good night to him, but she doesn't usually have to get him into bed."

"I don't care about Gabe's nanny," Sarah said. "I want to talk to you, Jon."

"Not here," Jon said. "We have a garage. Let's go there."

"The garage?" Sarah asked.

"It's private," Jon replied. "I don't want Lisa to hear us."

"You don't even know what I'm going to say!" Sarah cried.

"I can guess," Jon said. "All right?" He walked out the front door, and Sarah followed him to the garage.

"This is awful," Sarah said. "Has anyone been in here in five years? Can you at least turn a light on?"

"I don't think there is one," Jon said. "Just say what you want, Sarah. I'm ready."

"Ready for what?" Sarah asked. "Ready to embarrass me some more? I thought you liked me. I didn't invite you to sit with me. Not at lunch, not on the bus. One minute I see you; the next minute you're gone. And the minute after that, you act like I'm invisible. You walk right past me like I'm not even there."

"I know," Jon said. "Sarah, I'm sorry. I do like you. I like you more than any girl since I moved here. But Zachary, my friend—well we're on the team together—and the thing is you moved into his grandfather's house. Your dad took his granddad's job."

"Do you know what that man did?" Sarah asked. "What he did to his patients?"

"No," Jon said. "I don't know, and even if you tell me, I won't believe you. Grubs lie, Sarah. They lie all the time. Zach says they lied about his grandfather, and I believe him. And my friends believe him. Try to see it from Zach's point of view. His grandfather was forced out of town, and you stole his home."

"Daddy didn't ask for the job," Sarah said. "And we sure didn't ask for that house."

"Tyler says you were thrown out of your enclave," Jon said. "That someone pulled strings and got your father this job."

"My father is a great man," Sarah said.

"That's exactly what Zach says about his grandfather," Jon replied. "I'd probably say it about my dad if he were still around. Sarah, I can't afford to let Zach hate me. Tyler's on his side, and his father's on the town board. Lisa's up for her evaluation. I have to protect her."

"Do you like them?" Sarah asked. "Zach, Tyler, all of them? Do you even like them?"

"Yeah," Jon said. "As it happens, I like them a lot. They're my friends, Sarah. My teammates."

"What would I have been?" Sarah asked. "If Tyler and Zach didn't hate me?"

Jon reached over and kissed her. Sarah kissed him back, then pulled away.

"Oh boy," she said. "Now I see the advantages of this garage."

Jon laughed. "I want to see you," he said. "Just not where it will upset the guys. Not until after Lisa's evaluation."

"When is it?" Sarah asked.

"In a week or two," Jon said. "Can we keep things quiet until then?"

Sarah stood there, absolutely still. Jon felt her slipping away. He kissed her again, but this time she didn't respond.

"We could walk to the bus together," he said. "Where do you live?"

"Elm Street," she said.

Jon thought about it. "That's eight blocks from here," he said. "I'll ask Val to wake up twenty minutes earlier and make my breakfast. That should give me enough time to get to your house."

"Why don't you wake up twenty minutes earlier and make your own breakfast?" Sarah asked.

"I can't," Jon said. "I don't know how."

"You've never made your own breakfast?" Sarah asked, and Jon could see she was struggling not to laugh. He took that as a good sign.

"Maybe when I was a kid," he replied. "But that's what Val's for, to make our meals and clean the house."

"That's not what she's for," Sarah said. "It's what she does."

"Fine," Jon said. "It's what she does. And she's grateful for the job. We treat her well, and she knows it. There's nothing wrong with me telling her to get up a few minutes earlier every day to make my breakfast."

"I wish you understood," Sarah said. "Working at the clinic,

I'm starting to see things differently. Maybe you would too if you knew any laborers."

"You mean grubs," Jon said. "And I know some."

"I don't mean your domestics," Sarah said. "I mean friends, family."

"My sister's a grub," he replied angrily. "She works in the greenhouses. Her husband's a grub. He's a bus driver, here in Sexton. You don't have to tell me grubs are people, the same as clavers. Are any of your family grubs? Any of your friends?"

Sarah was silent.

"I'm not the only claver with family in White Birch," Jon said. "Most everybody has someone there. Maybe their dad was selected but their aunt and their cousins weren't. So they settled in White Birch, hoping things would get better. And maybe things will get better, and there won't be clavers anymore or grubs. But like it or not, that's how things are."

"How things are stinks," Sarah said.

"I don't see you moving into a grubtown," Jon said. "You had your chance, but you chose an enclave."

Sarah turned away from him. Jon touched her face, and felt her tears.

"I'm sorry," he said. "I'll make my own breakfast. Can we walk to the bus together?"

She faced him, and he kissed the tears off her cheek. "I know I sound awful," she said. "I didn't used to. It's just I feel so alone."

Jon nodded. "I know how that feels," he said. "We all do. Clavers, grubs, all of us. We all feel alone. We all feel exactly like you."

Jon tried making his own breakfast, but he burned everything.

When he got home from soccer practice, he asked Val if she'd mind getting up twenty minutes earlier to make his breakfast. He didn't bother to explain why.

Val told him it was no problem, exactly as Jon had known she would. He couldn't figure out why Sarah had made such a fuss.

Jon had spent the week eating lunch and joking with his team-mates, rebuilding their relationship. Sarah was a prime target of their ridicule. He told himself it didn't matter since she couldn't hear what they were saying. She knew he liked her, and that was what counted.

He was always a good student, mostly because he was afraid of the consequences if he wasn't, but he worked particularly hard that week. He was the first to raise his hand when his teacher asked a question. He participated actively in the discussions. He did everything short of licking ass.

That he saved for soccer practice. No one did more reps, no one pushed harder, no one took practices more seriously. He apologized again to Coach, and nodded thoughtfully when Coach lectured him on the importance not merely of winning but of winning big. Ryan and Luke snickered, but Jon acted as though he'd never truly understood all that, but now he did. Grubs had to be kept in their place, and it was his job to see to it they were. His job, except, he hoped, for the upcoming game.

Even if Matt wasn't going to be in White Birch that Sunday, Jon would have been reluctant to play. The Sexton team was scheduled to play against the York grubs. York was a backcountry town. It could be reached only by driving over untended roads, and the trip took at least four hours.

If that wasn't bad enough, the York grubs didn't seem to understand they were grubs. None of them commuted. Instead clavers came to them. York was the chief manufacturer of potka. They grew runty potatoes, the kind no one would ever have eaten before the bad times, and they fermented them into the only alcohol readily available in the area. They had a long history of moonshining, and they knew what they were doing.

Jon had played in two games against them. Both times the Sexton bus carried twice as many guards as usual. Both times the York team played for blood, and the only way the grubs were appeased after their defeat was by the enormous amount of potka the Sexton clavers purchased from them. Both times Coach proclaimed the clavers had taught them their place, and both times no one cared because they were too drunk to listen. The only sober one was the driver, and that was because he was a grub and knew better than to get drunk in front of clavers.

Even if Jon weren't the top scorer on the team, Coach would want him there on Sunday, partly because he was a slip and partly as punishment for his lousy play the week before.

But Jon asked anyway. He was scared of Coach, but he was more scared of Mom.

"No," Coach said. "Forget it, Evans. No special privileges for you."

Tyler walked over to them. "Excuse me, Coach," he said. "I'm scheduled for this Sunday off, but I'd like to play."

Coach snorted. "No one wants to play York," he said.

"Yeah, I know," Tyler said. "But my father has family around there. He'd like them to have a chance to see me play."

"You put him up to this?" Coach asked Jon.

"No sir," Jon said. "It's news to me."

"It would mean a lot to my father," Tyler said. "I know I'm not as good as Evans, but I'll have extra incentive. Dad hates that side of his family. He wants me there when we kick their ass."

Coach grinned. "All right," he said. "Buy me an extra bottle of potka. Evans, you got the day off."

"Thanks, Coach," Jon said. "Tyler, thanks."

Tyler shook his head. "That's what friends are for," he replied. "Don't forget who your friends really are, Evans."

Friday, May 8

Jon was in his room, studying chemistry, when Lisa knocked on his door.

"Come in," Jon called. He'd been sprawled on the bed, so he sat upright as Lisa sat on the desk chair.

"I was wondering if you'd like to take some food on Sunday," Lisa said. "We could manage with one less chicken next week, and I'm sure that would be a real treat for them."

Jon had known Lisa was going to suggest this. Every time he visited Mom, Lisa made the same offer. "I asked Val to pick up some grapes for me to take," he said. "Thanks anyway."

Usually that was enough, and Lisa would get up to leave. But this time she stayed seated.

"I woke up early, Jon," Lisa said. "I found Val in the kitchen. She said you'd asked her last week to get up earlier to make your breakfast."

"Just twenty minutes," Jon said. "Val said it would be no problem."

"You know what my job is," Lisa said. "I'm head of domestic

placements. Do you know what a mess it would be if Val filed a complaint against me? There are things other clavers can get away with that I can't. That we can't. Especially with the evaluation coming up."

Sometimes Jon felt like a slip in his own home. He loved Lisa, and he knew she loved him, but she was his stepmother, and his father was dead. "I'm sorry," he said.

"Is an early breakfast that important to you?" Lisa asked.

Jon nodded. "I've been feeling rushed," he said. "And when I have breakfast with Gabe, we both get distracted."

"All right," Lisa said. "I'll tell Val. Next time, though, ask me first. All right, Jon?"

"Thanks, Lisa," Jon said.

Lisa left the room, but Jon found it impossible to concentrate on his chemistry lesson.

Grubs weren't the only ones who lied, he thought. Slips were good at it, also.

But Sarah was worth the lies. And once the evaluation was over, the lies would be, too.

Saturday, May 9

"I'm going into White Birch tomorrow," Jon told Sarah as they walked to the bus stop. "My brother's in town. I thought maybe we could take the bus together."

"Dad and I leave at five a.m.," Sarah replied.

"Five a.m.?" Jon said. "I didn't know there was a claver bus that early."

"We have a private driver," Sarah said. "Daddy opens the clinic at six o'clock on Sundays. He says we should keep the clinic open all night Saturdays because there's a lot of fighting Saturday nights—knife wounds, domestic violence—but the town board won't let him. They say it would encourage even more fighting if the . . ."

"Grubs," Jon said.

"If the people know they can be taken care of right away," Sarah said. "Not that it is right away. Did you know there's not a single ambulance in White Birch?"

"Ambulances take gas," Jon said.

"Sexton has an ambulance," Sarah said.

"Yes," Jon said. "And it's mostly used for grubs who get hurt at the job. There's an entire wing at the hospital just for them. The grubs who get hurt in White Birch bring it on themselves."

"Not the wives who get beaten half to death," Sarah said. "And then have to walk miles to the clinic for treatment."

"There are buses in White Birch," Jon said. "They could take a bus."

"They charge for the buses," Sarah said.

"Sure," Jon said.

"We don't have to pay," Sarah said. "Not for the buses in town or the ones that go to White Birch. But the . . ."

"Grubs," Jon said.

"The laborers, the ones who come in every day from White Birch, they have to pay. That's so unfair, Jon. Can't you see that?"

"But it isn't unfair," Jon said. "Buses cost money, for fuel and maintenance and drivers. Clavers pay for all that. We pay for their schools and the clinic, too. I'd say grubs have it pretty easy."

"It doesn't have to be this way," Sarah said. "It wasn't like this in my old enclave."

"How do you know?" Jon asked. "Did you ever ask your domestics if they paid for their bus rides? Did you ever leave the enclave to see what things were like for the grubs?"

"No," Sarah said.

"Then don't make assumptions," Jon said. "Maybe things could be better for the grubs, but things could be better for clavers, too. We're in this together. We're all making sacrifices so things will be better, if not for us, then for Gabe and all the children to come."

"Do you think things will get better?" she asked. "Do you really think that?"

Jon had no idea what he thought, but he knew what the answer was supposed to be. "Yes," he said. "Things will get better for all of us."

Sarah took his hand and squeezed it. "Let's make it better," she said. "You and me. Promise me, Jon, we'll work to make things better."

"I promise," he said. "Okay, go."

"There's no one at the bus stop," Sarah said. "No one would see us walking together."

"I don't want to take chances," Jon said. "You go first."

"I can't wait for Lisa's evaluation to be over," she said.

"Me neither," Jon said. "And Sarah? Don't talk to the other kids the way you talk to me. Bus fares and ambulances. You won't convince them, and it'll only make them mad."

"All right," she said. "Jon, there's nobody looking."

Jon made sure she was right. And then he kissed her.

Chapter 2

Sunday, May 10

Jon was surprised to find Alex driving the claver bus to White Birch. "You driving Sundays now?" he asked as he boarded the bus.

"Picking up extra cash," Alex replied. "I'll be home before Matt leaves."

Jon nodded and took his seat. It was nice of Alex to give the family some time alone with Matt, especially since Matt had never much liked him.

Smart of Alex, Jon thought, and then out of nowhere, he could hear Julie saying, "But my IQ is higher than his."

Jon grinned. Julie had loved her big brother, but they fought all the time. One day, when Jon and Julie were alone, she told him that she'd overheard her parents talking about their kids and what would become of them.

Carlos, they felt, would either end up in jail or in the military. Fortunately for everyone he chose the military.

Her parents thought her older sister, Briana, might become a nun. Julie knew better. Bri was devout, but she loved babies and wanted to have a dozen or more.

Alex, everyone knew, would go to college and become somebody important. Their dad might grumble about him, but even he knew Alex was destined for greatness.

That left Julie, the youngest. It was then she heard her father say, "Don't forget, her IQ is even higher than Alex's."

But her mother replied, "We'll find an older man for her, one that can control her."

Jon couldn't believe any mother would wish that, but Julie assured him her mother meant no harm. The important thing was that her IQ was higher than Alex's, even though he was the golden one and she was the troublemaker.

He'd asked her if Alex knew, and Julie shook her head. "He must never know," she said. "Promise me you'll never tell him."

"I promise," Jon had said, although he couldn't understand why it was such a big deal. So what if Julie was smarter? That didn't mean Alex couldn't achieve his dreams.

But the world had come to an end, and Alex was a grub bus driver and Julie was dead. What difference did their IQs make now?

Jon watched as some of the clavers gave Alex tips. It was nice of them, he thought. They had no obligation. Each time one did, Alex tipped his cap and said, "Thank you, sir; thank you, ma'am." Jon grinned. Alex had always had good manners.

Alex pulled the bus over to Jon's stop. Jon walked to the front. "See you later," he said.

Alex nodded, and Jon got off. Mom's apartment was three blocks away. It was in a good neighborhood, as White Birch went. The houses had been converted into two- and four-family apartments. There were no drunks or corpses on the street, and the only guard Jon saw was more interested in flirting with a grubber girl than protecting visiting clavers.

Matt opened the door and gave Jon a hug. "You look great!" he said. "You've grown. More muscle."

Matt was thinner than Jon remembered, but it wasn't sickness thin. It was the leanness of someone forever in motion. "You look great yourself," Jon said. "How's Syl?"

Matt shrugged. "She took the last miscarriage hard," he said. "But she's back to work, and we keep hoping."

"Give her my love," Jon said. He and Miranda found it wildly amusing that Syl was working as a domestic. When she and Matt had first married, Syl did nothing but stay in their bedroom while the rest of the family did all the cleaning and washing. Not that Jon had done so much. Maybe that's why he was so comfortable having Val do the housework. He was used to others taking care of him.

Mom grabbed Jon from Matt and hugged him even harder. She'd lost weight, too, Jon noticed. It would be like Mom to eat less so Miranda could eat more. Jon wondered if Matt had noticed and spoken to Miranda about it.

Miranda glowed. The last time Jon had seen her, he could hardly tell that she was pregnant. But now there was no mistaking it.

"How are you feeling?" he asked her.

"Fine," she said. "I get a little tired at work sometimes, but otherwise I feel great. They even doubled my food allotment. I'm going to be the fattest person in White Birch."

"There's not a lot of competition," Jon said. "I saw Alex. He drove my bus in."

Miranda nodded. "He's working seven days a week," she said. "He says he'll stop when the baby is born. I don't know. I won't be able to go back to work for a couple of months, so we won't have my salary. It's going to be hard getting by on just his and Mom's pay."

"We'll manage," Mom said. "Look at us. My three children

together, all grown, all beautiful. It's almost four years since everything happened. And we're still here, still together."

"Remember Crazy Shopping Day?" Miranda asked. She and
Jon burst out laughing at the memory of their elderly neighbor,
Mrs. Nesbitt, attacking some poor guy who'd tried to steal her
shopping cart.

Matt hadn't been there for Crazy Shopping Day, but soon
they were reminiscing about their lives. Jon had learned not to
think about the past any more than he had to, but it was wonderful talking about Christmases and birthdays and even fights they'd
had growing up. Mom told how pleased Matt had been when Jon
was born and he had a little brother, and how angry Miranda had
been since she was convinced she'd been promised a sister of her
own.

"What are you going to name the baby?" Jon asked Miranda.
"Have you decided?"

Miranda laughed. "It had better be a girl," she said. "Alex and I
keep fighting over boy names. If it's a girl, it's Liana. The 'li' is from
Julie and the 'ana' from Briana."

Miranda hadn't even known of Briana's existence, Jon
thought. Julie had told him about her, but when they began the
long walk to Sexton, Jon had mentioned Bri to Miranda, only to
have Miranda ask who he was talking about. Miranda and Alex had
had a terrible fight after that, Miranda enraged that Alex never
told her he had a sister who'd died.

That was the first of their two terrible fights. There were
squabbles after that, but they all squabbled. The trip was a nightmare. It would have been impossible to stay in good spirits through
those long terrifying months. But the second fight Alex and Miranda had was something far beyond a squabble. No one could tell

what the fight was about, but a day later Alex left. Miranda said he was going to Texas to see Carlos and tell him of Julie's death. But Jon knew—they all knew—it was something more than that, something far deeper.

Jon had actually been surprised when he learned Alex had returned to Miranda in White Birch. By that point Jon had slipped into Sexton. But he came for Alex and Miranda's wedding, and now, in a matter of months, he'd be an uncle.

As they sat down for lunch, Jon knew Mom was giving up supper for a couple of days so the table would be full. Even so, Jon noticed the food was nowhere near as good as what he was used to in Sexton. He felt like he was seeing things through Sarah's eyes. The apartment Mom shared with Miranda and Alex seemed smaller than Jon remembered, and grimier. The only heat came from a coal stove in the kitchen. That's where they ate, but when they were through and went back to the living room, Jon felt a dank cold.

He also noticed that, at different moments, each one of them coughed. White Birch homes didn't come with air purification systems.

Jon had been to his family's apartment maybe ten times. He tried to remember if he'd noticed the cold before, the dirty air, the just adequate food. Maybe he hadn't cared because it was so much better than what they'd had in Pennsylvania, where the four of them slept in the sunroom, all of them near death from starvation.

No, that wasn't true. Jon had never been that close to death. The others had given their food to him. He'd been hungry, and he'd been tired from the endless labor of chopping firewood, but they'd seen to it that he would survive.

He looked at his mother, his brother and sister and thought

about how he alone was living in the enclave, with its well-heated homes with breathable air, and fresh vegetables, chickens, and eggs. Before, somehow it had felt right. He was the youngest. He was the closest to Lisa. When they'd learned that one of the three passes Alex had given to Miranda would have to be used for Gabe, it made sense that Jon be the one to live with him and Lisa. They'd talked it out. Miranda, holding on to the thought that Alex would return, had refused to move to Sexton. Matt and Syl had decided to make a home somewhere else. Mom said it wouldn't work for her and Lisa to live together. They got along remarkably well, given they'd both been married to the same man, but enough was enough.

So, just as they'd given their food to Jon, they gave him their chance at a decent, comfortable life.

The passes had been meant originally for Alex, Bri, and Julie.

"Julie would want you to have her pass," Lisa had said. Lisa had loved Julie and been closer to her than any of them, except Jon.

But Jon knew something Lisa didn't, something Lisa would never know. Julie might still be alive if it weren't for him. Taking the pass was like stealing from the dead.

Still, he took it. Miranda and Alex, who could have used the passes for themselves, were grubs now. Their baby was coming into a world of inequality at best, hunger and cold at worst.

"How's the teaching going, Mom?" Matt asked.

Mom shook her head. "Sometimes I don't know why I even try," she said. "I teach three classes, fifty kids in a class. Most of them don't care. They're killing time until they're sixteen and can start working in Sexton. But there was this boy. I've never seen a kid that intelligent. Not book-learning smart. He hasn't had the chance. But he grasped concepts faster than I could discuss them.

Brilliant kid. I thought maybe he could get into Sexton University. There's no rule against it, and a boy that smart should be able to find sponsors." She sighed. "He left two weeks ago. He was nice enough to tell me, which is more than most of them do. His father got arrested, and his mother is dead, and he has two younger brothers. The kid is fifteen. He's going to work in the mines. You don't have to be sixteen to work in the mines. He'll send the money home to support his brothers until the older one is sixteen and can go to work."

"These are hard times, Mom," Matt said. "The important thing is not to quit."

"I'm not quitting," she said. "Just despairing." But she laughed, and Jon knew things were all right again.

"The moon crash anniversary is a week from Monday," Miranda said. "I guess I should look at it as a day off, but I dread it."

"Sunday night will be worse," Mom said. "Matt, will you be on the road?"

Matt shook his head. "I'll get home Saturday afternoon. I won't be going out again until Tuesday."

"Mom, do you remember that first anniversary?" Miranda asked. "When you and Syl and I had that crazy ceremony?"

"What are you talking about?" Jon asked.

Mom and Miranda had just finished telling the story of their ceremonial sacrifice to the moon goddess Diana when Alex came in. He hugged Miranda and Jon and shook Matt's hand.

"You look tired," Matt said to him.

Alex shrugged. "I am," he said. He sat next to Miranda and squeezed her hand. "But it's worth it."

"I've been waiting until you got home before I mentioned something," Matt said. "It involves you and Miranda. Mom, too."

"What is it?" Mom asked. "Is everything all right?"

"Everything's fine, Mom," Matt said with a grin. "It's something good. Or at least something to consider."

"I'm listening," Alex said.

"You know how much I travel," Matt said. "Mostly from enclave to enclave, but I spend the nights in lots of different places. Keep this confidential, but there's a group of people who've set up their own community. Not an enclave, no government involvement, but not . . . well, not a place like White Birch either."

"Not a grubtown," Alex said.

"I hate that word," Mom said.

"Laura, that's what this is," Alex said. "You'd rather I called it a slavetown?"

"The point is, this new place won't be any of those things," Matt said. "Remember communes? Kibbutzes? That's what they're planning. They're starting small, but they figure to expand. Syl and I are talking about joining, but we're not ready to make a commitment yet."

"What will they do for food?" Jon asked.

"Grow their own," Matt said. "They've put together the money for two greenhouses, and they'll build from there. It's going to be rough, a lot rougher than White Birch, to start out with. But they won't be dependent on the whim of some enclave. They'll be independent."

"Where do we fit in?" Alex asked.

"I told them my brother-in-law is a mechanic," Matt said. "That you'd passed the mechanic's test, but you're not connected enough to get the promotion. A place like that is going to need mechanics. They love the fact that Miranda's pregnant. Actually, they're so pleased with the thought of you two, they are willing to take Mom, also."

"That's very gracious of them," Mom said.

"We know you're essential," Matt said. "But you don't bring a lot of skills to a community like they're planning. Alex does."

"What about me?" Jon asked.

"I didn't ask," Matt said. "You're fine in Sexton."

"What do you think, Alex?" Miranda asked.

"I don't know," he said. "Carlos and I have been saving money for our own truck," he said to Matt. "In another year, eighteen months, we should be able to buy one. We figure that's the only way, to go independent."

"But you'd stay in White Birch," Matt said.

"There are some pretty nice sections in White Birch," Alex replied. "And there's no law against fixing our home, buying more food if we can afford it." He grinned. "Living the middle-class life."

"We can't go anywhere until the baby is born," Miranda said. "But if we did decide to move, Mom, you'd have to come with us. I'd worry about you if you were here alone."

"Yes," Alex said. "If we go, you come with us, Laura."

"I'll come, too," Jon said.

"No, you won't," Mom said. "Whatever happens, you're staying in Sexton."

"Why?" Jon said.

Mom stared at him. "Look at your sister, Jon, and your brother and Alex," she said. "Matt's a courier and Miranda works in the greenhouses and Alex is a bus driver. You call them grubs. Well, you're not going to be a grub. You'll graduate high school and college. That's the whole point of your living in Sexton, so you can get an education, make something of yourself."

"What if I don't want to?" Jon asked.

"I don't care," Mom said. "In case you haven't noticed, none of us are doing what we want. We're doing what we have to, and we expect the same from you."

"Matt?" Jon said, but Matt just shook his head.

"Listen, Jon," Alex said. "You have a chance Miranda and I will never have. But it's not just us. It's Bri's chance and Julie's. You're the survivor, Jon, and survivors have responsibilities. If you walk away from your chance, you make all that loss, all that sacrifice, meaningless."

"All right," Jon said. "But don't go without telling me. Let me know where I can find you."

"Of course we will," Miranda said. Then she laughed. "The baby's kicking. Here, Jon. Feel." She put his hand on her belly, and he felt the movement that promised life.

"Soccer player," Jon said. "Takes after me."

For a moment they laughed, and for that moment they were a family again.

Chapter 3

"He's looking at her again," Zachary said as they sat in the cafeteria.

Ryan snapped his fingers in Jon's face. "Earth to Evans," he said. "Come in Evans."

"What the hell does that mean?" Luke asked.

Ryan shrugged. "I don't know," he replied. "But my father says it sometimes."

"What?" Jon said. "What about your father?"

"What about you?" Ryan said. "Why do you keep staring at Goldman that way? She isn't even pretty."

"You could have any girl you want," Luke said.

"No, I can't," Jon said.

"Okay, some of the girls won't go out with you," Luke admitted. "Their parents won't let them. But most of the girls would, if you asked them. Instead, you keep staring at *her*."

Jon tried not to look at Sarah, who sat silent and alone, while the other students were laughing and talking. "You'd think she'd have friends by now," he said.

"No one likes her because of what she did to my grandfather," Zachary declared.

"She didn't do anything to your grandfather," Jon said.

"She's living in his house," Zachary said angrily. "She's worse than a slip."

"Look, Evans, if you feel sorry for her, be her friend," Tyler said. "Go sit with her. Just don't expect to sit with us again."

"Her or us," Zachary said. "Get that, slip?"

"I get it," Jon said, and stayed where he was.

Thursday, May 14

"What's going to happen Sunday?" Sarah asked Jon as they began their walk to the bus stop.

"I have a soccer match," Jon said. "In Longley. It's about an hour, hour and a half from here."

"I mean Sunday night," she said.

"Some of our neighbors are having a party," Jon said. "Carrie and Val will be in White Birch, so Lisa's taking Gabe to the party with her."

"You can't stay with him?" Sarah asked.

"I'm going to White Birch after the match," Jon replied. "Luke says it's like Mardi Gras. The one chance a year we have to blow off steam. What about you? Will you be closing the clinic early?"

"Daddy wanted to keep it open all night," Sarah said. "In case anyone gets hurt from all that steam you'll be blowing off. But the town board said no, it might give the grubs bad ideas. They're making Daddy stay at the clinic anyway, in case some clavers get hurt."

"You're not going to be there, are you?" Jon asked. "It can get pretty crazy that night."

"I'll be home," Sarah said. "Daddy won't let me anywhere near White Birch on Sunday. Jon, you're not going to do anything too crazy, are you?"

Jon shook his head. "Just have some fun," he said. "Then church and fasting on Monday."

"I hate anniversary day," Sarah said. "I hate it so much."

"It's just one day," Jon said. "Then it's back to normal."

"There's no normal anymore," Sarah replied. "Normal got lost four years ago. It's never coming back."

"I know," Jon said.

"Oh, I'm sorry," Sarah cried. "I know how lucky we are. How lucky I am. I just wish I could be luckier. Is that wrong of me, Jon? To wish I could be luckier?"

Jon checked to see no one was around. Then he embraced her. "It's not wrong," he murmured. "It's just not going to happen, that's all."

Saturday, May 16

"Matt gave me five quarters before he left," Mom said. "He picks up whatever change he finds on the road when he's biking. It's amazing there are any coins left, but he says if you look hard enough, you can still find some. Five quarters. We'll be able to talk for fifteen minutes."

"Isn't there a line?" Jon asked. "Usually someone's shouting at you to get off the phone."

"I'm using one in a bad neighborhood," Mom replied. "People are too scared to use it."

"Is that safe?" Jon asked.

"I'm fine," Mom said. "The neighborhood isn't really that bad.

Just a lot of drunks who'll be spending their quarters on potka, not pay phones. So tell me, Jon, how did your week go?"

"It was okay," Jon said. "Mom, I don't like the idea of your being in a bad neighborhood. Why don't we just say hello, and you can call me next week, at your regular phone booth."

"There isn't any place in White Birch that's really safe," Mom said. "Remember, back home, how I'd make sure the doors were locked all the time? I can't even do that here. None of the doors have locks."

"I know, Mom," Jon said. All the locks were removed when laborers had been moved into White Birch. That way, the people who used to live in White Birch couldn't use their homes as barricades. Once the grubs were resettled, no one saw much point in giving them locks and keys. Grubs didn't have anything worth stealing.

"I hope Alex and Miranda leave," Mom said. "I'd rather never see my grandchild than have her grow up in a place like this."

"White Birch is a lot better than most of the grubtowns I've seen," Jon said. "There are schools and the clinic. Police, too, for protection."

"Police," Mom said. "I lost another of my boys to the mines this week. He was arrested for public intoxication. Thrown into jail and carted off to the mines. Half the men in this town are publicly intoxicated, but the police only take the young ones, the ones who'll last a little longer in the mines."

"We all need the mines," Jon said. "You use coal to heat your apartment, Mom. Where do you think it comes from? The coal fairy?"

"I don't know you anymore," Mom said. "I don't."

"You know me, Mom," Jon muttered.

"I never see you," she said. "I see Matt more often than I see you. You're a bus ride away, Jon. But you never visit."

"I play soccer most Sundays," Jon said.

"Then quit the team," Mom said. "Get a different afterschool. Something where you'll do some good."

"I'm not quitting the soccer team," Jon said. "It's the only thing I have."

"You have family," Mom said. "You have a roof over your head and food to eat and a school where you can get a real education. You have a future. My students don't have any of that. They get just enough food to keep them alive, just enough education so they can be trained for their jobs. It's an outrage. And you say the only thing you have is soccer. I don't know you anymore, Jon. I don't know who you've become, what the enclave has made you. Matt, Miranda, they haven't lost who they were. If anything, this whole experience has made them better, stronger."

Jon listened as Mom took a deep breath.

"I know I spoiled you," Mom said finally. "You were the baby in the family. And back, back when things got bad, well, I put all my hopes on you. Matt and Miranda let me, but I shouldn't have done it. It gave you a sense of entitlement, and living the way you do has only exacerbated that. So a lot of it is my fault. Not all of it, though. You're old enough, Jon, to see the world as it really is, not the way you want it to be."

There was nothing Jon could say. It was her choice. She had her world, Matt, Miranda, Alex. She had her students. She no longer had him.

"I'm getting off now," she said, understanding his silence. "I have better use for these quarters."

"Look at 'im," Tyler said in drunken indignation.

Jon looked at the old man sprawled unconscious on the pavement.

"He's drunk," Luke said.

"A bum," Ryan said.

"All grubs are bums," Zachary said. "Don't deserve to live." He took a slug from his bottle of potka, then passed it around for the other boys to drink.

Jon couldn't remember ever being this drunk before. It was part of the fun of the night, that and grubber girls and breaking windows and getting in fights. It seemed like every man from Sexton was there, but the grubs were enjoying themselves, too. There was potka and girls enough for all of them.

Zachary pulled out his knife. "Whaya think?" he asked.

"I think it's a knife," Luke said. "Whaya think it is?" He laughed at his own joke, and the guys joined in, except for Zachary.

"You know wha I mean," Zachary said. "Let's cut him up."

"Yeah," Ryan said. "Teach 'im a lesson. Teach all the damn grubs a lesson."

"Good idea," Tyler said. "Gimme the potka."

The bottle was passed around again. How many had they gone through? Three, Jon thought. Not that it mattered. There was plenty of potka left. That trip to York had been good for something.

"Cut 'im up," Zachary said. "Let 'im bleed. Let all the grubs bleed for what they did to my granddad."

"Wait," Tyler said. "Gotta better idea." He searched through his pockets and pulled out a small box of matches.

"Where'd ya get that?" Ryan asked.

"Stole it," Tyler said.

There'd been small fires burning all around White Birch. They must have been started by matches, Jon thought. Now they could start their own fire.

"Burn 'im," Tyler said.

"I wanna cut him," Zachary said.

"Cut 'im first," Tyler declared. "Then burn 'im."

Ryan laughed.

"Not a joke!" Tyler said. "Cut 'im. Burn 'im. Grubber bum don't deserve to live."

Jon wasn't sure why, but he didn't think cutting the bum and setting him on fire was a good idea. "Guys," he said.

"Wassa matter?" Ryan asked. "That your daddy, Evans?"

"Least I know who my daddy is," Jon said, relieved when the other guys laughed.

Luke took another drink from the bottle. "So what if we kill him?" he said. "No one'll know. He's a bum. Let's do something people will see. Not just burning a drunk."

"Do what?" Tyler asked. "Better be good."

Luke looked around. "Up the block," he said. "The high school. Let's trash it."

"Trash and burn," Zachary said. "Set it on fire."

Ryan nodded. "That'll make a difference. They'll notice that."

The boys turned to Tyler. "Better than knocking off some bum," he said. "People'll talk about it. Let's go."

Jon followed the others up the street. As they passed the bum, Zachary gave him a kick. The bum slept through it.

"He wouldn't've felt a thing," Luke said. "Waste of matches."

Jon had never been to the high school. Mom taught there,

but she had never bothered to show it to him. Talked about her students, though. Cared more about them than she did about her own son. Cried when they went to the mines.

"Damn school should burn," he muttered.

Tyler slapped him on his back. "Burn the damn school down!" he shouted.

When they got to the building, they found its windows had already been shattered. "Someone got here before us," Zachary complained. "Let's go back to the bum."

"Sure, they trashed it," Jon said. "But we're the ones who're gonna burn it down."

Tyler leaned over one of the broken windows. "Someone brush the damn glass off," he said.

"Job for a slip," Zachary said.

Jon took his jacket off and used it to brush the slivers of glass away. Tyler hoisted himself through the window and the others followed.

"Big mess," Ryan said.

He was right. Desks and chairs had been overturned, books ripped to shreds. The room stank of piss and puke. Might as well burn it, Jon thought. Too much of a shithole even for grubs.

"Got an idea," Zachary said. "Gimme the potka."

Ryan handed him the bottle.

Zachary took a deep gulp, then poured potka over the shredded books. "Lighter fluid," he said. "Get the fire goin' faster."

"Let's try," Tyler said. He pulled one of the matches from the box, struck it, and threw it into the book pile. Sure enough, the fire blazed hot and fast.

"Next room!" he shouted, and they followed him. Room by room they made piles of paper and watched as they burned.

"We did it," Luke said. "Whole school's on fire. Better go before we get hurt."

Laughing and congratulating themselves, the boys climbed out a broken window. They stood in front of the school and watched as the fire spread, until they could see flames coming out of the second-story windows.

"That'll teach those damn grubs," Tyler said. "Come on, guys. Let's find ourselves some more girls. The night's still young."

Monday, May 18

Jon got in at 4 a.m. By nine o'clock he was sitting in church, Lisa on one side, Gabe on the other. There was no law saying you had to go to church on the eighteenth, but everybody did.

He looked around and had no trouble spotting Luke and Ryan. Zachary and Tyler went to a different church, so he didn't expect to see them. But no matter how much he searched, he couldn't find Sarah in the crowd. He knew she and her father didn't attend church, but he thought they might show up for the eighteenth.

It was hard to keep Gabe distracted, but between Jon and Lisa, they managed to make it through the service. Jon hoisted Gabe and draped him around his shoulders for the walk home.

Jon and Lisa were fasting, but Gabe ate enough for both of them. He demanded Jon play with him, and Jon obliged until it was time for Gabe's nap.

"Let me get him to bed," Lisa said. "I need to talk."

A few minutes later Lisa joined him in the living room. "Val and Carrie are wonderful," she said, "but there are times I'm glad they're not here. They don't need to know how worried I am about the evaluation."

"Have they set a date?" Jon asked.

Lisa nodded. "Friday."

Friday, Jon thought. He and Sarah would have to keep waiting after that, until the results were in, but how long could that take? In a week or two they'd be taking the bus together, eating lunch together, letting everyone know how they really felt.

"Lisa, you'll be fine," he said. "You've got nothing to worry about."

"Oh, Jon," she said. "There's always something to worry about. Especially for me. Slips have to work twice as hard. You know that. And there's so much politics. So much I don't know. Factors. So many factors."

"Like what?" Jon asked.

"Like some claver's relative wanting my job," she said. "Or some claver not liking me because I don't smile enough or I smile too much. Or Gabe."

"What about Gabe?" Jon said. "What does he have to do with it?"

Even though the house was empty, Lisa lowered her voice. "If I don't pass my evaluation, I'll have to leave Sexton," she said. "You know that."

Jon nodded.

"If that happens, I'll have to decide what to do about Gabe," she said.

"I don't understand," Jon said. "You'll take him with you."

"To what?" she asked. "To some roach-infested tenement? No medicine, not enough food? If I'm lucky, I'd get a job in Sexton. I'd be away from home six days a week, twelve hours a day. And that's if I'm lucky. If no one will hire me, then where do I go? Where do I take him?"

Jon pictured Mom's apartment: it was a good one because she was a teacher. But still it was cold and miserable, and even Mom had given up trying to kill the roaches.

"You'll pass the evaluation," he said.

"Jon, there are a lot of people in Sexton who'd adopt Gabe," Lisa said. "Couples who lost their children. Couples who haven't been able to conceive or who've miscarried or had stillborns. If I don't pass the evaluation, there'll be a lot of pressure on me to give Gabe up for adoption."

"You wouldn't, would you?" Jon asked.

"I don't know," Lisa said. "What's best for Gabe? Living with me? I love him more than life itself, but what could I give him? Maybe he'd be better off living with another family who can give him a good life, safe, with a future. Your mother let you go. Maybe I should do the same."

"It's not the same and you know it," Jon declared. "You're family. And I get to see Mom." He pictured her school burning down and forced himself not to think about it.

"I'm terrified, Jon," Lisa said. "What if I fail my evaluation because someone wants Gabe? It could happen. Then what?"

"We'll figure something out," Jon said. "Maybe you could work as a domestic and keep Gabe with you. Or he could stay with me. I won't get evaluated for another year. If I pass, he can keep living with me."

"Mommy!"

Lisa got up. "Gabe must have had a nightmare," she said. "Thank you, Jon. I feel a little better, a little less crazy."

"Is it okay for me to go out?" Jon asked. "Do you need me here anymore?"

Lisa bent over and kissed him on his forehead. "Be home by suppertime," she said. "We'll break fast then."

Jon waited until Lisa left the room. Then he grabbed his jacket and ran out of the house. He didn't stop running until he got to Sarah's house.

He found her sitting on the porch. Even from a distance he could tell she was crying.

"Sarah!" he yelled, racing toward her.

"Oh, Jon," she said, reaching out to him.

He held her in his arms until she stopped crying. Then they sat on the wicker love seat, Jon putting his arm around her. "What is it?" he asked. "What happened?"

"Nothing," she replied. "Everything. Jon, my sister died four years ago today. I miss her all the time, but it's always worse on the anniversary."

"You never told me you had a sister," Jon said.

"We talk fifteen minutes a day," Sarah said with a sniffle. "And most of that time we're arguing."

Jon wanted to laugh. Instead he held Sarah a little closer. "Do you feel like talking about her?" he asked.

Sarah rubbed the tears off her cheeks with her fists. "Her name was Abby," she said. "She was sixteen. I'm older now than she was."

Jon nodded. "Time stood still," he said. "But not for us."

"We lived in Connecticut," she said. "On the Long Island Sound. We had a sailboat. It was beautiful, Jon. We spent so much time on it. Abby was a wonderful sailor."

"She went sailing that night?" Jon asked.

"With some of her friends," Sarah said. "They thought it would be great to see the meteor strike from the boat. One of her friends washed ashore a couple of days later. Do you remember how horrible things were then, how crazy? We kept hoping Abby was okay but couldn't make it home. We hoped that for a week, maybe more. Even after we knew better, we kept hoping. When Mom was dying, she told me she still was waiting for Abby to find her way home."

"I'm so sorry," Jon said.

Sarah began crying again. Jon knew there was nothing he could say that would make things better. Instead he held on to her so tightly he could no longer tell if it was his heart or hers that was broken.

Thursday, May 21

Luke looked around the locker room, then edged closer to Jon. "We did the right thing, didn't we?" he whispered.

Jon stared at him.

"The other night," Luke said, so softly Jon could hardly hear him. "Tyler would have killed that guy. They all would have. We had to give them something to distract them. The grubber school doesn't matter, does it?"

Now that he was sober, Jon knew what they'd done was very wrong. But it would have been a lot worse to kill a man.

"We did the right thing," he whispered back.

Luke looked around again. "I hate this sometimes," he said.

"I know," Jon said.

"What do you know, Evans?" Tyler asked, walking toward them.

Jon forced himself to grin. "I know how lucky I am," he said.

"Damn straight," Tyler said. "Luckiest slip around."

Chapter 4

Carrie came out of the hearing room and smiled wanly at Jon and Val. "Come, Gabe," she said. "Let's go home now."

Gabe had been playing with Jon and was unwilling to stop. "Sorry, cowboy," Jon said, handing him over to his nanny. "I'll see you later."

"No!" Gabe screamed.

A woman had come out of the hearing room and was gesturing for Jon to enter. Gabe grabbed Jon's leg and continued screaming.

"He never does this," Carrie said apologetically to the woman.

Grubs do lie, Jon thought. Gabe constantly had tantrums.

Val helped pull Gabe off, and Carrie picked him up. They carried him out while Jon followed the woman into the hearing room.

He didn't know what to expect, but he felt better seeing Tyler's father sitting behind a table, with a man on one side and a woman on the other.

The woman who'd escorted Jon picked up a Bible. "Put your right hand on the Bible," she said. "Do you swear to tell the truth, the whole truth, and nothing but the truth, so help you God?"

Jon nodded. "I do."

"Do you swear that you will never repeat or report anything that is said in this room, so help you God?"

"I do."

Mr. Hughes smiled at him. "Sit down, Jon," he said, turning to the people seated next to him. "Jon Evans is a friend of my son. Because of that, I'll turn the questioning over to Mr. Delman and Mrs. Haverford. Remember, Jon, you've sworn to tell the truth. If you aren't certain about the answer to any question, don't guess. Say you don't know."

"Thank you, sir," Jon said.

"For the record, what is your name?" Mr. Delman asked.

"Jon Evans," Jon said. "Jonathan Mark Evans."

"And where do you live?"

"In Sexton," Jon replied. "Twenty-seven Pierce Drive."

"How old are you, Jon?" Mrs. Haverford asked.

"I'm seventeen."

"What is your relationship to Mrs. Lisa Evans?" Mr. Delman asked.

"She's my stepmother."

"And how long have you known her?" Mr. Delman continued.

Jon thought about it. He was nine when Dad married Lisa, and he'd met her a couple of times before then. "Nine years," he said.

"And your father is dead?"

"Yes sir."

"How did you come to live in Sexton?" Mr. Delman asked.

"We had passes," Jon said.

"How did you come to have those passes?"

"A friend of ours gave them to us," Jon said.

"Do you know how he came to have those passes?" Mr. Delman asked.

Jon hesitated. "I was told he was given the passes by someone he knew. His friend's father. But I don't know that for a fact."

Mr. Delman nodded. "So you and Mrs. Evans and Mrs. Evans's son, Gabriel, moved into Sexton," he said.

"That's right," Jon said. "Gabe's my half brother."

"When did your father die?" Mrs. Haverford asked.

"Two years ago," Jon said. "Right before we got here."

"So for the past two years you've lived with Mrs. Evans and Gabriel," Mr. Delman said. "Does anyone else live with you?"

"No," Jon said. "Well, our housekeeper and Gabe's nanny."

"And their names are?"

"Val and Carrie," Jon replied. "I'm sorry. I don't remember their last names."

Mr. Hughes smiled at him. "Relax, Jon," he said. "You're doing fine."

Jon smiled back at him. "Thank you, sir," he said. "This is kind of nerve-racking."

"How would you describe your relationship with Mrs. Evans?" Mrs. Haverford asked.

"Good," Jon said. "Good. Very good."

"Does she ever hit you?" Mrs. Haverford asked.

Jon laughed. "No. Absolutely not."

"Does she ever hit or spank Gabe?"

"No ma'am," Jon said.

"Do the domestics ever hit or spank Gabe?"

"I don't know," Jon said. "I'm at school and then there's after-school and I'm on the Sexton soccer team. So I'm not home very much. But I've never seen Carrie or Val hit Gabe. I know he loves both of them."

"Does Mrs. Evans go out in the evenings?" Mrs. Haverford asked. "Is she romantically involved with anyone?"

"No ma'am," Jon said. "She took my dad's death pretty hard. And she doesn't have much spare time. There's her work, and Gabe and me."

"Does she ever speak about her job?" Mr. Delman asked.

"Well, I know what she does," Jon said. "But she doesn't go into details."

"Does Mrs. Evans go to church on Sundays?" Mrs. Haverford asked.

"Yes ma'am," Jon said. "She takes Gabe with her. I go with them when I can, but if I have a soccer game I go to the seven a.m. service instead."

"Just a couple more questions," Mr. Hughes said. "Then we'll be through."

"Thank you, sir," Jon said. He hoped no one could see how much he was sweating.

"Does Mrs. Evans ever hit the domestics?" Mrs. Haverford asked.

"No ma'am," he said.

"Does she give the domestics an adequate amount of food?" Mr. Delman asked.

"I guess so," Jon said. "I mean, yes. Well, I don't eat with them, so I can't swear they're getting enough, but they seem healthy. I've never heard either of them complain. As a matter of fact, they've both told me how grateful they are to work for us."

Mrs. Haverford smiled at Jon. "Is there anything else you'd like to tell us about Mrs. Evans?" she asked. "Before we call her in for her examination?"

"She's great," Jon said. "She didn't have to give me the pass, but she said she wanted me to live with her, that it would be wonderful for Gabe to have a big brother. And I know she works hard at her job. I really think she should be allowed to stay in Sexton." He stopped. "I hope that's okay," he said. "Thank you."

"Thank you, Jon," Mr. Hughes said. "You playing in Sunday's game?"

"Yes sir," Jon said, getting up.

"Give 'em hell," Mr. Hughes said. "Show them who's boss."

"I'll try, sir," Jon said. "Thank you, Mr. Delman, Mrs. Haverford."

Their nods indicated that he could leave. Jon realized he was shaking. He wasn't sure what they were trying to find out about Lisa. He could only hope he answered in the right way.

He didn't want to think about the consequences if he hadn't.

Saturday, May 23

"I'm sorry," Mom said as Jon answered the phone. "I never should have talked to you that way."

"It's okay," Jon said. "You were upset about your students. I understand."

"I'm still upset," Mom replied. "Maybe even more so. Did you hear what happened to the high school?"

Jon swallowed. "Yeah," he said.

"Destroyed," Mom said. "Someone's idea of a joke. It makes me sick."

"But you're still teaching," Jon said. "Right?"

"I'm trying," Mom replied. "They moved us to the elementary school. The whole high school is crammed into three rooms. They moved the chairs and desks out, and the kids sit on the floor. It's the only way they could fit everybody in."

"Where's the elementary school?" Jon asked, trying not to picture the high school as it burned down.

"On Maple," Mom replied. "It's about a ten-block walk."

"Well, that's good," Jon said. "At least you don't have that long walk anymore."

"It's so unfair," Mom said. "I know it's not your fault, Jon, but the whole system is so wrong."

"Hey, lady, you're not the only one who wants to talk," Jon heard a man shout.

"I've got to go," Mom said. "I'll talk to you next week. I love you, Jon."

"Love you, too," Jon mumbled, and hung up.

They'd done the right thing, he told himself. Mom wasn't there. She couldn't understand what it was like that night.

Besides, what difference did a couple more years of education make to a grub? Miranda and Alex had both gone to high school, and look where they were now.

They all had work to do, grubs and clavers. Jon would finish high school and go to Sexton University to learn whatever the board thought would be most useful to the enclave. He wouldn't have any more say about his future than a grub.

Maybe the system was wrong. But it was the only system they had. It was the system that kept them, clavers and grubs both, alive.

Sunday, May 24

It was a three-hour bus trip to Worley, and the air was particularly foul.

Jon didn't care. He played as though he were the only man

° 58 °

on the Sexton team. He didn't just steal the ball from the Worley players. He stole it from his own teammates. He made thirteen shots, and nine of them went in. Sexton won 11–2.

"Nice job, Evans," Coach said.

"He hogged the ball," Tyler declared. "Didn't give the rest of us a chance."

Coach paused. "You're right, Tyler," he said. "Evans, this is a team sport. Let the grubs see who the real clavers are."

It was a balancing act, Jon told himself. Everything was a balancing act. "I did hog the ball," he said. "Sorry."

"Just remember which side you're on, slip," Tyler said.

"I'll remember," Jon said. As though he'd ever be allowed to forget.

Monday, May 25

Jon was playing horsey with Gabe when the phone rang. Val answered it.

"It's your mother, Jon," she said.

Jon eased Gabe off his back and walked over to the phone. Mom called only on Saturdays. It was Miranda, he thought. Something bad must have happened to her.

"Is everything all right?" he asked before Mom had a chance to say hello.

"Everything's fine," she said. "Miranda went to the clinic for her checkup on Sunday, and it turns out a friend of yours works there. Sarah Goldman. Her father's the doctor."

"I know," Jon said.

"I had this idea," Mom declared. "I'll invite Sarah and her father—and you, of course—for dinner. They could come over from the clinic, and you could take the bus in with Miranda and Alex. Nothing fancy. What do you think?"

Jon thought it was a terrible idea, but he knew better than to say so. "Sarah's father is very busy," he said. "He probably wants to go right home at night."

"Well, we won't know until we ask," Mom said. "So why don't you ask Sarah? Find out what day would be best for her and her father. One day next week. You can tell me on Saturday."

"Can you afford it?" Jon asked. "Food's not cheap, Mom."

"I know what food costs," Mom said. "Better than you. And yes, we can afford it. Jon, ask Sarah, all right?"

"All right," Jon said. "I'll talk to you on Saturday."

"Have a good week, honey," Mom said. "I love you."

"I love you, too," Jon said.

He did love her, he told himself. She was his mother. She'd starved for him.

So why did he dread the idea of Sarah meeting her?

Tuesday, May 26

Jon woke up at the near sunless dawn. He hated the thought of inviting Sarah and her father to Mom's apartment. Not because he thought Sarah would be offended. On the contrary. He knew Sarah well enough to know what she'd say. She'd be delighted. All part of her everyone-is-equal attitude.

But Jon knew better. Maybe everyone was equal, or had been before, but everyone didn't live equally. That was the way the system worked. Clavers had more because they deserved more. Grubs had only as much as they needed to survive, because their survival was important. Not essential, the way claver survival was, but important enough to justify their being fed and sheltered.

Grubs could be replaced easily enough. Clavers, except for Zachary's granddad, were irreplaceable.

Julie should have been the slip. That had been the plan. He'd be the grub, working in a factory most likely. Maybe even in the mines. If Sarah had met him, and there'd be no reason why she would have, she wouldn't have looked twice at him. For all her talk about everyone being equal, she was a claver girl, and claver girls never looked twice at grubs.

But it hadn't happened that way. He lived in Sexton, on Julie's pass. Julie, who had died because of him.

He tried to fall back asleep, but it was impossible. Instead he got dressed and stared out the window until he knew it was time for Val to be making his breakfast.

"I guess I should thank you," he said, sitting down at the table. Val had already poured him a glass of goat's milk, and he took a sip.

"For what?" she asked as she scrambled his eggs.

"For not telling the board how I make you get up earlier," he said. "You didn't tell them, did you?"

"I didn't," Val replied. "But you don't have to thank me. Around here, it's better to keep your mouth shut." She served Jon his eggs, two slices of potato bread toast, and a small bowl of strawberries. A claver breakfast. Sarah was probably eating pretty much the same in her kitchen.

He didn't want to think about Mom's breakfast, or Miranda's or Alex's. What did Val and Carrie have for breakfast? He'd shared a house with them for two years and had never seen them eat.

Had he ever been told their last names?

"Why aren't you eating?" Val asked. "Is there something wrong with the eggs?"

"No," Jon said, taking a mouthful to prove it. "I was just thinking. Are you from Sexton, Val?"

"What makes you ask that?" she replied.

"Just curious," he said.

"I'm from Nevada," she said.

"My grandmother lived in Las Vegas," Jon said. "We don't know what happened to her."

"I got out early," Val said. "My boyfriend was a geologist. We were out of there by the end of May." She paused. "Four years ago," she said. "It feels more like four decades."

"Were you a domestic?" Jon asked.

Val laughed. "I was an assistant professor of philosophy," she said. "Not a lot of jobs for philosophy professors these days."

"But your boyfriend must be okay," Jon said. "Geologists were selected. Does he live in Sexton?"

"He died from the flu," Val said. "We were in an evac camp. I kept going east because I didn't know what else to do. Then I heard there were jobs around here. They like domestics to be college educated. Carrie was a marriage counselor before."

"Do you mind being a grub?" Jon asked, picking at the strawberries.

"I mind the term," Val said. "It's offensive."

"But everyone calls you that," Jon said. "Why be offended?"

"Everyone can call you ugly," Val said. "That doesn't mean you can't be offended."

Jon stared at her. Val burst out laughing.

"I'm sorry," she said. "You're not ugly, Jon. You're a nice kid and you're nice looking and I don't know how we got onto this subject. Eat your breakfast, and don't think so much."

Jon took a bite of his eggs. He'd wait until tomorrow to invite

Sarah. He'd had enough socializing with grubs for one day without having to hear Sarah go on and on about how everybody was equal.

Sarah wouldn't stop talking on the way to the bus stop. The clinic was understaffed. It was impossible to give the people the care they needed. There were children with rickets. Did Jon know what caused rickets? A lack of calcium and sunlight. People in Sexton took vitamin pills and calcium supplements and drank goat's milk while children in White Birch had rickets.

"Do you drink goat's milk?" Jon asked. "Do you take vitamins?"

Sarah scowled. "Daddy makes me," she said.

"And does he drink goat's milk?" Jon continued. "Does he take vitamins?"

"He has to," Sarah said. "He's the only doctor for all the people in White Birch. It's important for him to stay healthy."

"Exactly," Jon said. "That's why clavers get goat's milk and vitamins. It's more important for us to stay healthy than it is for the grubs."

"I hate you, Jon Evans," Sarah said.

Somehow it didn't seem like the right time to invite her to dinner.

Sarah was unusually quiet that morning, and Jon took advantage by inviting her and her father for dinner at his mother's. He had to know by Saturday and waiting until Friday was too risky.

"My mother says you met my sister Miranda at the clinic," he began. "You never told me."

"I can't talk about patients," Sarah said. "But I wanted to tell you. I liked her a lot. She's so proud of you."

"She is?" Jon asked. It hadn't occurred to him that Miranda thought about him at all.

"She couldn't stop talking about you," Sarah said. "How you're great with Gabe and so good at soccer. How brave you've been, living with Lisa and not with your mother." She paused. "I never think about it, what it must be like for you. I'd hate it if I had to live apart from my father. I'm sorry, Jon. I always tell you when you drive me crazy, which is practically every day, but I don't give you enough credit for who you are, what you go through."

"It's okay," Jon said. "I talk to Mom every week. And sometimes I see Alex, when he's driving the bus I'm on. Besides, they want me to be here. It was their choice. Miranda insisted I take the pass." Julie's pass, he thought. What would Julie have wanted?

"Still," Sarah said. She reached over, turning Jon so he was facing her, and then she kissed him.

Jon held on to her, trying not to think of Julie. He'd dated a few claver girls and enjoyed himself with plenty of grubber girls. He never thought about Julie, what he'd done to Julie, when he was with any of them.

Only Sarah. Because Sarah was the only girl he'd ever cared about. The only one other than Julie.

"Listen," he said, breaking away. "My mother wants you to come to dinner. Any day you want. You and your father. I'll be there. Ask your father, okay?"

He expected Sarah to look pleased, not just because it would give her a chance to go slumming but because it was his family and he was important to her.

Instead Sarah looked doubtful. "I don't know," she said.

"What do you mean you don't know?" Jon said. "We're not good enough for you?"

"No, of course not," Sarah said. "I mean, of course you are. You know what I mean. It's wonderful your mother wants to have us over for dinner. But Daddy hasn't done anything since Mother died except move here and work. It's been less than four months, Jon. It feels like forever, but it really hasn't been that long."

"It's just dinner," Jon asked. "He has to eat. Ask him, okay? Mom'll kill me if you don't."

Sarah laughed. "I'll ask him," she said, and she kissed Jon again. "I'd love to meet your mother. I'll let you know tomorrow, I promise."

"Promise," Jon said, and kissed her. But in the distance he could hear Julie crying, "No."

Friday, May 29

"Daddy says yes," Sarah said as soon as she saw Jon. "He thinks it's a wonderful idea. Monday, all right? We'll go straight from the clinic to your mother's."

"Monday," Jon said. "I'll tell Mom when she calls tomorrow."

He tried to feel happy, but all he could think of was Mom's miserable apartment. Sarah's home — Zach's grandfather's home — was a ten-room Victorian with a wraparound porch, a greenhouse, and three domestics. Sarah might bandage grubs, but she'd never eaten with one.

"It won't be fancy," he said.

"It doesn't have to be," Sarah replied. "It's family."

Jon knocked on Val's door.

"What is it?" she asked. "I'm leaving for the bus in a minute."

"I know," Jon said, handing her two books. "I took these out of the library. They're philosophy books. I thought maybe you'd like to read them."

Val looked the books over. "Aristotle," she said. "William James. That's quite the combination."

"The library didn't have much of a philosophy section," Jon replied. "I know we keep you pretty busy, but I thought you could read them before you went to bed. You can keep them as long as you want. The library works on an honor system."

"That's very sweet of you, Jon," Val said. "Thank you. I appreciate it."

"Well, you want to keep your hand in," Jon said, "so when they're looking for philosophy professors again, you'll be ready."

"Any day now," Val said. "Thank you, Jon. I'll start reading them Monday night. But now I've got to run if I want to catch the bus to White Birch."

It was funny, Jon thought. Monday night he'd be in White Birch.

He didn't think that all the philosophy in the world would make the evening any easier.

Chapter 5

Jon had never taken a grubber bus before, and he hoped he never would have to again. It was an old school bus, and it was crammed with fifty or more grubs, their stench so strong he could hardly breathe.

His claver ID badge indicated he had the right to sit wherever he wanted. He grabbed a seat, then offered it to Miranda, who took it gratefully. Jon stood, shoved between Alex and a burly grub who looked like he'd beat all the clavers to death if he ever had the chance.

There was one guard on the bus, standing next to the driver. One guard with a semiautomatic to protect him against fifty grubs. Of course if he started shooting, Jon was as likely to be killed as any of them.

Never again, he promised himself. One grubber bus trip in to appease Mom. After this he'd take a claver bus or not come in at all.

The grubs stampeded out of the bus when it reached the White Birch terminal. Miranda waited until it had emptied before getting out. Alex helped her down the steps and embraced her.

"How do you feel?" he asked. "Up to the walk?"

Miranda grinned. "What if I say no?" she replied. "You going to carry me home?"

Alex laughed. "Jon'll do the carrying," he said. "I'll navigate."

"How far is it?" Jon asked. He had never thought about how the grubs got from the terminal to their homes.

"It's not bad," Alex said. "About three miles."

"Three miles?" Jon said. "You walk that every day?"

"Twice a day," Alex replied.

"You get used to it," Miranda said. "It would be okay if the air was cleaner. Us pregnant women are supposed to get our exercise."

"You're on your feet all day long," Alex said. "When Carlos and I get our truck, you'll stay home, Miranda. You and Laura. You'll be ladies of leisure."

"What about that place Matt talked about?" Jon said.

Alex shook his head. "Not here," he said softly. "Not with so many people around."

"We haven't decided anything," Miranda said. "No decisions until the baby's born."

"Do you have a boy's name yet?" Jon asked.

Miranda laughed. "Tell him your latest one, Alex," she said.

"Francis Patrick Xavier Mulrooney Morales," Alex said.

"What?" Jon said.

"See," Miranda said. "I told you, darling. It's a ridiculous name. Worse than Harold."

"Father Mulrooney saved my life," Alex said. "My sanity and my life. I owe him everything."

"You don't owe him your firstborn's name," Miranda said. "It better be a girl."

"You really thinking about Harold?" Jon asked. That had been Dad's name, but everyone called him Hal.

"As much as we're thinking about Francis Patrick Xavier Mulrooney," Miranda said. "I like Daniel. I think it sounds good with Morales. But Alex doesn't want me to name the baby for an old boyfriend."

"You don't see me suggesting an old girlfriend's name," Alex said.

"You don't have any old girlfriends," Miranda said. "Except me."

"She's right," Alex said to Jon. "I was saving myself for her. I just didn't know it."

"Speaking of girlfriends," Miranda said, "Sarah seems very nice. Are you serious about her, Jon?"

"There's no point being serious about anyone," Jon said. "If Lisa doesn't pass her evaluation, I'll leave Sexton with her."

"Mom would hate it if you did," Miranda said.

"He won't have to," Alex said. "One of his friends would take him in. Gabe, too. They'd find a home for him in Sexton."

"That would be awful for Lisa," Miranda said. "Gabe's her life. If she had to leave him behind, it would kill her."

"Well, we won't have that problem," Alex said. "No one's kicking us out of White Birch. Little Mulrooney is stuck with us."

Miranda ignored him. "Is Lisa worried?" she asked. "When will she hear?"

"Pretty soon," Jon said. "And yeah, she's worried. She hasn't decided what she'll do about Gabe if she has to leave."

"There's no choice," Alex said. "Take Gabe away from Sexton? If she really loves him, she'll let him be adopted. There's no life for kids here."

"Our kid is going to live here," Miranda said.

"Our kid doesn't have a choice," Alex said. "Jon, tell Miranda what Gabe's life is like. The food. The toys. The clean clothes."

"Gabe's lonely," Jon said. "He has Carrie, but that's it. There are so few kids in Sexton, little ones, I mean."

"But the women must be having babies now," Miranda said.

"I don't see pregnant women on the claver buses," Alex said. "Do you, Jon?"

"I don't know," Jon said. "I never really thought about it."

"I thought claver women could have as many babies as they wanted," Miranda said. "They eat so much better. And didn't you say once, their houses have air purification systems? I thought I remembered you saying that, Jon."

Jon nodded.

"It's still a hard world," Alex said. He gave Miranda a squeeze. "We're the lucky ones."

"We'll all be lucky," Miranda said. "Lisa will pass her evaluation. And you'll get your truck, Alex. Carlos is coming for a visit, Jon. You'll have to come and meet him."

"When's he coming?" Jon asked.

"In a few weeks," Alex replied. "I keep telling Miranda he'll love her, but she's nervous about meeting him."

Julie had loved Carlos, her oldest brother. She'd been his favorite. Spending time with Alex was hard enough. Jon wasn't eager to face Carlos, even though there was no way Carlos could know what Jon had done.

"How much longer before you can get your truck?" Jon asked.

"Months," Alex replied. "Years."

"First we have to save the money," Miranda said. "And after I have the baby, I won't be able to go back to work right away."

"There's talk they won't reopen the high school next fall," Alex said. "In which case, Laura will be out of work, also."

"Mom said they'd moved the high school to the elementary school," Jon said. "Why can't they keep it there?"

"Maybe they will," Miranda replied. "It's all rumors."

Jon had resented how deeply Mom cared about her students. But he'd never intended the school to be closed permanently, for her to lose her teaching job. Would she have to get a grub job? Miranda worked ten hours a day in the greenhouses, with an hour commute each way and a three-mile walk to and from the bus terminal. How could Mom survive that?

"If I had the money, I'd give it to you," he mumbled.

"Thanks, Jon," Alex said. "But we'll need more than money. There's paperwork to be filled out, and we have to be approved."

"You will be," Miranda said. "Your record is perfect, darling. Carlos was a Marine, and now he's a guard. You're just the kind of people who should own a truck. They'll have to give you the permit."

"Unless some claver's fat-ass brother-in-law wants one," Alex said. "Then it's 'Wait your turn, grub.'"

Jon had never heard Alex speak that way before. It didn't seem to shock Miranda, though.

Instead she patted Alex's arm. "You'll get your truck," she said. "And we'll make a good life for ourselves. And for little Mulrooney."

Alex stopped and gave her a hug. "Daniel," he said. "Daniel Mulrooney Morales."

Miranda laughed. "See, Jon?" she said. "Alex pretends to be such a tough guy, but I've got him wrapped around my little finger."

Alex kissed her little finger. Jon felt jealous. He would never love a girl the way Alex loved Miranda. That was the price he'd pay for what he did to Julie.

They walked most of the way in silence, except for Alex's occasional coughing. They slowed down a couple of times so Miranda could catch her breath. It was hard on Jon, too. He was used to running around in fetid air, but this time there was no oxygen tank to cleanse his lungs with.

The baby will never survive, he thought. Alex might not either, the way he was coughing. And what would that do to Miranda?

She seemed to read his thoughts. "You're not used to this," she said. "But after a while you don't notice. We're really very lucky, Jon. We have each other and Mom, and we know Matt and Syl and Carlos and Gabe are all right. And we have a future. I tell the baby that every day. Things are going to get better. Alex will get his truck, and we'll find a safer, healthier place to live."

Alex laughed, but there was no humor in it. "Miranda pictures the world as some great big enclave," he said. "Room enough for everybody."

"Maybe not tomorrow," she said. "Or a year from now or even five years from now. I know everything that's happened can't be changed. But look at Jon. See how healthy he is, how strong. That's how our baby is going to be. Gabe started out in much worse conditions, and he's doing wonderfully. It can happen. We'll make it happen."

"Or die trying," Alex said. "Or die not trying."

"Don't," Miranda said. "Alex, please. Jon's here, and we're going to a dinner party." She managed a small laugh. "Mom and her parties," she said. "She spent all of yesterday cleaning and shopping. I've never seen the apartment look so good."

"It helped take her mind off of things," Alex said. "So what's this Sarah like, Jon? How long has she lived in Sexton?"

They spent the rest of the walk talking about Sarah, Lisa, school, soccer. Jon felt much better about things—until he got to

Mom's apartment and saw her sitting at the kitchen table having an animated discussion with Sarah and her father.

It made perfect sense that they would have gotten there before him. The clinic was only a few blocks away, while he had the commute and the three-mile walk. But Jon had imagined himself there when Sarah arrived, to reassure her that she shouldn't be uncomfortable, that soon she'd be back in Sexton where she belonged.

Sarah didn't look remotely uncomfortable. She and her father rose when Jon, Miranda, and Alex entered the room. Jon could see the resemblance right away. Sarah and her father shared the same sandy hair and inquisitive green eyes. Introductions were made, hands were shaken, and before Jon knew it, Mom was fussing at the stove while continuing her conversation.

"Wine?" Alex asked, seeing the bottle on the table.

"My contribution," Dr. Goldman said. "I brought a red and a white, since I didn't know what dinner would be. Laura's agreed to keep the unopened bottle for next time."

"White with chicken," Mom said. "Isn't it amazing the things you remember?"

Clavers didn't have to pay for their groceries, so Jon could only guess how much the chicken had cost. He saw Alex and Miranda exchanging glances, and Alex shrugging. Dinner for six, Jon thought. Who knew when Mom would eat next?

"I borrowed the table settings from our downstairs neighbors," Mom said as she began serving the chicken and vegetables. "The apartment came with service for four. White meat or dark, Jeffrey?"

"White," Dr. Goldman said.

Jon couldn't get over the fact that Mom was already on a

first-name basis with Sarah's father. Or that Sarah was chatting with Miranda like they were old friends.

"We kept all our old china when we moved to Sexton," Sarah said. "Daddy insisted. I have no idea why."

"It was your grandmother's," Dr. Goldman replied. "And very important to your mother." He took a bite of chicken. "You know, we never used the good china back home. My wife didn't want to risk putting it in the dishwasher. But now, with the domestics washing the dishes, that's not an issue. Sometimes I feel like we've gone from the twenty-first century back to the nineteenth."

"The nineteenth wasn't that great," Alex said, helping himself to a slice of potato bread. "Child labor. No universal suffrage."

"No indoor plumbing," Miranda said. "I'll take our twenty-first century with all its problems as long as I have a bathroom." She laughed. "Oh, Mom. Alex's agreed to Daniel. Daniel Mulrooney Morales."

"It's a girl," Mom said. "I just know it. My first granddaughter."

"It is kind of nineteenth century not to know if it's a boy or a girl by now," Miranda declared.

"I can't wait to have babies," Sarah said. "Dozens and dozens of them."

"You can wait," her father said. "High school, then med school, and then babies. As many as you want."

"I'd like to have more than one," Miranda said. "Maybe because there were three of us growing up."

"I was one of four," Alex said. "Let's see how we do with one before we start adding on."

"It's natural for girls to want to have children now," Mom

said. "Like the baby boom after World War Two. Offering life, after so much death."

"But the 1950s were a time of prosperity," Alex pointed out. "Now we don't know one day to the next if there'll be enough food to survive."

"Stop it," Miranda said, putting her hands on her belly as though to keep her baby protected. "Jon, do you remember when Dad and Lisa came to visit? She was pregnant with Gabe, and we got to talking about the future, how bad things might be, and she walked away from the table? She couldn't bear to listen." She shook her head. "I didn't understand. I didn't understand anything in those days. But now I know just how she felt. My baby, Daniel or Liana, is going to live in a better world. I won't hear otherwise."

"You're right," Dr. Goldman said. "We can't accept that things will always be bad. If we do, we won't fight to make things better."

"I'm sorry," Alex said. "But that's easy for you to say. You have your family china and the domestics to wash them. You have college for your daughter. You'll be driven home in a private car to a house with clean air. Sure, you'd like things to get better. But we dream of what you have now. And we know we'll never have it."

"I know we're spoiled," Sarah said. "Jon and me and everyone in Sexton. But I really think we'd give up some of what we have so everyone could live better. Wouldn't you, Jon? Eat a little less so your family could eat more?"

"You're putting Jon on the spot," Dr. Goldman said. "What's he supposed to say, no, he won't? And even if he would give up some of his food, how would his family get it? We're not there yet, Sarah. We're not at a point where we can make those kinds of sacrifices work."

"You're right," Alex said. "Right now all the sacrifices go one way."

"Alex," Miranda said sharply. "Dr. Goldman, I'm sorry. Alex is tired. He hasn't had a day off in weeks."

"It's not slave labor," Alex said with a grin. "Just making as much money as we can before the baby's born."

"You're working too hard," Mom said. "Take Sunday off."

Alex shook his head. "They tip better on Sundays," he replied. "I'll take a few days off when Carlos comes."

"Daddy works too hard," Sarah said. "He'd be at the clinic on Saturdays if I'd let him."

"One doctor for all of White Birch," her father said. "I'd clone myself if I could."

"They're doing a lot with cloning," Jon said. "Plants mostly, but chickens and goats, too. The animals we need to survive."

"I wish they'd clone cows," Mom said. "I really miss hamburgers."

Everyone laughed.

"You miss the strangest things," Alex said. "I miss the smell of a bodega. My uncle owned one. I never liked going there, but now I think about all the different smells, the fruits, the spices, even the beer and the cigarettes."

Miranda nodded. "I miss my high school cafeteria," she said. "If you'd told me four years ago I'd ever be nostalgic for the cafeteria, I would've said you're crazy. But we were so alive in there. So much drama, so much laughing."

"I will never ever miss the Sexton cafeteria," Sarah said so solemnly that everyone burst out laughing. "All right. It's not the worst place in the world. It only feels that way. What do you miss most, Jon?"

"Baseball," Jon said, without even thinking about it.

"Well, that's flattering," Miranda said. "You miss baseball more than your family?"

"Jon has his family," Mom said. "Right here."

"I thought you might say Julie," Alex said. "The two of you were pretty close."

I don't miss Julie, Jon thought. She haunts me. But all he said was, "I think about her a lot. But if you start listing all the people you miss, you'll never stop."

"Speaking of missing, we're going to miss the car they're sending us," Dr. Goldman said, standing up. "Come on, kids. We need to get going."

"I hope you'll come again," Mom said. "And not just for the wine."

"I'd like to," Dr. Goldman said. "I haven't enjoyed myself so much in a long time. Alex, Miranda, hang in there. Better times are ahead."

Jon hugged Mom and Miranda. He'd be riding back with Sarah and her father in a chauffeured car, back to Sexton, to school, to vitamin supplements and purified air, chicken twice a week, and domestics to do all the cleaning. Back to the life Julie had given him in exchange for her own.

"Your mother's wonderful," Sarah said as they sat in the car, driving out of White Birch. "I like Alex, too. I wish he and Miranda could have what we have."

"Someday they will," her father said. "As long as you and Jon and all the young people work toward it."

"We will," Sarah said. "Jon promised me we would."

Jon nodded in the darkness. It was easier to agree than to tell the truth. They'd never give up what they had. Sarah was the only person he knew who thought grubs were entitled to a better life. And for all her talking, Jon didn't think she'd trade places with

anyone in White Birch. She liked her purified air and vitamin supplements as much as the rest of them.

"Someday," he said because he knew Sarah wanted to hear it.
And what difference did another lie make? He was living a life of
them. That's why Julie haunted him day and night.

Chapter 6

"Who's Julie?" Sarah asked first thing that morning.

Jon wasn't surprised. He knew Sarah would be asking. You promise her to solve the world's problems, and she still wasn't going to be satisfied.

"Alex's sister," he replied.

"Is that how Miranda met Alex?" Sarah asked. "You knew his sister?"

"No," Jon said. "It's complicated."

"I'm listening," Sarah said, and Jon knew she was. Whether he wanted her to or not.

"We lived in Pennsylvania," he said. "Well, you know that. Dad and Lisa had tried to make it west, but they couldn't, so they came back. Gabe was a baby. They met people on the road, this really nice guy named Charlie, and Alex and Julie. They all came east, to our house."

"And you and Julie became close?" Sarah said.

"Everyone paired off," Jon replied. "Matt had married Syl a few weeks before, and Dad was with Lisa. Miranda didn't give Alex a chance to say no. Even Mom hung out with Charlie. So it felt natural, Julie and me. She was just a year younger. I liked her a lot." He paused at the memory. "Maybe I loved her. I said I did. I was almost fifteen. Can you be in love that young?"

"We didn't have a chance to be young," Sarah said.

"No," Jon said. "We didn't."

"So you loved Julie," Sarah said. "What happened to her, Jon?"

There was more than one answer to that question, but Jon knew what he would never tell Sarah, never tell anyone.

"Dad and Lisa and Alex and Julie and Charlie moved into an empty house," Jon said. "I was there all the time, or Julie was at our place. Mom and Dad got along, and Mom was fixated on making sure Lisa had enough to eat so she could nurse Gabe."

Sarah nodded. "I can picture that," she said. "And Miranda and Alex falling in love."

"The town we lived in was still getting food," Jon said. "Every Monday you could go in and get a few bags. So Julie and I went together. On our way back . . ."

This was hard. It didn't seem to matter that he'd rehearsed what to say, how to say it. The words didn't want to come out.

Sarah touched him gently on his arm. "It's okay," she said.

It wasn't okay. It would never be okay. "There was a tornado," Jon said flatly. "We got caught in it. I tried to hold on to Julie, but the wind picked her up. Remember plastic bags, how the wind could make them dance? It was like that. Julie fell wrong. I don't know. She broke her neck or her spine. She was paralyzed. She was conscious, but she couldn't move."

"Oh, Jon," Sarah said.

"We took her back to our house," Jon continued. "Dad and Matt and me. Alex got lost in the storm. It took him a couple of days to get back to the house." He forced himself not to think of Alex.

"Did Julie die?" Sarah asked softly.

"Not right away," Jon said. "She lived another day or so, and then she died in her sleep. Miranda was with her. Julie couldn't do anything for herself. Someone had to be with her all the time. Everyone took turns."

"That must have been horrible for you," Sarah said. "Staying with her, seeing her lying there, helpless."

"I never saw her," Jon said. "The house Dad and Lisa were living in collapsed in the storm. Lisa and Gabe and Charlie were stuck in the cellar. Then Charlie died, so it was just Lisa and Gabe. We had to pull all the rubble off the cellar roof before it collapsed on them. That was all we did, pull the rubble away. I didn't see Julie. I worked on saving Lisa and Gabe."

"That had to be done," Sarah said. "You did what had to be done."

"No," Jon said. "I mean, yes, we had to get Lisa and Gabe out. But that wasn't why I didn't sit with Julie. I was scared to. I'm a coward, Sarah. Deep down, that's all I am. A coward. I told Julie I loved her, but when she was helpless and dying and her brother was missing, I couldn't make myself see her. Lisa was an excuse. Mom and Matt and Miranda were used to treating me like a baby. They probably felt they were protecting me by not making me say good-bye to Julie. And I let them. I let Julie die without seeing me."

"Jon," Sarah said, and he could see how much she wanted to comfort him.

"No," he said. "You know why I'm here today, why I'm walking to the bus with you? I took Julie's pass. Alex had three. He gave two to Lisa, for her and Gabe. Julie was supposed to live with them. Lisa loved Julie like a daughter. Only Julie died, and everyone said I should use the last one. Because I was the youngest, and they were all in the habit of protecting me. I'm here on Julie's pass. I couldn't even face her when she was dying, and I get to live here and eat the food and go to school, and Miranda's going to have Alex's baby in that hovel."

"Jon, the apartment isn't that bad," Sarah said. "And Miranda and Alex won't live there forever. You loved Julie?"

Jon nodded.

"Did she love you?"

He nodded.

"Then she'd want you to have her pass," Sarah said. "She'd want you to have the chance she couldn't have."

"That's what everyone told me," Jon said. "So I wouldn't feel bad about living in Sexton while they were stuck in White Birch."

Sarah stood on her tiptoes and kissed Jon on his cheek. "I'm sorry Julie died," she said. "I'm sorry for Alex and for you and Lisa. But I'm glad you're here. You're my lifeline, Jon. I need you so much."

You don't know me, Jon thought. Nobody does.

The only one who had was Julie. And she wasn't around to tell everyone who Jon really was.

Thursday, June 4

Dr. Carlyle had been a professor of political science at Baumann Christian College, previously located twenty miles east of White Birch. The college, like most of the colleges in America, had ceased to exist four years ago. Dr. Carlyle, like the rest of the teachers, was not a claver, and so he kept his home in White Birch and was now forced to commute to Sexton, like a grub, to teach civics to the claver teenagers.

Jon understood why so much of the school time was devoted

to the sciences—botany and biology, chemistry, even physics. He understood the math they were taught was practical, intended for engineering. If you were lucky enough to be a Sexton teenager, it was presumed you'd go to Sexton University and learn all that you could to further their agriculture. New and better greenhouses needed to be built, water supplies to be expanded, and better sources of electrical power to be designed.

English was taught because no matter what field of science they went into after graduation, they'd be expected to be literate. Jon liked the English classes. Mom had been a writer before it all happened, and Matt loved reading sci-fi. There were always books in the house. English classes helped Jon feel connected to the world and the family he no longer lived with.

But civics was a waste of time. For three years now Dr. Carlyle had lectured them on his particular view of history, complaining to them about the repulsive nature of grubs. His quarrel wasn't with the government that hadn't selected him to be a claver. It was with the unwashed, uneducated grubs who had taken over White Birch and made every day of his life a living hell.

Jon had more sympathy for him now that he'd ridden a grubber bus, but even so, Dr. Carlyle was a bore and the class a waste of time.

It was, however, the only time during the school day when the students were given the opportunity to talk. So Jon wasn't surprised to see Sarah raise her hand, although he dreaded hearing what she had to say.

"Miss Goldman wishes to speak," Dr. Carlyle declared. "Yes, Miss Goldman, what is it?"

"I do my afterschool at the White Birch Clinic," Sarah said. "It's terribly understaffed. I was hoping some of you might consider changing your afterschools to clinic work. We can use all the help we can get."

Amber Healey raised her hand but didn't wait for Dr. Carlyle to call on her. "You actually expect us to work in White Birch?" she asked. "Touching those filthy grubs?"

"I work hard at my afterschool," Jennifer Egan said, "tutoring the first and second graders here. That's valuable work. The children are our future."

"There are children in White Birch, too," Sarah said. "With diseases claver kids don't get, like asthma and pneumonia."

"That's not our fault," Zachary said. "We breathe the same lousy air they do."

"That's right," Elizabeth Jenkins said. "But we know enough to take care of our children, not let them grow up like wild animals."

"Most grubs wouldn't even go to church if the guards didn't make them," Amber said. "They'd rather get drunk."

"I'd rather get drunk, too," Ryan said, and everyone except Dr. Carlyle and Sarah laughed.

"Why do we even have a clinic for the grubs?" Tyler asked.

"Because they're human beings," Sarah said.

"I don't know," Ryan said. "You ever see a naked grubber girl?"

This time even Dr. Carlyle laughed.

"Maybe there shouldn't be a clinic," Tyler said. "We need the strong, healthy grubs to do the manual labor, and we pay them enough for their food and rent and potka. But the weak grubs, the useless ones, are a drain on all of us. Why not let them die naturally so there'd be more resources for the ones who actually work?"

Half the kids in the class burst into applause.

"It's an interesting question," Dr. Carlyle said. "I won't ask your response, Miss Goldman, because I know what it is. Let's hear from someone else. You, Mr. Evans. As our resident slip, do you think there should be a clinic for grubs?"

"I can't give an objective answer," Jon replied. "I have family in White Birch. They use the clinic."

"Evans is half grub," Ryan said. "You can smell it."

The kids laughed.

"What if you didn't have family there?" Mr. Carlyle persisted. "Would you think there should be a clinic?"

What Jon thought was he hated Mr. Carlyle's guts, and he wasn't too fond of his friends, either. The clinic was important to Sarah, and Sarah was important to Jon.

But Lisa hadn't heard about her evaluation yet. She and Gabe had to be his first priority. Sarah and her ideals would have to wait.

"I think if we lived in a perfect world, everyone would have health care," he said. "But this isn't a perfect world. People who are a lot smarter than me make the decisions. If they think the clinic is a good idea, I'm not going to disagree with them. If they ever decide the clinic isn't a good idea, I won't disagree with them, either."

"So what you're saying is you'll just go along with whatever you're told," Sarah said. "Follow the rules and don't question."

"Are you suggesting, Miss Goldman, that you are smarter than the people who make the rules?" Dr. Carlyle demanded.

"Don't you think you're smarter than they are?" Sarah asked.

"Miss Goldman, you are very close to treason," Dr. Carlyle said.

"I don't see why," Sarah persisted. "You're a college professor. You have a PhD. You complain about the way you're treated."

"I complain, as you call it, about the people I am forced to share my hometown with," Dr. Carlyle said. "The dregs of humanity, looking for nothing but handouts."

"They work ten hours a day six days a week," Sarah said.

"So do clavers," Jennifer said. "My father works longer than that. I never see him. And he's doing real work, valuable work. Our domestics eat our food and sleep in our homes, and if they had their way, we'd be serving them."

"That's right," Amber said. "Grubs wouldn't have anything to eat if it weren't for us. And now you're saying we should give up our afterschools to hold some grub's hand and tell her not to work so hard."

"You're not from around here, Sarah," Jennifer said. "You don't understand how things are. You should keep quiet, not tell us what we should do."

"You're right," Sarah said. "I'm not from here. Maybe because I'm not, I understand things better than you do."

"You have some nerve," Amber said. "Thinking you're smarter than we are because you're from back east."

"It's not hard to be smarter than you," Sarah muttered.

Jon willed her to shut up. But he never could make Sarah do what he wanted.

"Let me explain something," Sarah said. "There is nobody, *nobody,* important living in Sexton. Not a senator or a judge or a governor. You think you're important because you have more than everyone else around here. But you have nothing compared to other enclaves. You know what those clavers think of you, those senators and judges? They think you're farmers, grub farmers. All those greenhouses that are going up? They're to feed the governors, not us. You're one drought away from losing your fancy homes and your domestics." She shook her head. "You have a lot more in common with the people in White Birch than you do with the people with power. Today's claver is tomorrow's grub."

"Are you calling me a grub?" Amber shrieked.

"I wouldn't insult grubs by calling you one," Sarah said.

"Grubby, grubby, grubby," Tyler started chanting. It was stupid and meaningless, but the rest of the class joined in, pointing at Sarah and calling her grubby.

Jon mouthed the word but didn't say it. It was a ridiculous compromise, but he didn't know what else to do.

The lunch bell rang as the class was getting louder and louder. Sarah was the first to grab her books and stand up. As she walked down the aisle, Zachary stuck his leg out, and she stumbled over it. Even Dr. Carlyle burst out laughing.

"Come on, Evans," Tyler said. "Let's see what happens to Little Miss Grub in the cafeteria."

Jon didn't want to see. But he had no choice.

Sarah went to the table where she always ate her lunch alone. Jon followed Tyler and his teammates to their table.

Amber walked over to Sarah and spit at her. The other kids in the cafeteria cheered, and Amber bowed.

Luke got up and, taking his lunch plate with him, walked toward Sarah's table.

"This'll be good," Ryan said. "Wanna bet he dumps his lunch on her?"

"Let's all do it," Zachary said. "Let her know what we think of grub lovers."

But all Luke did was stand by Sarah's side and ask if he could join her. Jon and his teammates watched in silence as Luke sat at Sarah's table and began talking with her.

"He's crazy," Tyler said. "Come on, guys. We've got soccer practice in a few minutes. Coach'll whip him back in shape."

Jon longed to join Sarah and Luke, but he didn't dare. When Lisa passes her evaluation, he promised himself. Then he'd be as brave as Luke.

Friday, June 5

When Jon arrived at Sarah's house after breakfast, he saw her standing on the front porch.

"Go away," she said.

"Sarah, I'm sorry," Jon said.

"I don't care if you're sorry," she said. "And I don't need to hear your excuses."

"It isn't an excuse," Jon said. "Lisa hasn't heard about the evaluation yet. I can't do anything that might hurt her chances."

Sarah shook her head. "Today it's the evaluation," she said. "Next week it'll be because you're a slip. You always have that one to fall back on, don't you, Jon?"

"I am a slip," Jon said. "You have no idea what that's like."

"It's an excuse, Jon," Sarah said. "You're a coward, just like you told me. When you didn't visit Julie, that wasn't because you were a slip or Lisa had an evaluation. It was because deep down inside you're scared. You're weak and cowardly, and I don't want to see you ever again."

"Sarah," Jon pleaded.

"Go away," she said. "And don't ever come back. I'll call for a guard, Jon, if you don't leave right now. I'm not kidding."

"I'm sorry," he said again, but he began walking away. He turned back once and saw Sarah standing there absolutely still.

Julie wasn't the only one who understood him, he thought. Sarah had known him for a month, and she knew him every bit as well, and now hated him just as much.

Chapter 7

Jon had never seen Lisa look so happy, so excited.

"You passed your evaluation," he said.

Lisa raced over and hugged him. "I passed!" she cried. "We're safe for another three years."

"That's great, Lisa," Jon said. "You deserve it."

"Oh, Jon, it's even better than that," she said. "Sit down. No, I'll sit down. No, I'm too excited to sit down."

Jon laughed. "We'll both sit down," he said. "Tell me what happened. How did you find out?"

"They called me in," Lisa said. "I can't wait to tell Gabe. I know he won't understand, but I want to tell him anyway. Jon, I didn't just pass. I got a promotion!"

"You're kidding," Jon said. "Lisa, that's amazing."

"I'm now head of domestic placements," she said. "My boss got transferred. I can't believe they hired me. I thought for sure they'd hire someone's sister or cousin. I thought they'd hire the relative and I'd be struck having to train some idiot, or worse still, they'd say no to my evaluation to justify not giving me the job. It doesn't matter. Maybe no relative wanted the job. Either way, I got it."

"What are the benefits?" Jon asked.

"They offered me a choice," Lisa replied. "I could have a bigger house, better neighborhood, but I love this neighborhood, so why should I want to move? And we don't need a bigger house. So I decided against that right away. Instead we're getting a personal greenhouse. Jon, we'll be able to grow our own fruits and vegetables. Herbs. Do you know how much I've missed fresh herbs?"

"That's great," Jon said.

Lisa laughed. "Don't worry, you won't have to work in it," she said, but then she lowered her voice. "Whichever I chose, I'd be getting a third domestic. I had this amazing idea, Jon. I'm going to arrange it so that Miranda gets the job."

"Miranda?" Jon said.

"Quiet," Lisa said. "Val might hear you."

"I'm sorry," Jon whispered. "But Miranda working here?"

"It makes a lot of sense, Jon," Lisa replied. "The baby could share the nursery with Gabe. Carrie can look after both of them while Miranda works in the greenhouse."

"What about Alex?" Jon asked, still trying to understand how it would work.

"He'd keep the apartment, I guess," Lisa said. "Miranda and the baby can take the bus Saturday nights with Val and Carrie. But Miranda wouldn't have to work nearly so hard, and she wouldn't have the commute, and she'd be able to look in on her baby at mealtimes. She'll eat better here, and the air would be better for the baby. You can see all that, can't you, Jon?"

Jon remembered what Alex had said about Gabe being better off in Sexton than with his mother. This wasn't exactly the same. Miranda would still be a grub, and her baby would be a grub's baby, not a claver's. But Lisa would treat them well, and things would be easier for them.

He wasn't sure how he felt about having his sister being a domestic where he lived. It felt weird, wrong. But if Miranda was in the greenhouse and he was at school or at practice, he'd hardly see her anyway.

"Where would she sleep?" he asked. "Is there room for her?"

"We'll convert the garage," Lisa said. "It's wired for electricity. We'll put a heater in and a bed, some furniture, a lamp. A crib, of course. It'll be nice and cozy for both of them."

The garage had been his place, his and Sarah's. And now that Lisa had passed her evaluation, there was nothing to keep him from getting Sarah back. She needed him as much as he needed her. He'd make her forgive him.

"How about if I move into the garage?" he asked. "Miranda could have my room."

Lisa shook her head. "That's sweet, Jon, but it wouldn't work. No one can know that she's family, or we'll all get in trouble. Besides, in a year you'll pass your evaluation and move into the Sexton dorm. Carrie will get transferred, and Gabe will move into your room. Miranda and her baby can have the nursery then."

"Have you talked to Miranda?" Jon asked.

Lisa shook her head. "I'll go there on Sunday and talk to all of them," she said. "Laura's going to be the hardest one to convince. She's so possessive of Miranda. But I'll talk her into it. It's what's best for Miranda and the baby. Laura will see that."

Good news, weird news, Jon thought. My sister the grub.

But Lisa was right. In a year, he'd either be in the Sexton dorm or thrown out of Sexton. And in a year Alex might have his truck. Or he and Miranda might decide to move to that place Matt had told them about. Or the moon might crash into the earth and they'd all be dead anyway.

"Congratulations," he said to Lisa. "Now go tell Gabe the good news."

Wednesday, June 10

Jon walked over to the table where Luke and Sarah were sitting. "Lisa passed her evaluation," he said to Luke, pretending not to notice that Sarah was there. "She even got a promotion."

"That must be a relief," Luke said. "I know you've been worrying about it."

Jon nodded. "She's feeling a lot better about things," he said. "I am, too."

Sarah kept still.

"That's it," Jon said. "Just thought you'd want to know."

But as he walked back to Tyler's table, he could sense Sarah looking at him.

Things are about to get better, he told himself. He'd learned from his lessons. He'd be the man Sarah wanted him to be and then she would have to forgive him.

Friday, June 12

Luke lived almost a mile away, but there was no bus that went through the neighborhoods, so Jon walked there. He'd been to Luke's a few times but never without an invitation. He didn't think Luke would mind, though.

He didn't mind, but he was surprised. "What are you doing here?" he asked. "Is something the matter?"

"I wanted to talk to you," Jon said. "I figured this was the best place."

"Come on in," Luke said. "We'll go to my room."

Jon thought about the offer Lisa had had for a bigger house. Luke's felt like a mansion. His brother lived in the Sexton dorm, so it was just Luke, his parents, and five domestics. Jon wondered how many of them were professors of philosophy.

"Okay," Luke said. "What's up?"

"Could you close the door?" Jon asked. "I need to talk to you in private."

Luke shrugged, but he closed the door, then sat down on a chair that faced Jon's.

Jon took a deep breath. "I can't stop thinking about the grubber school," he said. "How we burned it down. Now that my stepmother's passed her evaluation, well, I could go to the authorities, tell them what happened. But I decided to talk to you first."

Luke got up and opened the door. "Marie!" he called. "Could you get my father for me? Ask him to come to my room."

"Yes, Mr. Luke," Marie said.

"What did you do that for?" Jon asked.

"Wait," Luke said. "We'll talk it over with my father."

Jon felt a sharp longing for a father of his own to talk things over with. Not that he hadn't keep secrets from Dad. But maybe if he were still alive, Jon wouldn't have made such a mess of things.

He and Luke sat in uncomfortable silence until Dr. Barner arrived. Jon rose, and Dr. Barner smiled and shook his hand. "This is a nice surprise," he said. "Are you joining us for supper, Jon?"

"Oh no," Jon said. "No, thank you. I came here to talk something over with Luke."

"Jon wants to go to the authorities," Luke said to his father. "To tell them about setting the school on fire."

"He knows?" Jon said.

"I know," Dr. Barner replied. "Luke told me after church on the eighteenth. He and I talked about it at great length."

"I asked Dad if I should go to the authorities," Luke said.

"I told him he should," Dr. Barner said. "But only if all five of you agreed. I'll tell you the same thing, Jon. Either all of you go or none of you goes."

"Dad said I'd have to tell them who was there with me," Luke said. "I couldn't lie and say I did it by myself. I'd never get away with it. They'd ask questions, like where did I get the matches. And there's no way I'd rat on my friends."

"I'm not saying what you did was right, Jon," Dr. Barner said. "But Luke was protecting the old man. The grubs who trashed the school before you got there had no such reason. They were simply drunken vandals."

There was no way of knowing who had trashed the school. Everyone was drunk that night, clavers as well as grubs. "The school was a mess," Jon said. "But it could have been cleaned up. What we did was irreversible."

"Exactly," Dr. Barner replied. "There's nothing you can say or do that will change matters. So why throw your life away? I'll say to you what I said to Luke. The important thing is to accept what you did was wrong and move on. I had him promise never to do anything like that again. I think you'll feel better if you make that same promise."

"I promise," Jon said, waiting to feel better.

"Very good," Dr. Barner said. "You're sure you don't want to stay for dinner, Jon? There's always room for one more."

"No, thank you," Jon said. "Lisa's expecting me. And Gabe'll be disappointed if I'm not there."

"Some other time, then," Dr. Barner said. "Come, Luke. We don't want to keep your mother waiting."

"I'll be there in a minute," Luke replied. "I'll see Jon out."

"Don't take too long," Dr. Barner said. "You don't want your dinner to get cold."

"I won't," Luke said. "Come on, Jon."

Jon followed Luke down the stairs and outside. "I didn't want to say this in front of Dad," Luke said softly. "But I talked to Tyler yesterday. I've wanted to for a while, and when you said Lisa had passed, I figured the time was right."

"What did he say?" Jon asked, knowing he wasn't going to like the answer.

"He said his father thinks the grubs burned the school down," Luke replied. "And Tyler wants to keep it that way. Tyler can't go after me. We're family. But he said if either one of us talks, he'll see to it you're sent to the mines. That family of yours in White Birch? They'll end up there, too, like those grubber women who complained about Zach's grandfather. Everyone knew they were telling the truth. That's why he got thrown out of Sexton. But the grubs were sent to the mines anyway."

Jon thought of Alex and Miranda and their baby. He had no right to destroy their lives. "I'll keep quiet," he said. "I swear it."

"There's something else," Luke said. "Sarah."

"What about her?" Jon asked.

"Look, I know about the two of you," Luke declared. "Sarah talks to me."

"I thought now that Lisa's okay, I'd try to make it up to Sarah," Jon said.

"That's what she wants," Luke replied. "But you can't let that happen. Tyler asked me if anything was going on between the two of you. I said no, but I don't think he believed me. He'll hurt her, Jon, just to show you he's in charge."

"But she wants to get back together?" Jon asked.

"She says she loves you," Luke replied. "If you love her, you'll leave her alone."

Jon knew he had one weapon left, and that was to let Sarah know the truth about him. "Tell her I want to see her," he said. "To come to my house so we can talk."

"Jon," Luke said.

"I know what I'm doing," Jon said. "I'll see to it Sarah never looks at me again. But I have to talk to her first. Tomorrow night, after the grubs go to White Birch. I'll be waiting for her."

"I hope you know what you're doing," Luke said.

"I do," Jon said. "Get her there, okay?"

"Luke!" Dr. Barner yelled. "What's taking you so long?"

"I'm coming!" Luke shouted. "I'll do what I can," he whispered, then turned his back on Jon and entered the house.

"The truth shall set you free," Jon told himself as he walked back to Lisa's. It would set Sarah free, at least. Not even the truth could do much for him at this point.

He'd be all right. He'd survived hunger, disease, the loss of his home, the loss of his father. He'd survive this as well.

But he'd need all the strength and courage he had to protect the people he loved.

His misdeeds had cost Julie her life.

He couldn't let the same thing happen twice.

Saturday, June 13

Val and Carrie had already left for White Birch when the doorbell rang. Lisa was upstairs with Gabe, so Jon answered the door.

"Sarah," he said, silently thanking Luke.

"Luke said you wanted to talk," she said. "That I should come over tonight."

Jon nodded. "I'll meet you in the garage," he said, looking around the street to make sure no one had seen her. "We can talk in private there."

Sarah nodded and walked away.

Jon called upstairs to Lisa to say he'd be out for a few minutes. Then he left the house, silently walking to the garage, making certain he wasn't spotted.

"I'm only here because Luke told me to come," Sarah began. "He's been a real friend to me."

"To me, too," Jon said. "Sarah, I know I can't make it up to you, the way I've behaved. I've thought about everything you said to me, how I was weak, a coward, and I know you're right. But I have to tell you that I love you. I was too scared to tell you that before, too weak, too cowardly. I know I'm just a slip; I'll never deserve your love. But I needed you to know."

"I don't care that you're a slip," she said. "Oh, I don't know. Maybe I did. Maybe I didn't understand what it feels like for you. After you came to our table and told us about Lisa and I wouldn't even look at you, well, Luke talked to me about you, what you've been going through. How rough you had it when you first moved to Sexton, how the only way you could make friends was by playing soccer so well. How you and Lisa will always be regarded as not quite as good as everyone else because you're slips."

"It's not an excuse," Jon said. "You told me that."

"Maybe I shouldn't have," Sarah said. "I get too righteous sometimes and I hurt the people I love. I love you, Jon. I love that you're protective of Lisa and Gabe. And I didn't even tell you I was glad she passed her evaluation. Oh, Jon, I am glad. I'm glad for her and I'm glad for you, and it's been killing me that I didn't say so."

"I love you, Sarah," Jon said, but in his mind he knew what he had to do. He walked over to her and kissed her, gently at first and then with more passion.

Sarah responded. Jon held on to her so tightly she could hardly breathe. When he knew he had complete control, he began pawing at her, trying to tear her blouse from her.

Sarah broke away. "Stop it!" she cried. "You're being too rough."

"I thought you loved me," Jon said.

"I do," Sarah said. "I'm not holding back from you, Jon. But don't treat me like that."

"Like what?" Jon asked. "Like a grubber girl?"

"Is that how you treat them?" she asked. "Take what you want without caring how they feel?"

"I know how girls feel," Jon said, sickening himself at the sound of his voice. "You're all alike. Julie was exactly the same way."

"Julie?" Sarah said. "What about Julie?"

"She pretended she loved me, too," Jon said. "She said it the way you said it. 'I love you, Jon.'" He spoke in a falsetto, not the way Julie had sounded, still sounded, in his memories, his nightmares. "It was going to be our last day together so I told her to prove it. The next thing I knew, she was screaming for me to stop."

"She screamed?" Sarah said, edging farther away from him.

"She wanted it as much as I did," Jon said. "I could tell. But she wouldn't admit it. She said it was a sin. She didn't care what I felt, how excited I was. What I wanted didn't matter."

"She was a kid," Sarah said. "Younger than you. Smaller. She must have been terrified."

"So what?" Jon said. "I didn't plan on hurting her. It was her fault for fighting me."

"Did you rape her?" Sarah shouted, her voice rising with rage. "Tell me the truth. Did you rape Julie?" Her voice rose as she grew more hysterical.

Jon kept absolutely quiet.

"Don't you touch me," Sarah said. "Ever again. If you even try to, I'll tell Alex what you did. Is that clear, Jon? I don't want to have anything to do with you ever again." She grabbed at her blouse, trying to pull it together, as she raced out of the garage.

Jon watched as she ran away from him. I love you, Sarah, he thought. But he'd thought the same about Julie. And she'd run away from him, also.

He knelt on the concrete floor. "I'm sorry!" he cried. "I'm sorry for everything."

Not even Julie's ghost seemed to hear him.

Sunday, June 14

Jon passed the ball to Tyler as much as he could without getting Coach mad at him. Sexton beat the half-starved, half-crippled Carmichael team 14–2. He drank his share of potka on the drive back and laughed at his share of jokes. Tyler made only one crude remark about Sarah, and Jon was careful not to laugh too loudly. Just enough so Tyler would see how little Jon cared.

Lisa was already home when Jon got in. "How was the game?" she asked.

"We won," he said. "Fourteen to two."

"There's not much left of Carmichael," Lisa said. "There's talk they're going to tear it down and build greenhouses."

Jon thought of the dozens of people who'd watched the game. "What becomes of the grubs who live there?" he asked.

Lisa shrugged. "Most of them will move to White Birch," she said, "hoping for work."

Jon sat down. He wasn't sure he was ready for the answers, but he knew he had to ask the questions. "How did your visit go?" he asked. "Did Gabe enjoy himself?"

Lisa laughed. "He loves it there," she said. "He's crazy about Alex. Alex is going to be a good father. He has a real tenderness. Miranda must have brought it out in him."

"Did they see how much he's grown?" Jon asked. It had been six months since Lisa had taken Gabe to White Birch to spend time with that side of his family.

"Of course," Lisa said. "And how handsome and brilliant he is. I used that as an argument. How healthy he is, I mean. How good it would be for Miranda's baby to grow up here."

"What did she say?" Jon asked.

Lisa rolled her eyes. "It took a lot longer than it should have," she said. "First Alex objected. He didn't like the idea of only seeing Miranda and the baby on weekends."

"You can't blame him for that," Jon said. "It'd be great if Alex could move into the garage with them."

"You know that's impossible," Lisa said. "Only domestics can live in Sexton, and I can't see Alex working as a butler. Not for us, at any rate. He'll be in White Birch while Miranda stays here. That's just how it is."

"Did he agree to it?" Jon asked.

"Eventually," Lisa said. "Laura was actually the least resistant. She's not happy with the idea of Miranda working for me, but she understands it would be best for the baby." She shook her head. "Laura tries so hard to keep that apartment clean, but there are roaches all over. And the air quality is so bad."

"They can't buy air purifiers," Jon pointed out.

"They aren't forbidden to," Lisa said. "They could put their names down on the list to buy one, but all they're interested in is that truck. In any event, it's no place for a baby, and Laura can see that. Miranda put up the biggest fight. She doesn't want to leave Alex or Laura, and she wasn't crazy about the idea of living in a garage. She even said she liked her work in the greenhouses."

"But you convinced her," Jon said. Lisa had to. Miranda would be safe working for them, as long as no one knew she was family.

"I can convince anyone of anything if I set my mind to it," Lisa replied. "I told Miranda the garage was only until you start college. In the meantime she'll eat better and the baby will be healthier and well taken care of."

"What if Alex buys his truck?" Jon asked. "Would Miranda keep working here?"

Lisa snorted. "I love Alex," she said, "but he's a dreamer. It'll take years before he and Carlos can afford a truck, and even then they'll have to get a license to run it and another license to buy diesel, and they don't have the connections, so they'll need some extra money to make it happen. It's going to take at least five years, if it ever happens."

Five years ago, Jon thought, he'd been living in Pennsylvania with Mom and Miranda and Matt. The sun shone and food was plentiful, and his biggest worry was if he'd ever learn to pull an inside fastball.

Five years from now, maybe Alex would get his truck. Or maybe he and Miranda and the baby would move to that place Matt talked about. Or maybe Miranda would settle in to live as Lisa's domestic, seeing Alex and Mom once a week. It didn't matter, just as long as Miranda was safe from Tyler.

"So she agreed?" Jon said.

"She'll start in about a month," Lisa said. "We have to get the greenhouse built and the garage ready, and I need to do the paper-work without anybody suspecting why I've picked her. Oh, Carlos is coming on Thursday. Laura wants you there on Sunday to meet him."

"I'll have to ask Coach," Jon said.

"Don't ask him," Lisa said. "Tell him."

Jon nodded. He could tell Coach things now. Lisa had passed her evaluation. Jon might be a slip, but Coach, like all the teachers in the high school, was one step up from being a grub.

"I'll tell him," he said.

"Good," Lisa said. "Now go say hello to Gabe. He wants to tell you all about his exciting day in White Birch."

Tuesday, June 16

"I won't be able to play in Sunday's game," Jon told Coach at prac-tice. "I have a family obligation." He waited for Coach to yell.

"I wasn't going to play you anyway," Coach said instead. "You've been looking a little tired, Evans. We'll play you against Hilton on the twenty-eighth. Get you sharp for the White Birch match."

The rest of the team gathered around. "We're playing White Birch?" Tyler asked.

"The Fourth of July," Coach replied. "It's the match we've all been waiting for. What are we going to do to those White Birch grubs?"

"Kill 'em," Zachary said.

"I can't hear you," Coach said.

"Kill 'em!" the boys shouted.

"What's that you say?" Coach said.

"KILL 'EM!" Jon and his teammates screamed. "KILL 'EM! KILL 'EM! KILL 'EM!"

Jon thought he might burst with excitement. Everyone from Sexton would bus down for the game, and everyone from White Birch would be there as well. Lisa could bring Gabe, and Mom, Miranda, and Alex would finally see him play soccer. Maybe not Alex, since he'd be driving buses. And Miranda might not feel up to it. But Mom would go, the way she used to go to his baseball games. Tyler wouldn't know who she was, but Jon would sense her presence. And she'd tell Miranda and Alex and Matt how well he played.

For the first time in weeks Jon felt almost all right.

Thursday, June 18

It was an accident. Jon swore to himself he hadn't intended to. But as he walked from the classroom to the cafeteria, he brushed against Sarah. Just the feel of her arm against him was electric.

"I told you never to touch me!" she shouted.

Luke gave Jon a shove. "You heard her," he said, putting his arm around Sarah. "Leave her alone, Evans."

"Sorry," Jon muttered.

He could tell from the sound of Tyler's laughter that he'd witnessed the whole thing.

That's good, Jon told himself. Sarah's safe now.

But even knowing that didn't stop him from feeling like he'd been kicked in the gut. Feeling the way he had those last moments with Julie.

It was after midnight, but Jon knew sleep was impossible. The west wind blowing made the air worse, but he couldn't bear to be indoors. He got up, threw his clothes on, and went outside.

The sky was a sickly gray. It must be a full moon, Jon thought, layered with ash and rain clouds. The wind felt like a punishment as he sat on the cold, hard ground and forced himself to think about Julie.

She was thirteen when he met her. Thirteen when she died. At thirteen her parents were gone, her sister dead, her home, her school, her life destroyed.

It had terrified Alex when Julie coughed. Their sister Bri had coughed and coughed, and died.

But Julie was tough. She wouldn't have given up. A cough wouldn't have killed her.

No, Jon had that privilege all to himself. Julie could have survived a cough. It was Jon she couldn't survive.

He was fourteen, a year older, a year bigger. Much stronger than she was. Julie had been on the road for months before he met her, months where Jon and his family had had shelter and food.

Had he loved her? He'd told himself he had. But maybe that was a lie. Maybe Julie had been convenient, the way grubber girls were convenient. Julie was there, and she was close enough to his age, and Jon was old enough to want what Matt and Syl were having, what Miranda and Alex were having.

Julie hadn't believed him when he told her about Miranda and Alex. "It's a sin," she'd said. "Alex doesn't sin."

But Alex was human. He was a teenage boy, and Jon was a teenage boy, and Julie was there. She was convenient.

Except that day was the last one she was going to be there. Dad and Lisa, Gabe, Julie, Alex, Miranda, and Charlie were going to leave the next day to make their way to Sexton. They had no idea what they'd find there. But it was an enclave, and Alex had three passes.

Jon and Julie had gone to town that day to get the bags of food they were entitled to. They'd been walking home when the weather turned bad, and they'd run for shelter into one of the many empty houses on the road.

The house was furnished. People left or died, but the houses stayed the same.

They put the bags down and began to kiss. They'd been kissing for over two weeks. Twice, when Julie was certain they were alone, she'd let him touch her breasts.

Alex had been talking for as long as they'd been in Pennsylvania about taking Julie away, but somehow it never seemed to happen. Tomorrow it was going to happen, though. Maybe it was because everybody was leaving, but Jon felt desperate. He'd be left alone with Mom and Matt and Syl while everyone else was going to have a chance to live with other people. He was trapped.

It wasn't enough to kiss, to touch. He was almost fifteen, and his life was over, and he'd never known a woman. This was his last chance, his only chance. He loved her. She had to let him just this once.

Julie broke away from him. "No," she said. "Jon. No."

He couldn't understand why she was saying that. She'd said she loved him when he'd touched her breasts. She must want him as much as he wanted her. This was her chance as much as it was his.

But she fought him, shouting for him to stop. Which he wouldn't do. Not then, their last day, his last chance.

Julie was tough. She clawed at him, tried kneeing him. But Jon was six inches taller, thirty pounds heavier, stronger, better fed. It was a fight he was bound to win, but he didn't want it that way. He loved her. Didn't she know that?

"I love you, Julie," he said, convinced that would make her quiescent. You told a girl you loved her, she'd agree to anything. That's what the guys at school had always said. You said the magic words, and the girl was yours.

But Julie didn't seem to understand the rules. She didn't say, "I love you, too," or "Oh, Jon, Jon," or not talk at all, but still let him have her.

Instead she kept trying to get away. The harder she tried, the angrier he got, the more he felt the need to make her his.

For three years this had been his memory of Julie. Her frantic cries for him to stop. Her struggle to escape.

Since he'd moved to the enclave, Jon had never taken a grubber girl by force. The other guys did without a second thought. That's what the girls were there for.

But Jon wasn't a rapist. Not in White Birch, not back in Pennsylvania. He didn't rape Julie, no matter what he had led Sarah to believe. He'd wanted Julie more than he'd wanted anything in his life, but he'd honestly believed she wanted him, too. He did love her. He would have stopped.

But Julie didn't know that. Somehow she broke away from him and ran outside, into the storm.

Jon had followed her, intending to calm her down before she went home and told everyone what he'd tried to do. Dad and Lisa loved Julie like a daughter, and Mom—well, Mom would have taken Julie's side. He had to talk to Julie before she ruined his life.

Once Jon got outside, he realized the only thing that mattered was getting Julie indoors to safety. The rain had turned to hail, the wind was tornado level, and in the distance Jon could see a funnel cloud.

"Julie!" he screamed. "Julie! Come inside!"

But she didn't listen, or if she did, she was more scared of him than the weather. She was a city girl. She didn't know the power of a tornado. All she knew was Jon was taller and stronger and didn't know what "No!" meant.

He managed to grab her just as the twister bore down. He flung Julie to the ground, lying on top of her, a human cross.

But Julie wiggled out from under him, not realizing that he was trying to protect her. She fought to stand up, but the wind pushed so hard against her that it bent her over.

Jon faced the same battle. It was a slow-motion chase, like in a cartoon, the wind a wall against which Julie and Jon struggled to free themselves.

"Hold on!" he shouted, grabbing hold of a tree. But Julie didn't hear him or wouldn't listen. She kept trying to run.

Then the wind got her. It lifted her and threw her down against the ground.

He held on to the tree until the wind lessened. Only then did Jon go to her body.

She's dead, he thought. She'll never tell.

But only her body was dead. Julie's mind was still alive. The terror in her eyes screamed of life.

She was completely helpless now, Jon realized. All she had was her mind and her fear.

"No," she said to him. "Jon, no."

He stared at her. All their friendship, all their love, had died along with Julie's arms and legs. She'd run into a storm and the storm had killed her, and still she feared what Jon would do to her.

"Julie, it's all right," Jon said, knowing it wasn't, it never would be. "I have to get help. I have to find Alex and get help."

"I can't move," she said. "I can't feel anything."

"I know," he said. "But I have to go. They don't know where we are, Julie. I have to tell them where you are."

"I'm scared, Jon," she said. "I'm so scared."

He wanted to pick her up, hold her in his arms, comfort her. But he'd lost the right to touch her.

"I'll be back," he said instead. "Pray, Julie. Pray."

He brought Matt and Dad back to her. Alex was missing, Miranda hysterical. Charlie was dead, and Lisa and Gabe were trapped.

Julie had lingered for two days. He'd never gone to see her, to beg forgiveness.

But she never told. Maybe it was because Alex didn't get back in time and Lisa couldn't get out to see her. The only people Julie saw in those hours before she died were his family, his father, mother, brother, sister. And none of them indicated to Jon that Julie had told them anything.

She'd said she loved him and she did. She protected him when she wouldn't allow him to protect her. She'd faced her death bravely. Perhaps she even forgave him.

But Jon could never forgive himself. He hadn't raped Julie, but he'd killed her.

The rain fell on him, but it couldn't wash away his sins. Nothing could. Julie would haunt him for the rest of his life. She controlled him in death as she never had in life. She was his hell.

Part Two

Chapter 8

Sunday, June 21

"I don't believe this," Mom fumed. "I spent three hours waiting to get into the store yesterday, and I forgot to buy soap."

"We can live without soap for a week," Miranda said. "Don't worry about it, Mom."

"We can't live without it," Mom said sharply. "Not with all those chemicals you work with. It's dangerous enough for the baby. You've got to wash them off you whenever you can. No, I'll go back. Maybe the line won't be so long today."

"Mom, it's always worse on Sunday," Miranda said.

"I'll go," Jon said. "Soap and what else?"

"I hate it when you go," Mom said. "It's taking advantage of the system."

"That's exactly what it is," Alex said. "And it's the one advantage we can take. Thanks, Jon. I don't think we need anything else."

"I'll go with you," Carlos said. "I could use a breath of fresh air."

"Good luck finding some," Alex said.

Jon didn't blame Carlos for wanting to get out. The tension was palpable. Mom's outburst about soap had felt like a volcano spewing steam.

"The market's about five blocks away," Jon told Carlos as they began the walk. "Mom does the shopping Saturday afternoons because her school day ends at noon."

"How many markets are there in White Birch?" Carlos asked.

"Two or three, I guess," he said. "At different ends of town." Sexton, with a third of the population, had four markets, although he'd never been inside of one.

Carlos grinned. "We were cleaning out a town," he said, "back when I was a Marine, and the townspeople, the ones who were left, got it into their heads to use a supermarket as a fortress. I don't know what they thought they were doing. There must have been a couple hundred people in there."

"How did you get them out?" Jon asked.

"Tear gas," Carlos replied. "Most of them surrendered. We made them scrub that supermarket down. Didn't want the clavers tasting tear gas in their lettuce."

"Do you miss the Marines?" Jon asked.

"A little," Carlos said. "The work was dirty, but there was a sense of, I don't know. Brotherhood, I guess. We were all in it together, no matter how bad things got. But being a guard's good, too. Fewer people to salute."

"My brother Matt is a courier," Jon said. "He seems to like it."

"It's a good job," Carlos said. "Any job's a good job nowadays." He laughed. "Never thought Alex would end up a bus driver. He was planning on being president."

"Well, that didn't happen," Jon said. "Now he'll be satisfied owning a truck."

"Doesn't look like that's gonna happen, either," Carlos said.

"Why?" Jon asked.

"You ever play poker, kid?" Carlos asked.

Jon nodded.

"You know how you can be hot? Every card you touch turns into a flush, an inside straight. You start with a pair and end up with a full house."

"I've never had that kind of luck," Jon said.

"It feels like it's never going to end," Carlos said. "It's magic. You keep upping the ante, especially if you need the money for a truck. And then the cards go cold on you. So you keep betting more, figuring your luck'll return, only it doesn't. It never does."

"You gambled away your share of the money," Jon said.

"That's Alex's attitude," Carlos said. "I prefer to think of it as an investment gone sour."

Well, Lisa will be happy, Jon thought. Miranda will be her grub for a long, long time.

The line for the market was two blocks long. "They'll be here till curfew," Carlos said.

Jon nodded. It was lucky Mom shopped on Saturday.

He and Carlos walked to the head of the line. Jon showed one of the guards his claver ID badge.

"Come on in," the guard said, escorting them into the store.

"I just need soap," Jon said.

"Where's the soap?" the guard shouted.

"Aisle four, on the left!"

The guard walked with Jon and Carlos to the shelf with soap. There were four bars.

"Take 'em all," the guard said. "You're entitled."

Jon hesitated. He could get any girl he wanted in White Birch for a bar of soap. A quick look at Carlos showed he was thinking the same thing.

"Three'll do," Jon said. He left one bar on the shelf and walked out of the store escorted by the guard and Carlos.

"Here," he said to the guard, handing him one of the bars. "Thank you."

"Thank you, sir," the guard said.

Jon handed the second bar to Carlos. "Have fun," he said.

Carlos took the soap, then pulled out his knife and cut it in quarters. "Four quarters, four girls," he said. "They'd probably take eighths, but I'll be generous."

"Just don't tell Mom," Jon said. "She sent me for one bar, and if she knew I took more, she'd get really mad."

Carlos laughed. "I like your mother," he said. "She's got guts. I like Miranda, too. That kind of surprised me."

"You mean because she's Alex's kind of girl?" Jon asked.

"I didn't even know Alex liked girls," Carlos said. "I always figured he'd bring some boy home to meet the folks."

Jon laughed. "He's crazy about Miranda," he said. "And he's never made a pass at me."

"No, I know," Carlos said. "I could tell how much he loved her when he saw me in Texas. Funny. He never needed my approval before, but he wasn't gonna marry her without my okay. Not after what she did to Julie."

Jon stopped, then clutched the bar of soap. If he asked what Miranda had done, Carlos would never tell him. And whatever it was Carlos knew, Jon had to find out.

"I didn't know you knew," Jon said, trying to sound casual.

"Oh yeah, I know," Carlos said. "Alex told me. It threw me. It still does. Miranda seems so sweet. You wouldn't expect her . . . Well, she's your sister. You know her better than I do."

"It surprised me, too," Jon said, burning with the need to know what Miranda had done. "When I found out. But things were desperate."

"That's what Alex said," Carlos said, rolling the soap quarters in his hand. "I gotta tell you, though. I've killed plenty of people, probably some kids, too. You get the order to shoot, you don't look to see who you're shooting. But I don't think I could ever kill someone the way that sister of yours did. So cold. Alex said she did it to spare Julie. Sleeping pills, so Julie wouldn't know what was gonna happen. Pillow over her mouth to smother her to death. Miranda swore to him Julie slept through the whole thing, that the last thing she did was pray, so she died in a state of grace. That kind of thing's important to Alex. At least it used to be. Now, I don't know. He married his sister's murderer. Not what they taught us in catechism."

"Alex would forgive Miranda anything," Jon said slowly.

"He said she got the pills from him," Carlos said. "The idea, too. You're right about those times being desperate. My sister Bri, the way she died? Completely alone, no one rescuing her. Maybe it's better what Miranda did. Julie paralyzed like that, she would have died anyway. Well, it's water under the bridge. Alex and Miranda expecting a baby. He'll get that truck eventually. Alex always gets what he wants."

Jon nodded.

"You know what I want right now?" Carlos asked. "A girl. A nice quarter-of-a-bar-of-soap girl. Wanna join me, Jon? There's four quarters here. I won't miss one."

Jon looked at his watch, hoping Carlos wouldn't see how hard he was shaking. "Better not," he said. "I want to get the next bus home, and I've got to drop the soap off with Mom."

"Tell them I'm still breathing the fresh air," Carlos said with a laugh. "Good knowing you, Jon. I'll think of you four more times."

Jon managed a laugh. He watched as Carlos walked back toward the center of town.

Five minutes, he told himself. Five minutes to go back to Mom's, hand her the soap, kiss her good-bye, say good-bye to Alex and Miranda, and catch the claver bus home.

Five minutes. He'd survived three years of Julie haunting him. He could survive another five minutes.

Monday, June 22

Sarah was in his bed. They were holding each other tightly, shutting out the world with the power of their love.

"I love you," he whispered to her.

"You killed me, Jon," she said.

It wasn't Sarah. It was Julie. And she wasn't holding him because she couldn't hold anything. She was lying there, still as a corpse. "You killed me," she said. "You kill everything you love."

Jon sat upright, his heart pounding. "You can't haunt me anymore," he whispered. "I didn't kill you. Miranda did."

He'd thought of little else since yesterday afternoon. He'd told Lisa about the visit, told her about Carlos gambling away the truck money. Lisa had tried not to seem pleased, but he could tell she was. She had a gift for knowing what was best for other people, and she knew what was best for Miranda and her baby.

He'd sat at lunch with Tyler, Zach, and Ryan and had hardly listened to a word they said. He'd bench-pressed, stretched, run, and practiced, his body knowing what to do while his mind was elsewhere, focused on Miranda, on Miranda killing Julie, on Miranda cold-bloodedly drugging Julie, then smothering the life out of her.

He'd tried to figure out who else knew and decided no one did. Dad and Lisa would never have forgiven her. Matt might have, but Miranda wouldn't have wanted Syl to know. And Mom . . .

Mom was closer to Miranda than she was to either him or Matt, but even if Mom could have forgiven her, she couldn't have kept it a secret. If Mom knew, they'd all know, and since they didn't, she couldn't.

No, the only person Miranda told was Alex. She told him on the road to Sexton, and Alex left her. Carlos was right. Alex loved Miranda, but he'd loved Julie, too, and felt responsible for her. If Carlos had said no to the marriage, Alex wouldn't have returned.

But Carlos had said yes, allowing Alex to marry his sister's killer. And Jon spent three years feeling responsible for something that had never truly been his fault.

He thought about that final day harder than he ever had before. Yes, he'd wanted Julie. He was a teenage boy and she was a teenage girl, and that was the nature of things. If Julie hadn't been so religious, or more to the point, if she hadn't been so scared of Alex, who was so religious, she would have had no reservations about making love. It had been their last chance, probably the last time they'd ever see each other.

Jon knew now he'd pushed too hard, and he understood why Julie had panicked. But panic was an irrational response. Julie knew him and loved him and should have understood that he would never hurt her. But her fear of Alex was stronger than her love of Jon. Which was pretty ironic, given that Alex loved her murderer.

Julie had panicked. Jon had gone out after her, had risked his own life to protect her, and she continued to panic. By that point, he realized, she must have been as terrified by the storm as she had been of him. The rain, the wind, the hail, must have driven her into a wild, irrational terror, and she was past the point of understanding that all he wanted was to keep her from harm.

Then the wind had lifted her and thrown her down. Jon had

done everything he could to protect her, but she'd resisted and paid the price.

Jon remembered everything about that moment. He acknowledged, as he never had before, that there'd been an instant when he thought, She's dead and she'll never tell what happened.

But she wasn't dead, and he didn't leave her there to die. He could have. The storm was raging. No one knew where they were. He could have risked it, gone back to the house, claimed they'd gotten separated, hoping she'd be dead by the time they found her. He'd thought of all that then. For a moment he'd considered it.

Instead he'd gone back and led them to her. Julie could have accused him of trying to rape her. She could have claimed she ran into the storm because she feared for her life in the house with him. Everyone would have believed her. Jon could have told the truth, sworn he never would have hurt her, and they would have turned against him anyway.

Julie hadn't told. She loved him enough not to. Maybe she was waiting for him to see her, waiting to have a chance to forgive him. If she'd lived only a few days longer, he would have gone to her. Saving Lisa and Gabe was his first priority, but after that he would have gone to beg for Julie's forgiveness, and he knew she would have forgiven him.

But Miranda killed her before he and Julie had that chance. All these years he'd blamed himself for Julie's death, but it was Miranda who was responsible.

Jon understood why Miranda had done it. Julie was paralyzed. Miranda believed there was no cure.

But maybe she was wrong. Maybe they could have gotten Julie to a doctor, somehow, somewhere. Or maybe Julie's prayers and Alex's and Lisa's and Syl's would have been answered, and a miracle would have happened, and Julie would have been cured.

Dad thought Lisa's survival, Gabe's survival, was miraculous. Maybe Julie could have had a miracle of her own.

Only Miranda hadn't let that happen. They were Alex's pills, but Alex hadn't told her to kill his sister. Miranda came up with that all on her own. Months later she'd confessed to Alex what she'd done. By then Julie was just a memory, a sister Alex had loved but one he'd fought with, one he thought of as a burden he'd been trying to be free of for over a year.

Carlos said, "Sure, marry our sister's murderer." Alex took that as a blessing and raced back to Miranda. It was as though Julie had never existed.

She existed for Jon, though. She haunted his dreams. She kept him from having any kind of chance with a girl like Sarah. Only grubber girls, who could be bought for a quarter of a bar of soap.

Miranda had done that to him. Miranda had murdered Julie, and she had murdered everything that was good in him.

And now Miranda was going to be living in his house. It was a fantasy to think he'd be able to avoid her. She'd work in the greenhouse, eat with Val and Carrie, sleep in the garage. But she'd be there. She'd be running in to check on her baby, the one Julie would never have. Officially she'd be a domestic, but she'd feel like Lisa's stepdaughter, Gabe's half sister. Jon's sister. Every time he'd see her, he'd picture her putting the pillow over Julie's face, holding it down until she could never breathe again.

"Jon! Wake up! I wanna play!"

Gabe had rushed into his room and jumped on top of him.

"Carrie!" Jon shouted. "Carrie, get in here!"

Carrie ran in. "Gabe, stop that," she said. "Jon will play with you later."

"I want to play now!" Gabe yelled.

Carrie walked over to the bed to pull Gabe away. But as she did, Jon rose, and by the time she reached Gabe, Jon's hand was up and he was ready to strike her.

Carrie froze. Gabe began crying. Jon pulled his hand back. He'd never hit a girl before, not even a grub, but he knew if he hit Carrie once, he would never stop. He would batter her with his fists until she was unconscious, until she was dead.

Gabe ran out of the room and Carrie ran right behind him. Jon stood absolutely still, trying to catch his breath, trying to regain his sanity.

It wasn't Carrie. He had nothing against Carrie. It could have been Val.

It could have been Sarah.

It was Miranda he wanted to kill. Miranda, who'd killed the girl he'd loved, leaving him to drown in guilt for the rest of his life.

Thursday, June 25

Jon answered the phone as soon as he walked in.

"Oh, Jon, I'm glad I got you," Lisa said. "I'm here at the hospital with Miranda."

"Miranda," he said, trying to sound like a loving brother. "Is she all right?"

"Yes, I think so," Lisa said. "She passed out at the greenhouse this afternoon. They sent her here by ambulance."

"And the baby?" Jon asked.

"Fine," Lisa said. "I'm sure Miranda is, also. It's hard to be eight months pregnant and on your feet all day long, and the greenhouses are so hot and humid. But they're not taking any chances. They're going to keep her in the hospital for the remainder of her pregnancy. Her blood pressure's very high, and they think it's better for her to be monitored. The paperwork's all done, so officially she works for me. That's why they called me."

"Have you seen her?" Jon asked.

"No, not yet," Lisa said. "It's been less than an hour, and they're still checking her out. Everyone tells me there's nothing to worry about, but of course I feel I should talk to her and make sure she's all right. I don't know how long that's going to take. Alex may not realize anything's wrong until he gets to White Birch, but he's bound to panic when he doesn't see her there. And Laura will be hysterical. My guess is they'll get to a phone before curfew and call us to see if we know where she is. I'll probably be home by then, but just in case, I wanted you to know what's happening. You can tell them Miranda's getting the best possible care."

"Will they be able to see her?" Jon asked.

"I'm not sure," Lisa said. "Laura won't be able to get a pass, I know that. I might be able to pull some strings and get one for Alex, since he works in Sexton anyway. But I can't be sure. The rules are very stringent about where grubs are allowed. If they ask, tell them you don't know, but I'll be visiting Miranda whenever I can and you will, also, and we'll keep them posted."

Jon knew he would never visit Miranda. The thought of seeing her repulsed him. But he wouldn't tell Lisa that, or Mom or Alex. He'd find excuses, just as he knew he'd find excuses when she came to work for Lisa.

"Jon, I've got to go," Lisa said. "Give Gabe a big kiss for me, and tell Val to have my dinner ready. If there's any more news, I'll call."

"Thanks, Lisa," Jon said, and hung up. He gave Val the message and went to the nursery to check in on Gabe. Carrie backed away when he entered. He didn't blame her.

Lisa got in before Alex called. She told him what she'd told

Jon, adding only that she'd seen Miranda briefly and she was feeling much better.

"I think I calmed him down," she said to Jon after she hung up. "Of course he wants to break every rule and rush to her side, but that's the worst thing he could do. It won't do Miranda any good if he's thrown in jail."

"They'd send him to the mines," Jon said.

"That won't do Miranda any good, either," Lisa replied. "But there's a chance I can get him a pass. Someone's been after me for a while for an Ivy League domestic. I may be able to do some swapping. One Yalie for two state-college grads and a pass for Alex as a thank-you. It might work."

Jon didn't care. Alex could end up in the mines as far as he was concerned, and Miranda and her baby could follow him there.

He felt bad for Mom, but that was it. Someday, he decided, he'd tell Mom the truth about Miranda. Mom would never forgive her. Miranda would be dead to her, just as she was to Jon.

Friday, June 26

"When Alex calls tonight, you take it, all right, Jon?" Lisa said.

"Okay," Jon said, although he had no desire to talk with Alex. "Why are you avoiding him?"

"I spent half of today trying to get him that pass," Lisa said. "But the family with the Yalie wouldn't give her up, and the family that wanted a Yalie wouldn't take anything else. I even offered Val to sweeten the pot, but Tulane wasn't good enough for them."

"You would have transferred Val?" Jon asked. He knew how much Lisa depended on her.

"Miranda and Alex are family," Lisa said. "Val isn't. If it weren't for Hal and me, Miranda would never have met Alex. In some ways, I'm more of a grandmother to their baby than Laura is."

Jon stared at her.

"Don't give me that look, Jon Evans," Lisa said. "Yes, I know I'm taking Miranda on as a domestic and that's not the same as what I've done for you. But it's the best I can do. A decent home with clean air for their baby. A year or two from now things could be completely different. Who knows. But the important thing is to stay alive and healthy. And the best way of doing that is playing by the rules."

"Even if the rules stink?" Jon asked.

"They're not that bad for us," Lisa said. "You might try to be more grateful for what you have. And don't get any ideas about beating up the domestics, Jon."

"Carrie told you?" Jon asked.

"Gabe did," Lisa said. "He was very upset. Carrie says you didn't hit her, but she was afraid you were going to. Jon, what's the matter with you? It's one thing to tell Val she has to get up earlier in the morning, even though you should have asked me first. But abusing the domestics? I don't care what your friends do. In this house everyone is treated with respect."

"I told her I was sorry," Jon said. "I'd been having a bad dream, and then Gabe waking me up like that, I couldn't tell what was real and what was nightmare."

"You'd better learn the difference," Lisa said. "I have enough problems around here without Carrie reporting you for battery."

"I was going to slap her," Jon said. "That's not battery."

"Carrie said you looked out of control," Lisa said. "Oh, Jon, I don't even know why we're arguing about this. I have a headache, and I'm going to bed. When Alex calls, tell him I couldn't get the pass, but I called the hospital this afternoon and they said Miranda is doing fine. He and Laura shouldn't worry. Miranda's getting excellent care, and it's much better for her to be in the hospital than working ten-hour days in the greenhouses. Oh, and Jon, you visit Miranda next, and keep it to yourself that she's family. Just say I asked you to check up on her because she's my domestic and I'm too busy to go."

Jon knew he wasn't going to visit Miranda, but he also knew not to argue. He'd go to the hospital and ask how she was doing, without actually seeing her. That should be enough to shut everybody up.

"Good night, Lisa," he said. "Feel better."

Lisa paused before going upstairs. "You're a good boy, Jon," she said. "Sometimes I think you lose sight of that fact. Give my love to Alex. Tell him things will seem better in the morning."

Saturday, June 27

"I'm here to see how Miranda Morales is doing," Jon said. "My stepmother asked me to. Miranda's one of her domestics."

"She'll be in the grubber wing, then," the nurse said. "Walk down the hallway to the left, and take the stairs up."

"Thank you," Jon said. He found the door to the stairway, climbed the two flights, and saw an immediate difference once he opened the door to the third floor. The floors were filthy, wastepaper baskets full, and only half the lights were on.

Jon knew Sexton prided itself on having a grubber's wing in the hospital, but it was clear the people who bragged about it had never actually seen it. He peeked into the various rooms. Almost all were empty, but in the handful of rooms that were occupied, there were six beds where four were meant to be.

"We don't encourage slackers," the only nurse on the floor said. "Make things too comfortable for grubs, they'll never go back to work."

Jon nodded. "I can see that might be a problem," he said. "I'm here to check up on Miranda Morales."

"Why?" the nurse asked.

"She's our domestic," Jon said. "My stepmother wants to see how she's doing."

"Tell your stepmother she's doing fine," the nurse said. "The baby's due in about three weeks. The grub should be back at work a day or so later."

"Do they usually recover that fast?" Jon asked.

"Grubs recover when we tell them they've recovered," the nurse said. "Everyone is making a big fuss over her because she's the only girl in here due to have a baby. No clavers, no grubs. Just her. She's going to be spoiled rotten by the time that baby comes, and your stepmother is going to have a lot of work ahead, whipping her into shape. I'm glad it's not my problem. You tell your stepmother that, and let me get back to work, all right?"

"All right," Jon said. "Thank you."

"It's my job," the nurse said. "A lousy one, but a job."

Sunday, June 28

It was a five-hour drive to Hilton, Tennessee, and by the time the bus got there, not even Coach seemed all that interested in the match.

Jon played the first half and scored three times. Sexton ended up winning 7–2, but there were no tirades on the drive back because of the low score. Instead all of them — Coach, the team, and the guards — got drunk on potka. Endless speeches were made about the complete and utter destruction the White Birch grubs were going to face on the Fourth of July.

"We'll leave them drowning in their own blood!" Tyler shouted, and everyone laughed and cheered, Jon included.

Better that way than drugged and smothered, he thought. At least the grubs would have a chance. That's more than Miranda had offered Julie.

Monday, June 29

"Hey, Evans," Ryan said in the locker room after practice. "Looking forward to Saturday?"

"Sure," Jon replied. "We'll slaughter the grubs. Make them beg for mercy."

Tyler laughed. "It's the grubber girls that'll be begging."

"Show them no mercy," Zachary said.

"The plan is to stay in White Birch after the match," Ryan said. "Right, Tyler?"

"Right," Tyler said. "Make the eighteenth look like a picnic. You with us, Evans?"

Jon knew there was only one way he could answer. "Can't wait," he said.

Tyler walked over to him and slapped him on the back. "That's a good slip," he said. "Now let's get out of here before Coach makes us run more laps."

Tuesday, June 30

The sound of a knock on the door startled all of them. Jon got up from the dinner table, walked to the hallway, and opened the door. There stood Sarah. *Sarah?*

"What are you doing here?" he whispered.

"I have to talk to you," she said.

Jon checked. There was no one standing outside. "It's not a good idea," he said.

"I'm sick and tired of your good ideas," she replied. "We're going to get things straightened out once and for all."

"Who is it?" Lisa called.

"It's Sarah," he replied.

"Invite her in," Val said. "There's plenty of food."

"Some other time," Sarah said. "Thank you anyway." She gestured to Jon. "Come on," she said.

Jon followed Sarah to the garage. There was a cot there now, one Lisa had found in the attic and had had Val carry in.

Sarah noticed it right away. "This is new," she said, sitting down on it.

"Lisa's getting a new domestic," Jon said. "She'll sleep in here."

"Cozy," Sarah said. "Oh, Jon, stop looking like that. You can sit down. I won't bite."

Jon made sure to sit at the other end of the cot.

"Your mother came to the clinic on Sunday," Sarah said. "She told us about Miranda, and asked Daddy if he could check up on her. Last night Daddy decided he'd ask for Alex to drive him to the hospital. He'll see if he can slip Alex in to see Miranda while he's there."

"Is that why you came here?" Jon asked. "To tell me that?"

"No," Sarah said. "I wanted you to know, but that's not why I'm here." She took a deep breath. "I like Luke, but he can't keep a secret. He told me all about you and Tyler, how you feel like you have to protect me. I wanted to slug him. No, I wanted to slug you and then him."

"Tyler isn't a joke, Sarah," Jon said. "He could hurt you."

"Tyler is an idiot," Sarah replied. "Which I'd think you'd know by now. Anyway, I explained to Mr. Can't Keep A Secret that my uncle is a United States senator and anyone who even breathes on me the wrong way is mine meat."

"Mine meat?" Jon said.

"That's what we called them in my old enclave," she said. "I'm sure Luke ran off to tell Tyler right away."

"I'm glad for you," Jon said. "I'm glad there's someone to protect you."

"There's something else," she said. "Jon, I've thought about you and Julie, what you told me, what you didn't tell me. I asked you outright if you'd raped her, but you didn't admit it. You didn't say anything. You wanted me to ask, didn't you? You wanted me to hate you so Tyler couldn't hurt me. Well, he can't, so you can tell me the truth. You didn't rape her, did you?"

Jon shook his head. "She thought I would," he said. "She ran into the tornado to escape. For a long time I felt like I'd killed her." He thought briefly of telling Sarah the truth, that Miranda had murdered Julie, but Sarah spoke before he'd decided what to say.

"I know what you feel like," she said. "I feel like I killed my mother."

"I don't understand," Jon said.

"My mother had kidney disease," Sarah said. "They tested my sister first, but she wasn't a match. Then they tested me and I was. Mother was on dialysis and that kept her going, but the sooner she had the transplant the better. Mother and I weren't close, not like she was with Abby. When Abby found out she wasn't a match, she cried. When I found out I was, I cried, too."

"How old were you?" Jon asked.

"Thirteen," Sarah replied. "You can't just walk in and donate a kidney when you're that young. It has to be approved. So they interviewed me away from my parents and asked if I was okay with it, and I burst into tears and said I didn't want to do it and I felt like I was being forced to."

"You were being honest," Jon said.

"At the cost of my mother's life," Sarah said. "They told my parents I was too young and Mother would have to stay on dialysis until another donor could be found. Five weeks later Abby died. My parents were devastated. I thought I could make things better by agreeing to the surgery, but by then they'd stopped transplants. Nobody was manufacturing the drugs you need to keep your body from rejecting the organs, so everyone who ever had a transplant died. There were a lot of deaths you didn't hear about, like the diabetics who couldn't get insulin and the people with cancer whose chemo was stopped."

"But your mother only died a few months ago," Jon said.

"My uncle pulled strings and got us selected for an enclave where she could get dialysis," Sarah replied. "Things were okay until they decided to close all the dialysis units. The people on dialysis weren't doing enough to justify the resources. It took Mother thirteen days to die. Daddy didn't leave her side the entire time, when he should have been working. The enclave board didn't like that, so they held a hearing and decided to expel him. My uncle got Daddy the job here."

"Even if you'd agreed to the transplant, your mother would have died," Jon said. "She might have died sooner."

"I know," she replied. "The way you know things in your head but not in your heart. I kept thinking Mother would have been the only person who never needed drugs. Or they might have kept making the drugs, or we would have found a supply big enough to last until they started making them again. And Abby was so angry with me for not agreeing. We hardly spoke the month before she died. I hold that in my heart, also."

"It wasn't your fault," Jon persisted.

"It doesn't matter," Sarah declared. "In my heart I'm always going to feel guilty. Just the way you do about Julie. I don't think there's anyone else in this world who could understand how I feel."

He could never tell her the truth. He could never say it was Miranda who killed Julie, who kept her from the kind of miracle Sarah dreamed of for her mother. She'd take it as a rejection, as his way of saying he was better than she was. She needed him to be guilty. It didn't matter if it was a lie.

"I love you," he said, because that was a truth she could accept.

"Hold me, Jon," she whispered. "I can't bear to be alone anymore."

Wednesday, July 1

"Daddy's arranged for Alex to drive him to White Birch today," Sarah told Jon as they walked to the bus. "They're going to stop at the hospital first so Daddy can check up on Miranda. He'll try to get Alex in to see her."

"That's nice of him," Jon said.

"Daddy likes your family," Sarah replied. "So do I."

"Are you coming to the match on Saturday?" Jon asked. "See me slaughter those White Birch grubs?"

"You make it sound so appealing," she replied. "But I'll be at the clinic all day."

"The clinic's closed on Saturdays," Jon said. "Besides, it's July Fourth."

"That's why we're staying open," Sarah said. "Laborers will have the day off. It'll give them a chance to come in. We're staying open until the last one leaves, and then we'll get a driver to take us home. What'll you be doing after the match?"

"Staying in White Birch to celebrate," Jon said. "We'll get home somehow."

"Will you burn any more schools down?" she asked.

Jon stood still. "You know about that?" he asked.

"It's true?" Sarah asked. "I thought maybe Tyler made it up."

"Tyler told you?" Jon asked. He grabbed Sarah by the shoulders. "When? What did he say?"

"Let me go," Sarah said.

Jon released her. "I'm sorry," he said. "But I need to know what happened."

"It was after lunch yesterday," Sarah said. "Tyler saw you eating with Luke and me. Then you left for practice. Tyler came up to me when I was waiting for the driver to take me to White Birch. Tyler said he had a problem, a moral issue, and he wanted to talk to me about it. I said that seemed weird since he hates me, and he said that was why he was asking me. He couldn't count on his friends to give him an honest answer."

"What was the problem?" Jon asked.

"He said he was with some of his friends that night, and they saw you with a bunch of other guys running into the high school," Sarah replied. "The next thing they saw, the school was on fire and you were all running away. He's been trying ever since to decide whether he should tell the authorities. His friends said no, but it's been bothering him."

"And you believed him?" Jon demanded.

"I didn't know what to believe," Sarah said. "I thought about asking Luke, but I couldn't trust him to keep his mouth shut. Tyler said the guys you were with looked like grubs. But you don't know any grubs, do you, Jon? Except for your family, I mean."

"They weren't grubs," Jon said. If he told Sarah the truth, she'd confront Tyler or go to the authorities. Either way, his family would be the ones to suffer. "They were clavers, guys from college probably. We were drunk. We didn't swap names and addresses."

"Was it their idea?" Sarah asked.

Jon wanted to say yes, he hadn't known what they were going to do until it was too late. But there were only so many lies he felt like telling. "One of them had matches," he said instead. "We thought it was a great idea. I thought it was a great idea."

"Why, Jon?" Sarah cried.

"I was angry at Mom," he said. "For caring more about her students than she does about me. But Sarah, if Tyler goes to the authorities, they'll blame her."

"You're the one they'll blame," Sarah said.

"Yeah, but I deserve it," Jon said. "Mom didn't do anything wrong, but they'll throw her out of White Birch. They'll punish Alex and Miranda, too. They'll say I lied about being with clavers, that it was my family's idea."

"You saw them a few days before," Sarah said.

Jon nodded.

Sarah took a deep breath. "I'll tell Tyler you said you were too drunk to remember what happened. Jon, if you turn yourself in, will they do anything to your family?"

"I don't know," Jon said. "I don't want to risk it. But if you want, I'll leave Sexton. I'll go to my brother's after Miranda's baby is born. But I won't come back. I won't be a claver."

"I don't want to lose you," Sarah said. "But I don't know that I've ever had you. How can I love you when I don't think I like you?"

"You were lonely," he said. "You're making friends now. You'll find someone else. I'll be gone. You'll be okay."

"I don't want to be okay without you," she said. "Jon, hold me."

Jon didn't move. "Go," he said. "Catch the bus. I'll walk to school."

"You'll be late," she said.

"Don't worry about me," he said. "Take care of yourself."

Sarah paused for a moment, but then she began running from him.

He'd had her and he lost her. He could blame whoever he wanted, whatever he wanted—Tyler, his family, the moon it-self—but none of that mattered.

He was alone. He would always be alone.

That was all he deserved.

Friday, July 3

Practices had been brutal all week. Coach drove them beyond their capabilities, calling them every name in the book when they came short of his expectations.

Each practice ended with chants, louder and more crazed, about what the Sexton players were going to do to the White Birch grubs. Nothing was too violent or obscene.

It was hard each day to go home and return to being Nice

Jon, Friendly Jon, Big Brother Jon. He tried his best, but mostly he thought about everything he'd done, everything he'd lost.

Mom called that night. He couldn't remember the last time he'd heard her sound so happy, so relieved.

"Alex gave me the complete report yesterday," she said. "He says he's never seen Miranda look so good. Miranda can't get over how well they're feeding her. Chicken and fish every single day. She walks around the ward for exercise, but mostly she lies in bed and gets pampered. The baby is thriving and everything's going wonderfully. She's really looking forward to working for Lisa. She says she hadn't realized how much the greenhouse work was taking out of her until she fainted."

Jon listened patiently, making the appropriate noises when Mom would expect to hear them.

"Jeffrey doesn't think he can get Alex in to see Miranda next week, but he'll try for the week after," Mom continued. "And he'll check in on Miranda after she's had the baby, and he'll get Alex in then, also. I wish Alex could see her daily, but it's better than nothing. Jeffrey's really being wonderful about it."

"The soccer match is tomorrow," Jon said. "Are you coming, Mom?"

"Oh, honey, I wish I could," Mom replied. "I was given a ticket. But one of the boys in my class is on the team. I gave him my ticket so his father can see him play. Lisa will be there? And Gabe?"

"Yeah," Jon said, knowing in Mom's eyes they were all the family he needed.

"I'll see you the next time," Mom said. "After Miranda has the baby. We'll all come, cheer you on."

"Okay," he said. "Take care, Mom."

Jon heard her say, "I love you," as he hung up the phone.

When he was a kid, his father used to go to his ball games. Jon loved to play, knowing his father was watching, cheering him on.

But after the divorce Dad lived too far away to get to the games. Jon used the anger he felt, and the disappointment, to make him play harder.

That's how he'd play on Saturday, he told himself. Harder than he'd ever played before.

Chapter 9

Saturday, July 4

Until the White Birch forward died, it was the best day in Jon's life.

After he died, it was the worst.

It had started better than Jon had imagined. Instead of a four- or five-hour drive on winding, rutted roads, it was a familiar twenty minutes. The bus was full. All the team members made the trip, plus Coach, the referee they always brought, and a couple dozen guards, who were there to circle the playing field for their protection.

Everyone was in a great mood, with a lot of yelling about what they were going to do to the White Birch grubs. The wilder and more disgusting the shouts, the more everyone cheered.

Finally Coach raised his hands to quiet the team. "If you lose, you can take a bus back after the game. Someone'll find room for you losers."

The catcalls were deafening.

"But if by some chance you manage a win, there'll be a bus for you at four a.m.," Coach said. "To the victors belong the spoils."

"What does that mean?" Zachary asked.

"It means do whatever you want to whoever you want," Tyler said. "No questions asked. Right, Coach?"

"I'm not asking," Coach said. "Just don't get killed."

Luke glanced at Jon, but Jon ignored him. Luke could do whatever he wanted. Jon was going to do whatever Tyler wanted.

The team got to the stadium a couple of hours before match time. They changed in the locker room, then looked around.

The high school stadium grandstands sat two thousand, and Jon knew it would be full. The lower half was reserved for clavers. Then there'd be a row of guards, and above them were the seats for the people from White Birch. Twenty buses would shuttle back and forth from Sexton, carrying the clavers and the guards. The grubs could walk.

Jon could see that playing so close to the burned-down high school bothered Luke. He told himself not to think about it. The high school was a remnant of a different time. The students still went to school, just in a different building. Back in Pennsylvania after the bad times had begun, they'd closed schools and no one cared.

Even in the locker room, Jon could hear the clavers getting off the buses and being seated. Close to a thousand of them coming to watch their team slaughter the grubs. An equal number of grubs witnessing the slaughter.

Eventually one of the guards knocked on their door and told them to come out for the "Star-Spangled Banner." Jon looked around as he walked onto the field. He was used to playing games almost every week, but they usually played on an empty field somewhere, and at most a hundred of the town's grubs showed up to watch.

This was completely different. Even with the scores of guards, it was still overwhelming to see hundreds of grubs waiting for the clavers to lose.

But then they started singing the national anthem, and everything felt right. Sure, the clavers were clavers and the grubs were grubs, but it was the Fourth of July and they were all Americans.

It was a hot seventy-five degrees, and if you squinted, you could see the sun. There was soccer to be played, a game to be won.

What Jon hadn't expected, what none of them had expected, was that the White Birch players would be good. None of the grubber teams they'd played had known what they were doing. The grubs only scored because the clavers let them. Jon and his teammates could easily win 20–0.

But the White Birch grubs played hard, never quitting, never gasping for air. The grubs had defenders. The clavers had never needed defenders, and all the players regarded themselves as forwards. Now they had to block passes shot by players who understood the game, and watch helplessly as their own passes were blocked. Jon had several of his passes taken from him, and he was outrun more than once.

To make matters worse, the grubs had a goalie who knew how to field. Jon was accustomed to scoring easily, the grubber goalies terrified at the speed and power of his kick. But this goalie blocked the kicks and saw to it that his teammates got the ball back.

The grubs in the stands were going wild, screaming and pounding against the bleacher floors. The clavers tried to show their enthusiasm, but they'd expected a rout, and Jon could sense they were starting to worry.

Coach was screaming on the sidelines, and the referee gave as many calls as he could to the clavers. Even so, at halftime, the score was 1–1.

The thing was, Jon loved it. Winning every week against a bunch of losers wasn't fun. It was a job, whether Sarah understood that or not.

But this was great. Win or lose, this was what sports were about. Soccer would never replace baseball in Jon's heart, but this time he understood what was fun about soccer, why even in a world of fear, hunger, and loss, this game alone had survived.

He didn't even mind listening to Coach in the locker room. He especially enjoyed hearing Coach scream at Tyler.

None of the other guys were enjoying themselves. Maybe he could because he was a slip. Sure he wanted to win. He'd come in determined to show the White Birch grubs what pathetic losers they were. He understood that there was danger if the grubs stopped fearing them. The clavers had to win, especially this game so close to home.

But this time they'd have to earn that win. The clavers had every advantage, but they were being outplayed by a bunch of loser grubs. Only they weren't losers. There was nothing loser about them.

With two minutes left, Jon was starting to wish the grubs would remember what losers they were. The score was tied 3–3, and both teams were exhausted. Even Coach had wearied of screaming. The fans in the seats were quieter, waiting for the decisive goal to be scored.

Luke kicked the ball to Jon. He could see a clear path to the goal. The White Birch goalie, who'd played a heroic match, was weakening. This was the chance Jon had been waiting for.

But before he had a chance to strike the ball, one of the grubber forwards collapsed on the field. For a moment they all stood still. Then the grubs ran over to check on their forward. No one thought to call a timeout.

"Kick the ball!" Coach yelled. "Score!"

Jon stood still. Tyler ran over and kicked the ball in for the score.

"He's dead!" one of the grubs shouted.

The White Birch coach ran onto the Sexton side of the field and began pummeling Coach. The next thing Jon knew, he was being attacked by two of the White Birch players.

Soon all the players were fighting. Jon felt sorry for the guy who'd died, but it was exhilarating to be swinging, hitting, pounding his fists against flesh and bone.

The guards started swarming the field. Shots rang out. Jon thought the guards were shooting in the air, to calm the crowd, until he saw one of the grub players fall to the ground. Then the barrier between the field and the grandstands collapsed, and clavers and grubs stampeded the playing field.

The screams grew louder and the gunshots more frequent. Jon tried to locate Lisa and Gabe, only to feel a hard punch to his stomach. He collapsed onto the field, the air knocked out of him, then heard a bullet and saw the grub who'd attacked him falling down. Jon managed to squirm away just in time to keep the grub from dying on top of him.

Guns were going off everywhere. Clavers who'd brought their guns with them for protection were shooting wildly. Jon ran, searching for Lisa and Gabe. It was Gabe he saw first. A man had hold of him and was lifting him up.

Jon couldn't be certain if it was a grub who planned on harming Gabe or a claver trying to protect him. At that moment it didn't matter. He climbed over the fallen barricade, pushing against crazed and frantic people, and reached the man.

He hadn't played soccer for nothing. Jon placed a hard kick on the man's shin, and while the man was hopping from pain and surprise, he kneed him in the groin.

The man dropped Gabe. Jon grabbed the boy, placing him on

his shoulders. Gabe was screaming for his mother, and Jon managed to spot her.

"Follow me!" he yelled to Lisa. He held on to Gabe's legs as tightly as he could and shoved his way through the hysterical crowd. At first he stepped around bodies, in case they were still alive, but after a couple of minutes he gave up caring. Gabe was the important thing, not some dead grub. Or some dead claver.

He tripped once, but Gabe was holding on to his hair, and Jon was able to keep him from falling off. It took a couple of terrifying minutes before Jon saw an exit sign, and he walked as swiftly as he could, carrying Gabe outside to safety.

Jon watched as people ran from the stadium, but he wasn't going anywhere until Lisa joined them. Gabe hadn't stopped crying, but he saw Lisa first, and began calling, "Mommy, Mommy," until Lisa found them.

"Let's get to the buses," Jon said.

Lisa nodded.

The farther they walked from the stadium, the safer Jon felt. A guard spotted them and escorted them to the parking lot.

Jon knew Lisa and Gabe would be taken home by any of the bus drivers, but still he was relieved when he spotted Alex. He raced to Alex's bus, with Lisa running by his side.

"I'll take him," Alex said, lifting Gabe off Jon's shoulders. "Get in, Lisa. The bus is full. We'll be leaving right away."

"Take them home," Jon said. "Lisa can show you where."

"Don't worry about them," Alex said. "Just make sure Laura's okay."

"She's home," Jon said. "She isn't here."

"Come on, you stinking grub!" a man shouted from the bus. "Get us out of here!"

"Check on her," Alex said, closing the bus door and beginning the drive out of the parking lot.

Alex worried too much, Jon told himself. The important thing was to get the other claver women and children safely to the buses. Jon told the guard to follow him, and the two of them ran back to the stadium a dozen or more times to rescue them from the chaos.

Eventually Jon was satisfied that the clavers who needed help had made it to the buses. The playing field and the bleachers were filled with bodies, some of them children's. One of the guards told him the bodies would be sorted, with clavers being taken back to Sexton for burial. The grubs would be thrown into a body pit on the outskirts of town.

"Better than they deserve," the guard said. "They should all be thrown in, dead or alive."

Jon didn't argue. Instead he walked to the locker room and showered. He was filthy with blood and sweat, but no matter how hard he scrubbed, he still felt death all over him.

He finished dressing and walked outside. He was hoping to see Coach or some of his teammates, but they weren't around. The buses were gone as well.

Jon found a guard. "Where is everyone?" he asked.

"A lot of the clavers are staying in town to teach the grubs a lesson," the guard replied.

"A lesson?" Jon asked, feeling like an idiot. "What kind of lesson?"

The guard laughed. "The kind even grubs won't forget," he said. "What happened here? Kid's play compared to what's going to happen."

Jon thought about the bum they hadn't killed that night. He

thought about Coach letting them know they could do whatever they wanted tonight. He thought about clavers and their guns. He thought about Alex telling him to make sure Mom was all right, and now he understood why Alex was worried.

"Do you know White Birch?" he asked, realizing he didn't. He knew the high school was three miles from where Mom lived, but he had no idea how to get to her apartment. "Broadway. Do you know how to get to Broadway from here?"

"I'd stay off Broadway if I were you," the guard said.

The market was on Broadway. If Jon got to the market, he'd be able to find Mom's apartment. "Broadway," he said. "How do I get there?"

The guard pointed. "It's about six blocks that way," he said. "The first traffic light is Broadway. But it's going to be a jungle. You armed?"

Jon shook his head.

"Stay off Broadway, then," the guard said. "Walk the side streets, parallel."

"I'm looking for the clinic," he said, knowing that was in Mom's neighborhood. "When I get to Broadway, do I turn right or left?"

"The clinic won't be open," the guard said. "It's Saturday."

"Please," Jon said. "Which way?"

"Left," the guard said. "Clinic's two or three miles from here. Why not wait for a bus to Sexton? Go to the hospital there."

"Left on Broadway," Jon said. "Thanks."

"Be careful," the guard said. "The grubs don't care who they kill."

Neither do the clavers, Jon thought, but he kept quiet as he began the walk toward Broadway. He turned left a block before the traffic light and ran down the side streets, hearing gunshots and screams only a few yards away. Across Broadway he saw an apartment house burning. Guards stood in front, shooting the grubs as they ran out the door.

Jon couldn't stop the slaughter. He was caught in a human tornado, with no choice but to run. Only when he reached a small deserted park did he pause to catch his breath. But when he looked up, he saw a man's body hanging from a tree, mutilated and lynched.

It's Tyler, Jon thought, but then he told himself it couldn't possibly be. Tyler's father was on the town board. No one, not even grubs driven to insanity, would kill Tyler. The body belonged to some other claver separated from guards, from friends, from protectors. He refused to believe it was Tyler.

Jon told himself that even with so many guards in White Birch, enough remained in Sexton to kill any grubs trying to force their way in. Alex would bring Lisa and Gabe home to safety. He could only hope Mom was safe as well.

Fires were burning all around him, but at Mom's end of town Broadway seemed quiet. Jon walked swiftly to the avenue, stepping around bodies lying in rivulets of blood.

Storefront windows were shattered, with glass everywhere. As Jon passed the market, he saw it had been destroyed. Shelves were knocked over, whatever food there'd been, taken. A bar of soap, he remembered. He'd left a single bar of soap for all the grubs in the neighborhood.

Jon knew where he was now, and he ran the remaining few blocks to Mom's apartment. Things were quiet, but in front of Mom's house there were three women's bodies, their faces slashed to ribbons.

Jon looked long enough to make certain none of them was

his mother, then raced into her building. No one had locks in White Birch. Grubs had no need for locks.

"Mom!" he screamed as he flew up the stairs to her apartment. "Mom!"

He burst into her apartment, still yelling at the top of his lungs. "Mom, where are you?"

"Jon!" she cried, rushing into his arms. "Oh, Jonny!"

Jon held his mother as tightly as he could. "You're all right?" he asked. "No one hurt you?"

Mom broke away. "I hid," she said. "When we moved here, we figured out the best places to hide. We had drills. Alex made us."

"He told me to come," Jon said. "He was worried about you."

"Is he all right?" Mom asked.

"He's okay," Jon said, hoping that was true. Who knew what they did to the drivers when they reached Sexton. "Mom, we'd better get out of here. It's safe now, but they could come back."

"I heard screams," she said. "It was like the tornado. I felt so helpless."

"I know," Jon said. "Come, Mom. Let's go."

"Where?" she asked. "Where can we go? Can we go to Sexton?"

"We'll go to the clinic," he said, knowing even in all the madness, his mother wouldn't be allowed into Sexton. "It's open today. We'll be safe there."

Mom nodded. "I'm sorry," she said. "I'll be all right. Oh, Jonny, I was so scared."

"Don't be," he said. "We're all okay. Miranda's safe in the hospital, and Alex took Lisa and Gabe home hours ago. But we'll be better off in the clinic. Dr. Goldman will know what to do."

Mom was still shaking, but she followed Jon out of the apartment and down the stairs. There was no protecting her from the sight of the bodies, though. Mom stood in front of them.

"Will they be buried?" she asked. "They had family in Georgia. Will anyone tell their family?"

"No," Jon said. "They'll be cremated. No one will tell their family."

"That could have been me," she said. "If I'd lived on the first floor."

"Don't think about it," Jon told her. "Let's go."

In the five-block walk to the clinic they saw dozens more bodies scattered around. This was a quiet residential neighborhood, Jon thought. If it was this bad here, it must be a hundred times worse a mile or two closer to the high school.

"What happened?" Mom asked. "What started this?"

"It was the soccer match," he said. "It started there."

"Soccer," Mom said. "A war started once because of a soccer match. Did you know that?"

"No, Mom," Jon said.

Mom sighed. "It was just an excuse," she said. "People kill for no reason whatsoever. That's never going to change."

"Things will get better," Jon said. "You always say that, Mom."

"No," she said. "I'm not saying that ever again."

They walked another block in silence until they saw a child's body on the pavement. Mom shook her head. "Why would anybody do that?" she said. "Slaughter a little girl."

Jon pulled at her sleeve. "We have to keep going, Mom," he said. "We can't stay here."

There were lights on in the clinic and two guards stood in front. Jon showed them his claver ID badge. "This is my mother," he said. "We're friends of Dr. Goldman."

"We're not supposed to let anyone in," one of the guards said, pointing his gun at Jon.

"Put that down," Mom said. "Hasn't there been killing enough?"

"Mom," Jon said. "Don't argue with the guards. Sarah! It's me, Jon!"

Dr. Goldman opened the door. "Jon," he said. "Laura. Guards, it's all right. They can come in."

The guards stood aside, and Jon and his mother walked into the clinic. As Dr. Goldman closed the door, Sarah raced into the room and threw herself into Jon's arms.

"I was so scared," she said. "I was so afraid for you."

"Laura," Dr. Goldman said, "Jon. Sit down. Sarah, get them some potka."

"No," Mom said. "We don't need any."

"Yes, you do," Dr. Goldman declared. "I'm sorry I don't have any brandy, but the potka will suffice."

Sarah left the room and returned with two glasses and a bottle. She poured a tiny amount into each glass. "Drink," she said. "Doctor's orders."

Mom took a swallow and grimaced. "How can anybody drink this stuff?" she asked. "It's rotgut."

"I don't see Jon having a problem with it," Dr. Goldman pointed out.

They turned to face Jon, who had finished his glass in two swallows.

Mom sighed. "It's a different world," she said, and then she burst into hysterical laughter.

They laughed so hard, one of the guards came in to see if they were all right. "It's the potka," Dr. Goldman told him.

"I could use some myself," the guard said.

"I'm sure you could," Dr. Goldman replied. "But not while you're on duty."

"Yes sir," the guard said, and went back out.

"I hope it's okay we came," Jon said. "I didn't know where else to go."

"You did the right thing," Dr. Goldman said. "What happened, Jon? All we know is we were ordered to keep the door locked and not let anyone in. I'm sure there are people who need assistance, but the guard said he'd shoot me if I left the building."

"There was a riot at the soccer match," Jon said. "Then the clavers decided to go into White Birch. Everyone went crazy. I saw a lot of bodies, fires everywhere."

"They killed my neighbors," Mom said. "I should have tried to stop it, but I hid instead."

"You couldn't have stopped them, Laura," Dr. Goldman said. "There's no point feeling guilty."

"You shouldn't feel guilty either, Daddy," Sarah said. "If you'd gone out, you would have been killed, too."

"Well, we're here," Mom said. "What happens next? When can Jon and Sarah go home?"

"Not until tomorrow," Dr. Goldman replied. "I called the depot to see if we could get a driver, and they said no one's allowed in or out of White Birch tonight. No, we're here for the night. I'll call again tomorrow to see if they can get Jon and Sarah out."

"If you stay, I stay," Sarah said.

"No," Dr. Goldman said. "We don't need guilt and we don't need nobility. You and Jon will go home together. Meantime, this is as safe a place as we can be. We might as well get some sleep. Laura, why don't you sleep on the examining table? The rest of us can use the floor."

"I can't do that," Mom said.

"Don't worry," Dr. Goldman said. "You'll be just as uncomfortable as the rest of us."

Mom climbed onto the examining table. "You sure this is all right?" she asked.

"Mom, go to sleep," Jon said.

Mom sighed. "A son's love," she said. "Nothing sweeter."

They all laughed. Then Jon, Sarah, and Dr. Goldman stretched out on the floor.

Jon reached out and touched Sarah's hand. They were safe, he told himself. They were protected. Whatever had happened, whatever would happen, for this night at least, they were safe.

Chapter 10

"Wake up, Jon."

Jon sat upright on the floor. His body ached all over. He was hungry and, for a moment, confused.

"Is everyone okay?" he asked as the memories flooded back in.

Dr. Goldman smiled. "We're fine," he said. "But it's time for you to get up."

"He always was a late sleeper," Mom said. "Even when he was little."

At least Mom acknowledged he wasn't little anymore. "What's happening?" he asked. "Does anybody know?"

"Things are better," Sarah said. "Calmer."

"For the moment, anyway," her father said. "I called the depot. They'll send a private car for us this afternoon. I said I preferred to stay, but they're insisting I go back with you."

"They're letting the fires burn themselves out," Mom said. "But this section is safe, and there are guards on the streets. So it's time for me to go home."

"Not alone," Jon said. "I'll take you there."

"You and a guard," Dr. Goldman said. "He'll escort you there and back, Jon, and you'll wait with us for the car."

Jon nodded. He excused himself and went to the bathroom. When he returned to the office, Mom was ready to leave.

Dr. Goldman walked out of the office with them, telling one of the guards what to do. There was still smoke in the distance, but Jon only heard one gunshot, and that seemed far away.

They walked in silence back to Mom's apartment. The three murdered women were still lying in front of the building.

"I heard they'll start moving the corpses tomorrow," the guard said. "Meantime, stay in your apartment, ma'am. A siren will ring three times, then stop, then three times again to let the grubs know they can go out again. Don't leave until then or you might get shot."

"Thank you," Mom said. "I'll stay in my apartment until I hear the sirens."

"I'm going upstairs with my mother," Jon said. "I'll be a few minutes. Wait for me here, all right?"

"Yes sir," the guard said.

Jon and his mother walked the flight of stairs to her apartment. "Wait here," he said, "while I check things out."

"Don't be silly," she replied, promptly walking ahead of him. "You must be famished. I know I am. I'll get us something to eat."

"I'm okay," Jon said. "I'll eat when I get back to Sexton."

"You'll eat right now," Mom said. They walked to the kitchen and saw it had been ransacked. Mom checked the cupboards, but all her food had been stolen. They looked around the apartment, but whoever had stolen the food was gone.

"Are you going to be okay?" Jon asked.

"I'll be fine," she said. "Come here."

They walked to Miranda and Alex's room, and Mom opened the closet door. "Our hidden stash," she said, pulling cans of food out of an emptied pillow on the closet shelf. "Alex's paranoia can come in handy."

Jon checked the supplies. "That should last you for a few days," he said. "Besides, they'll start getting food to you in a day or two."

"I'm not so sure," Mom replied. "They'll feed the workers in Sexton. But I don't think they'll send food to White Birch. They're not putting the fires out. They closed the clinic when it's most needed. I don't think they're going to send us any supplies until they think we've suffered enough."

"I'll bring you food," Jon said.

"Jon, thank you," Mom said. "We're all right for the time being. Sit down. I want to talk."

They sat on the bed. Mom reached out and touched Jon's hand. "We may never see each other again," she said.

"Mom!" Jon said. "Don't say that."

"I have to," she replied. "Things are bad, Jon. Not the way they were before. Everything else — the earthquakes, the diseases, all of it — no one's been at fault. We've suffered together. But what's happening, what's going to happen, is man-made. Sexton's a bully, Jon. It's a frightened bully. You know me. I'm the one who always believes if we can just hold out, things will get better. I don't believe that anymore. Not after yesterday. The enclave will let us die. They'll bring in new laborers and work them to death and then bring another batch in."

Jon turned away.

Mom grabbed his arm and forced him to look at her. "I love you," she said. "And I want you to know the decision to let you live with Lisa was one of the hardest I've ever made in my life. Harder than divorcing your father. Harder than letting Matt and Syl move away. Every day I've asked myself if I did the right thing, and I still don't know. You're healthier than you would have been here, and you're better educated, and you have a real chance at a future. But I know it hurt you to live away from your family. I know you feel like I haven't been there for you."

"I've wanted things to be different," he said. "Like they were before, back home."

"We'll never have that again," Mom said. "It's gone, not just for us, for everybody. We're the lucky ones, Jon. Think of it. You have your brother and your sister. Gabe, too, and Lisa. Lisa's been wonderful, and I want you to tell her how grateful, how eternally grateful I am to her. Love them, Jon, because they're your family and they're good, loving people. Your father loved you so much, and I love you so much. Never forget that."

"I know," Jon said. "I love you, Mom. And I need you. Promise me you'll be all right."

"All I can promise is that I'll try," Mom said. "Promise me you'll try, also, Jonny."

"I promise," Jon said.

Mom kissed him and then got up. "The guard's waiting for you," she said. "Do whatever Dr. Goldman and Lisa tell you. Please see Miranda, and let her know I'm all right. I don't want her to worry about me."

Jon stood and embraced his mother. "We'll make it through this," he said. "I promise."

"Go," Mom said. "And remember how much I love you."

Jon left Mom in the bedroom. He walked out of the apartment, down the stairs, past the dead bodies. The guard followed him as he walked.

In a couple of hours he'd be home. Back to the house in Sexton where there were domestics to look after him and always enough to eat. Back to the life everyone had sacrificed for so that he might have a home and food and a real chance at a future.

I'll be good, he promised them all, he promised himself. I'll make you proud.

Monday, July 6

Jon found Carrie in the kitchen when he went downstairs for breakfast.

"How do you like your eggs?" she asked. "Scrambled?"

"Yeah," Jon said. "Where's Val?"

"I don't know," Carrie said. She broke two eggs into a bowl, poured some goat's milk in, and began beating them.

"I thought you and Val took the bus together Mondays?" Jon said.

"Look," Carrie said, turning to face him. "I walk to Val's house Monday mornings and we take the bus together. Only this morning I couldn't. The guards herded us like cattle to the terminal. They frisked us before we got onto the buses, and I was stopped four times walking from the terminal to here. That's all I know."

"Did you tell Lisa you don't know where Val is?" Jon asked.

Carrie poured the eggs in the pan. "Yes, I told her. She said I should assume Val wouldn't be coming, and for the time being I should do her work as well as mine."

Lisa had been in a terrible mood when Jon had gotten home the day before. She'd yelled at Jon because he hadn't let her know he was all right. Then she said work was going to be a nightmare because, from what she was hearing, there were hundreds, possibly thousands dead in White Birch, and that meant any number of houses in Sexton would be without one or more of their domestics, and they'd be calling her to demand she replace the ones who were gone.

Jon began to eat. If Val was missing, then Carrie was their only domestic, at least until Miranda had her baby. And if Lisa had to send Carrie to some other claver's home, then Miranda would be their only one, cleaning the house, doing the cooking, looking after Gabe and her own baby.

There'd be no avoiding her then. She'd sleep in the nursery and clean Jon's room and make his meals and be some bizarre combination of his domestic and his sister.

It was one thing for Mom to tell him to love Miranda. It was another to want her in his home, reminding him, without saying a word, that he had all the advantages she didn't, her baby didn't.

And he'd never be able to forget Julie with her killer in his home.

He walked over to Sarah's house, trying not to think about any of that. But Sarah's mood didn't make things better.

"They won't let us open the clinic," she said. "No one from Sexton is allowed into White Birch."

"They've let the grubs come here," Jon said. "Carrie's here but not Val."

"Two of our domestics are missing," Sarah said.

"Missing isn't dead," Jon said.

"Yes it is," Sarah said. "Oh, I don't know. Maybe not. I don't know anything about them. They've been working for us, living with us for months, and I don't know anything about them."

"They don't want you to know," Jon said. "They hate us. We give them just enough food to live, and we make them do whatever we need, and they have no choice but to put up with it. The only thing left to them is a little bit of privacy."

Sarah stared at him. "You've changed," she said.

"Trust me," Jon said. "I liked it the way it was. I liked having Val do all the housework and Carrie taking care of Gabe so I didn't have to. I liked feeling it was okay for me to eat real food and have clean clothes and clean air to breathe. Okay? That's how it was when I was a kid. Without the grubs, but all the rest of it: food and clothes and air. Then for two years I lived in hell. Everyone did, I know that. But I got offered a way out and I took it, and got food and clothes and clean air. I'm not going to apologize for liking it. You like it. We all like it."

"Do you think someday everyone will have that?" Sarah asked. "Will there ever be enough for all of us?"

"I don't know," Jon replied. "Maybe someday if we figure out how to share. Mom thinks things are going to get worse around here, though."

"Daddy won't say it," Sarah said. "But I can tell that's what he thinks."

"They're afraid for us," Jon said. "They have been for four years now. They don't know how not to be afraid."

"I'm afraid, too, Jon," Sarah said.

Jon held her tight. "We'll make it," he said. "I promise you."

But when they got to school, Jon began to doubt he could keep that promise, any promise. He'd never seen the school so heavily guarded. And none of the students were laughing, or even talking.

They were told to go directly to the auditorium. Luke saw Jon and Sarah and walked in with them.

The middle school students were there along with the high schoolers, seated in their own section. Jon looked around. Tyler wasn't there, and neither was Zachary.

The students stood and sang "The Star-Spangled Banner." Then Mr. Morrow, principal of all the Sexton students from kindergarten through high school, told them to continue standing for a moment of silence in memory of all who had died on Saturday.

"These are difficult and frightening times," Mr. Morrow said after everyone was seated. "The Sexton school system has suffered great loss. Miss Wilkins, the second grade teacher, is missing and presumed dead. Mr. Donnelly, who teaches English in middle school, is known dead. He died saving the lives of our students. His courage will long be remembered."

Jon took Sarah's hand and held on to it.

"Four students died on Saturday," Mr. Morrow continued. "Jennifer Simms, a fourth grader, was trampled to death at the stadium. Seventh grader Michael Davies was separated from his parents. He was found shot to death on the playing field."

The guards killed him, Jon thought, but he knew no one would ever admit that.

"Tyler Hughes and Zachary Wright, two of our most popular students, were murdered," Mr. Morrow said. "It seems a mob grabbed Tyler, and when Zachary ran to get help, another mob found and killed him." He paused. "I've been told there will be funerals for all who died, but not until the end of the week. Their bodies have been recovered and are in Sexton, but with so many deaths, it will take time before all the arrangements can be made."

"They need grubs to dig the graves," Luke whispered.

Jon thought of all the bodies he'd seen in White Birch, grubs who'd be tossed in body pits and cremated without anyone to witness and grieve. Then he thought of Tyler and what his parents must have felt when they saw what had been done to their son.

"I want to take a moment to praise the many students who stood their ground against the mob and helped women and children make their way safely back to Sexton," Mr. Morrow said.

"Five of the Sexton soccer team were students here. Now there are three. Would those three fine young men please stand? They represent what's best in Sexton."

Jon had no desire to stand, and he could see how uncomfortable Luke was. But Ryan, in the row ahead of them, stood, and reluctantly Jon and Luke rose as well.

It was a nightmare hearing the students and faculty cheering for them. Jon sat as soon as he possibly could, and Luke joined him. A moment later Ryan also sat.

"I didn't do anything," Luke whispered. "I got on a bus right away. Ryan did, too. We were too scared to stay."

"It doesn't matter," Jon said. "They need heroes. We're it."

"After this assembly, guards will escort you to your buses," Mr. Morrow said. "School will be closed until next Monday so that you can attend the funerals of your friends and fellow students."

Jon spotted Alex on one of the buses. It made him feel better. But when he got home, he found Carrie on her hands and knees scrubbing the kitchen floor while Gabe jumped up and down, screaming for attention.

"What's going on?" Jon asked.

"Val's not here," Carrie said. "Someone has to do the work."

Gabe turned his attention to Jon. "Play with me!" he screamed. "I hate Carrie! She won't play with me!"

"Stop it," Jon said sharply. "Carrie, your job is to take care of Gabe."

"You think I don't know that?" she said. "I'm doing what Mrs. Evans told me to do. I don't have four hands."

"I'm sorry," Jon said. "It came out wrong. You take care of Gabe. I'll do the scrubbing."

Carrie stared at him. Gabe continued to scream.

"I'm getting the best of it," Jon said. "Give me the scrub brush."

Carrie stood up. "Do you know how to scrub a floor?" she asked.

"No," Jon said. "But it's about time I learned."

Tuesday, July 7

"I want you to go to the hospital," Lisa said at breakfast.

Jon wanted to whine, "Do I have to?" but knew better. Lisa was exhausted. She'd gotten home from work at ten o'clock the night before and had told Jon she expected to keep those hours for the rest of the week at least.

"Four hundred twenty-two domestics didn't show up for work yesterday," she said. "Roughly three hundred families are short at least one grub, and trust me, they need their grubs. Air purifiers can do only so much. Nineteen families don't have working washing machines, and they each need one grub just for laundry. Carrie, this floor is filthy. I thought I told you to wash it."

"I washed it," Jon said. "I'll do a better job today."

"It's not your responsibility to scrub the floors," Lisa said.

"It's not Carrie's, either," Jon said. "It's Val's, and she's not here. I don't have school until Monday. I can do some housework until then."

"Do it better, then," Lisa said. "And visit Miranda. That *is* your responsibility. Carrie, for the time being, you're the only domestic in this house. You want to eat? You do the work."

"Yes, Mrs. Evans," Carrie said.

Lisa sighed. "I know Gabe's a handful," she said. "I know I've spoiled him rotten. His father's gone, and I'm at work six days a week, and I can't bring myself to say no to him during the little time we have together. And you've done wonders with him. You, too, Jon. He's a sad and lonely little boy, and I don't know how to make things better for him."

"I don't think you can," Jon said.

"Probably not," she said. "I've got to go. Tell Gabe I love him, and I'll see him tonight. Only I won't. I won't get back here until after his bedtime. Tell him when I get home, I'll wake him up with a kiss." She got up to leave. "Jon, go to the hospital. Find out how Miranda is doing," she said again. "And help Carrie out. Play with Gabe so she can do the housework."

"I will," Jon said. "I'll see you tonight."

Lisa bent over and gave him a kiss. "You're a good boy, Jon," she said. "Give Miranda my love. Tell her we're counting the minutes until she gets here."

Jon went upstairs, woke Gabe, and helped him get dressed. He brought him to the kitchen and sat with him while Carrie made his breakfast. When Gabe was through eating, he and Jon went upstairs and played every game Gabe could think of. Carrie cleaned the house and made their lunch.

"I'm going to the hospital," he told Carrie, after putting Gabe to bed for his afternoon nap. "I'll stay with Gabe when I get back."

"Thank you, Jon," Carrie said. "See you later."

Jon got a bus that took him to the hospital neighborhood. He couldn't get over how many guards were in town. Did they really think the grubs were going to rise up in revolt? Or was it just to make the clavers feel safer?

Miranda was lying in bed when Jon got there. She looked good, better than Carrie and Lisa did.

"Jon!" she said. "Oh, I'm so glad to see you. I know something's going on, but I don't know what, and I haven't seen Lisa since last week. Is everyone all right? I've been so worried."

"Everyone's fine," Jon said. "I saw Mom on Saturday. Sunday, too. And I saw Alex yesterday, driving a bus."

"Lisa?" Miranda said. "Gabe?"

Jon laughed. "They're fine, too," he said. For a moment Miranda was just Miranda, his big sister, the one who'd teased him, the one he'd driven crazy. Just for a moment, though. Then he remembered Julie and what Miranda had done to her. He didn't want to, but he edged away.

"What's the matter?" Miranda said. "Sit down, Jon, and tell me what's going on. I know you're keeping something from me."

Jon sat on a straight-back chair against the wall. "Things went crazy in White Birch this weekend," he replied. "Bad crazy. But Mom's fine. Nothing happened to her. And Alex is on the job, so he's okay, too."

"The nurses used to pop in on me all the time," Miranda said. "Orderlies, too. The past couple of days I've hardly seen anyone. Oh, they're taking good care of me, and I know how lucky I am to be here. But something's wrong. Things are too quiet."

"A lot of people who live in White Birch are missing," he replied. "Some of them died, but a lot of them probably packed their bags and left. Lisa's going crazy trying to replace the domestics. That's why she hasn't seen you. She got home after ten o'clock last night, and she says it's going to be like that all week."

"But Mom's all right," Miranda said. "And Alex."

"I spent the weekend with Mom," Jon said. "She sends her love. She wishes she could be here, but there's no way she can get a pass. And Alex is back at work, so he's okay, too. We all are, Miranda. We're just waiting for you to have the baby."

"Is it okay with you?" she asked. "Me working for Lisa?"

It wasn't, but there was nothing Jon could say. "Lisa thinks it's a great idea," he said. "Val's missing, so things are kind of hard. We could use a helping hand."

"I like Lisa," Miranda said. "Gabe's a handful, but he's my brother and I love him. I'm hoping to be out of here in a week. The baby's kicking up a storm. It's ready to be born, I'm sure of it."

Jon looked at his watch. "I told Carrie I'd be home soon," he said. "She has all the housework and Gabe, and that's too much for her. I'd better go."

"Will you come back?" Miranda asked. "Will I see you again?"

"I don't know," Jon said. "With school and soccer and helping out with Gabe, I don't have much time."

Miranda smiled, but there was no warmth in it. "You're a good claver, Jon," she said. "You do all the right things."

"This isn't my fault," Jon said. "I didn't ask for any of this."

"I didn't, either," Miranda said. "Okay, Jon. Go. You did your duty. The next time I see Mom, I'll tell her what a good boy you are."

"Go to hell," Jon said. He walked out of the room, paying no heed to Miranda calling his name.

Wednesday, July 8

When the phone rang, Jon figured it was Lisa calling from work. Carrie was putting Gabe to sleep, but Lisa probably wanted to wish him good night over the phone.

But it was Alex.

"Miranda's all right," Jon said. "I saw her yesterday."

"That's not what I'm calling about," Alex said. "Do you know where Laura is?"

"Mom?" Jon said. "Why? What's the matter?"

"I don't know," Alex said. "Maybe nothing. But I got home from work and she wasn't there. That's not like her. I thought maybe you'd gotten her into Sexton."

"You know we can't," Jon said. "Maybe Mom's visiting people." He remembered the dead bodies in front of the apartment and started to feel sick. "Look, Alex, if Mom comes home, could you let me know?"

"Not today," Alex said. "Curfew's in five minutes. I'm already taking a chance calling. I'll talk to you tomorrow night. Or if Laura gets back, I'll have her call you tomorrow."

Jon could hear sirens in the background. "Gotta go," Alex said. "Curfew."

Alex was a worrier, Jon told himself. Even Mom thought he was paranoid.

But Mom also thought she might never see Jon again. Someone had gone into her apartment and stolen her food. Someone had slaughtered her downstairs neighbors.

He picked up the phone and called Sarah.

"Is something the matter?" she asked as soon as she heard his voice.

"Yes," Jon said. "No. I don't know. Look, is your father going to White Birch tomorrow? Is the clinic open?"

"Yes," Sarah said. "I'm going, too. It's a good excuse not to go to Zachary's funeral."

"The funeral," Jon said. He'd almost forgotten. Zachary's was scheduled for Thursday and Tyler's for Friday.

People wouldn't care if Sarah wasn't at the funerals. They didn't like her or trust her, and they'd figure she'd skip out on something that important.

But Jon was different. He was their classmate, their teammate, their friend. It would seem strange if he wasn't there. It would be one more mark against him, one more indication that he was just a slip, not really a claver.

But Alex was scared and Mom was missing. "I need to go to White Birch," Jon said. "How do you get there? Are the claver buses running?"

"No," Sarah said. "Clavers aren't allowed in. Daddy goes by private car. And when we're there, we're not allowed out of the clinic except to go home."

"Mom's missing," Jon said. "Alex called. Maybe it's nothing, but I've got to find out. I'm going with you. What time do you leave?"

"Seven o'clock," Sarah said. "But Jon, even if you get there, you can't walk around. It's too dangerous."

"I have to," Jon said. "I'll be at your house at six thirty. Tell your father."

"Jon," Sarah said, but he hung up.

It'll be okay, he told himself. He'd get to Mom's apartment somehow and find her there. She'd hug him, the way she used to when he was little.

It'll be all right. This one time, it had to be all right.

Thursday, July 9

"Drop him off here," Dr. Goldman said to the driver.

"You sure?" the driver asked. "My orders are to take you to the clinic."

"Your orders are to do what I tell you," Dr. Goldman said. "I brought this boy along to run errands. Now do as I say and let him out here."

"Watch out for the guards," the driver said as he pulled to the curb in front of Mom's apartment. "They'll shoot first, ask later."

Sarah grasped Jon's arm. He looked at her and smiled. "I'll be fine," he said. "See you soon." He opened the car door and let himself out.

The bodies were still there, but Jon felt an absurd sense of relief when he saw there were no new ones. He opened the door and ran up the stairs, calling for Mom. But there was no answer.

Jon checked the apartment, continuously calling Mom's name. He even checked where she hid her food. There were still cans there.

If someone had broken in and demanded to know where the food was, Mom would have told him. She wouldn't die for the sake of a few cans.

So where was she?

Before, when things were normal, when things were the way they were supposed to be, Mom would have left a note. But now she lived in a world with no paper, no pencils or pens. They'd brought nothing like that when they'd come from Pennsylvania. They hadn't even brought copies of the books Mom had written.

No paper. No pens. Only a pay phone a half dozen blocks away.

Feeling like a fool, Jon searched the apartment one more time. There was no sign of Mom, of anybody. Alex had even made the bed that morning. Somehow that didn't surprise Jon. It was the kind of thing he would do. His wife was hospitalized, his mother-in-law missing, and Alex made the bed.

Unless Mom wasn't missing.

Jon thought about it. She hadn't been home when Alex got home, and then he went to the pay phone to call Jon. But maybe

Mom was home when Alex got back. He couldn't leave the apartment to call. It was past curfew.

The curfew ran until 5 a.m., when the dayworker grubs, like Alex and Miranda, began their walks to the bus terminal. Alex took a 6 a.m. bus. He wouldn't have had time to call Jon before leaving for work.

Jon remembered Carrie saying guards had herded them Monday morning. The grubs needed passes to get on the buses, and Mom didn't have a pass, because she didn't work in Sexton. She wouldn't have risked going to the pay phone while the grubs were walking to the terminal.

Mom could have waited until seven o'clock to call him, when he was already on his way to White Birch.

He grinned. Mom was fine. She was at school, helping those precious students of hers. He was the one risking his life while she was safe and sound.

He thought about waiting in the apartment until Mom got home, but he knew Sarah would go crazy if he did. No, the thing to do was go to the school, see Mom, and go from there to the clinic.

Jon made sure he had the note Dr. Goldman had written claiming he'd been brought to White Birch to run errands. Of course the guards might shoot him before they saw the note. But Jon didn't think that would happen. He'd seen only a few guards on the drive through White Birch. Things had quieted down. He'd be safe.

Still, he took care as he walked the few blocks to the elementary school. The one time he saw a guard, he stood back, hardly breathing, until the guard was a few blocks away.

Except for the guard, Jon saw no one but corpses. He wondered when the grubs would be allowed to cart the bodies off.

Bullies. That's what Mom had called the clavers. She was right. There was no reason to leave the bodies except to rub the grubs' noses in it. The way Coach had wanted them to do.

Sunday's match had been canceled. It was an official day of mourning for Sexton. All the claver bodies would be buried by then. Maybe after that they'd let White Birch take care of theirs.

Jon knew roughly where the school was, but he didn't know exactly, so he walked for a few blocks before he spotted it. Taking care there were no guards around, he approached the school.

He could never be sure just when he saw her. A block away maybe? Two blocks? How far could you be before you saw a body hanging from a tree? How near did you have to be to know the body belonged to your mother?

Jon no longer cared about guards. He ran to the schoolyard, to the tree, to Mom's lifeless body, her feet dangling over a drying pool of blood.

She'd been shot. Jon couldn't guess how many times, but her clothes were ripped with bullet holes, and half her face was gone.

He wanted to scream, but that might bring the guards. The same guards who had killed her. He moaned instead and took his mother's hand, holding the cold, dead flesh for as long as he could bear. Then he stormed into the school. The grubs would know what happened. If he had to beat it out of them, he'd find out why his mother had been slaughtered.

He broke into one of the classrooms and grabbed the teacher. "I'm her son!" he screamed. "Laura Evans's son!"

The kids in the class didn't look much older than Gabe. They began crying. Their teacher broke away from Jon.

"I'm sorry," she said. "So sorry. There was nothing we could do."

"What happened?" he cried. "Why?"

The teacher shook her head. "Not here," she said. "Go to Mrs. Brunswick's office, by the front door. She can tell you."

He left the classroom and ran to the office. He'd passed it when he came in, but he hadn't realized there was someone in there.

She sat quietly behind a battered desk.

"Mrs. Brunswick?"

The woman nodded.

Jon took a deep breath. "I'm Jon Evans," he said. "What happened to my mother?"

"I'm sorry," she said. "Please, sit down."

"Mom didn't come home last night," Jon said. "I came here looking for her. Tell me what happened." He was using his claver tone, he realized, and for a moment Mrs. Brunswick reacted like a grub.

But then she exhaled, and Jon saw she wasn't a grub, any more than his mother had been.

"I'm sorry," he said. "I thought I'd find Mom here, teaching. Please. I have to know."

Mrs. Brunswick nodded. "Your mother was in her classroom," she said. "A half dozen guards came in. They told me they'd come for the high school students. There's a labor shortage, because of the riots. All the high school students had to start work immediately, the boys in the factories, the girls as domestics."

Jon thought about Lisa trying to find domestics for all the claver homes. He knew she wouldn't have asked for the high school students, but he also knew she wouldn't have argued against it. A month ago he wouldn't have, either.

"The guards went into your mother's classroom, and Laura, well, she put up a fight," Mrs. Brunswick continued. "She stood up to them."

"And they shot her," Jon said.

Mrs. Brunswick shook her head. "I wish they had," she said. "I wish it had been that quick, that clean. Two of them grabbed her, dragged her outside. The others went to the classrooms, told everyone they had to go out. We knew they'd kill the children if we didn't. We had no choice but to do what they said."

"I know," Jon said. "I know this isn't your fault."

"They used one of their belts for a noose," Mrs. Brunswick said, her voice quivering. "They told Laura to say her prayers. She said . . . she said she'd see them in hell. They made it tighter, but she still wouldn't beg like they wanted her to. Then they used her for target practice."

She was sobbing by then, but Jon didn't cry. There was no point. Dead was dead. His father had died of hunger and disease. Was that better than being hanged and shot?

"They said they'd come back for the belt," Mrs. Brunswick added. "They said they'd kill our children if she wasn't still there when they came back for the belt."

"The students," Jon said. "The high school students?" The ones Mom died for, he thought.

"They took them," Mrs. Brunswick said. "I don't think they hurt them. Sexton needs the workers."

Jon stood. "I have to go," he said. "There are people expecting me."

Mrs. Brunswick rose. "I'm so sorry," she said. "I only met your mother after the high school burned down, but I could see what a wonderful woman she was. She was devoted to her students."

Jon nodded.

"To her family, also," Mrs. Brunswick said. "She was . . . It was an honor to know her."

"Yes," Jon said. "Well, I have to go."

"There's a back door," Mrs. Brunswick said. "Down this hall-way. If you leave through that door, you won't have to . . . It might be easier for you."

"Thank you," Jon said, but when he left the office, he went out the front door. They wanted people to see Mom. They wanted people to understand what they were capable of doing, what they enjoyed doing.

Jon stood absolutely still by his mother's body. He wanted to take her home, back to Pennsylvania, back to life as it had been. He wanted to be twelve again, to hear Mom cheering him on as he played shortstop for his Little League team. He wanted Mom to see the sun again, to see the grandchild she'd been so eagerly awaiting. He wanted to kill.

A guard walked up to him. "You have business here?" he asked.

"I'm here to run errands for Dr. Goldman," Jon replied. "I have a note." He pulled it out of his pocket and handed it to the guard.

"I'll go with you," the guard said. "You're not supposed to be here, you know. Some of my pals are a little trigger happy."

"Thank you," Jon said. "I appreciate it." He began walking away from his mother, trying not to think that this was the last time he would see her.

"Grubs," the guard said, shaking his head in disgust. "Ani-mals. You should have seen the stadium on Saturday."

"Bad?" Jon asked.

"The game was okay," the guard replied. "Soccer's not my game, though. I played baseball. Third base. Made it to Double A for the Red Sox."

"I was a shortstop," Jon said. "Little League. Phillies fan."

"Good team," the guard said. "Wouldn't have minded being traded to them."

"Double A's good," Jon said. "Would you have made it to the big leagues?"

The guard nodded. "I was drafted out of high school. I was only twenty when everything happened. Killed that dream, let me tell you."

"Mine, too," Jon said. And my father's. And my mother's.

The guard laughed. "We all started somewhere," he said. "I made it to Williamsport one year. Little League World Series. We were knocked out second round, but it was great. One of the best times of my life. I felt like a star."

"I would have liked that," Jon said.

"I feel bad for you kids sometimes," the guard said. "Well, you have it all right, being a claver. But the ones here? Once things turned bad, well, they turned bad right along with it. You should see what they did to each other Saturday." He paused. "I killed a bunch of them Saturday night. I'd never killed anyone before then. I could have a few times, but I didn't. I was a ballplayer, you know? I wasn't aiming to kill people. But Saturday there was no choice. And after the first few, it didn't feel so bad anymore. That woman? The one you were looking at? She had to be shut up. We had to make an example of her. And the guard in charge, he gets ideas. Everything has to be bigger. He's my boss and I guess he knows what he's doing. I didn't second-guess my manager or the hitting coach. I did what they told me. Same thing, really."

Jon had been beaned once. The ball had hit him flush on his helmet. The world had swirled around him as he'd fallen to his knees.

It was the same sensation now. He'd been walking, talking,

with one of his mother's killers. And he was as helpless now as he had been when the fastball had struck him. The guard was armed, and Jon wasn't. Even letting the guard know it was Jon's mother he'd killed could be fatal.

Mom wanted him to live. He could hear her telling him to swallow his rage.

"The clinic's over there," he said, pointing to the building. "I'll be okay from here."

"Pleasure meeting you," the guard said, shaking Jon's hand. "Us ballplayers got to stick together."

Jon nodded. He walked to the clinic door. The two guards protecting the clinic let him in.

Sarah rushed into his arms. "Did you find her?" she asked. "Is she all right?"

"No," Jon said. "I mean yes. I found her. She's dead." He felt his knees giving in.

Dr. Goldman grabbed him. "Sit down," he said. "Sarah, get the potka. Now."

Jon made it to a chair, and when Sarah brought him the drink, he swallowed it in one burning gulp. "She was killed yesterday," he said. "I saw her body."

Sarah looked at her father, who nodded. She poured another drink.

Jon sipped it this time. "I have to tell people," he said. "Alex will want to know. Miranda. Matt." He started to laugh. "I don't even know how to tell Matt. He delivers mail but he doesn't get any."

"Get a blanket, Sarah," Dr. Goldman said.

Sarah got one and wrapped it around Jon. The warmth felt good, but he couldn't stop shaking.

"You're in shock," Dr. Goldman said. "You wouldn't be human if you weren't. Sarah, get another blanket. Jon, I'm going to give you a shot."

"A shot," Jon said. "That's what Mom got." His laughter grew even more out of control.

"Get up, Jon," Dr. Goldman said. "Keep the blanket wrapped around you. You're going on the examining table. I'm giving you a sedative."

Jon did as Dr. Goldman told him. That's what you were supposed to do. You didn't second-guess. It was wrong to second-guess.

Dr. Goldman rolled up Jon's sleeve. "This will put you out for a couple of hours," he said. "Your problems won't go away, but you'll be able to handle them better." He injected Jon's arm.

"Whatever you say," Jon mumbled. "I don't second-guess."

In a moment he was asleep. Now it was Mom crying, "No. Jon. No."

Chapter 11

"You're going to have to tell Miranda," Lisa said, serving Jon breakfast so they could talk privately. "This morning. The sooner you get it done, the better you'll feel."

"Do you think that's a good idea?" Jon asked. He thought it was a very bad idea, but more for himself than for Miranda.

"Eat something, Jon," Lisa said. "I know you don't feel like it, but you'll need your strength. And no, I don't think it's a good idea, but it has to be done. Miranda's going to want her mother. I know how much I wanted mine when Gabe was born." She paused. "I can't imagine a world without Laura," she said. "I'll never forget how kind she was. It can't have been easy, being so good to your ex's wife. She was an amazing woman. Jon, just a bite, all right?"

Jon took a bite. He missed Val's eggs. Val was probably dead. He wondered if her family would ever find out.

"Miranda would never forgive us if we kept it from her," Lisa said. "Go to the hospital and tell her."

"Can I bring Sarah?" Jon asked. She'd told Jon she wouldn't go to the clinic in case he needed her.

"No," Lisa said. "Miranda's met Sarah what, two times? Three? Her baby's due any minute and she's about to learn her mother died. She doesn't need to have a stranger in the room. When you come back, I want you to look after Gabe while Carrie does the housecleaning. Sarah can keep you company then. Eat some more, Jon. You know how lucky you are to have a breakfast like this?"

"Very," Jon muttered.

"Oh, Jon," Lisa said. "I know I'm not your mother. I'll never replace Laura. But you're going to eat breakfast and you're going to see Miranda and you're going to take care of Gabe."

"Tyler's funeral is this afternoon," Jon said.

"You're not going," Lisa said. "You don't need it, and they don't need you. I need you. Gabe needs you. Miranda needs you."

"How did Alex take it?" Jon asked. Alex had called the night before, but Lisa had spoken to him.

"Not much better than you," Lisa replied. "You know Alex. He feels everything is his fault, he should have been able to protect her." She shook her head. "He couldn't protect his sisters, either. I just hope he'll find the strength to protect Miranda and the baby. Now one more bite and out you go. Give Miranda my love. Tell her I'll do whatever I can and that we're waiting with all our hearts for her and the baby to move here."

Jon knew he wouldn't say any such thing. But he finished his eggs, gave Lisa a kiss good-bye, and left for the bus that would take him to the hospital.

Miranda seemed very happy to see him. "I thought after our fight you wouldn't come," she said. "The baby's due any day now." She laughed. "I've got to be the only girl looking forward to labor. But I want to see Alex so much. And Mom. I want to see her holding the baby. Her first grandchild, Jon. Do you know how much that's going to mean to her?"

"Mom's dead," Jon said. "She died."

"What?" Miranda said. "What do you mean? How can she be dead? You just saw her. You told me you saw her, Jon. You said she was fine. What are you talking about?"

The image of Mom's dead body washed over him. What she'd looked like, how the guard had spoken so easily about killing her. Miranda would never know. Matt wouldn't, either. That memory was his alone.

"Jon!" Miranda cried. "Tell me!"

"I'm sorry," Jon said. "It came out wrong."

"You mean she isn't dead?" Miranda asked. "It's someone else? Is she sick? What, Jon? Tell me."

"Mom was killed," Jon said. "Day before yesterday. Alex called that night after work because he was worried about her; she wasn't home. So I went to White Birch yesterday, to her school. The principal told me what happened. Guards went into Mom's classroom. Someone decided the grubber kids should go to work in Sexton. A lot of grubs died over the weekend. Lisa's been going crazy trying to get replacements."

"I don't care about Lisa!" Miranda shouted. "What happened to Mom?"

"She put up a fight," Jon said. "They shot her."

"I don't believe it," Miranda said. "Did you see her?"

"I saw her," Jon said. "It's true, Miranda. I'm sorry."

"NO!" Miranda screamed. "NO!"

A nurse ran into the room. "What's going on here?" she asked.

"I just told her her mother died," Jon said. *Our mother,* he thought.

"She doesn't need a mother," the nurse said. "We're taking good care of her. She's going to have a fine, strong baby. Now, get out, whoever you are, and leave us alone."

Jon had no desire to be there, but he knew how wrong the nurse was. Miranda needed Mom. They all needed Mom.

Miranda was crying hysterically, and the nurse was trying to quiet her. "I told you to leave," the nurse said. "Get out before I call the guards."

"Miranda, I'm sorry," Jon said as he left the room. He didn't know if she heard him.

He understood now why Lisa had insisted he take care of Gabe. All he wanted was Gabe's love and Sarah's comfort. That was all he wanted, and all he had left.

Saturday, July 11

"In here," Dr. Goldman said to Alex, who was walking behind him, carrying two large suitcases.

"What are those?" Jon asked.

"Props," Dr. Goldman replied. "A way of getting Alex in here. Is your stepmother around?"

"She's at work," Jon said. "Where's Sarah?"

"Home," Dr. Goldman said. "Studying. Something she hasn't done for a week now. Who else is here, Jon?"

"No one," Jon said. "Carrie took Gabe to the market. They left a few minutes ago."

"Good," Dr. Goldman said. "Jon, why don't you take Alex someplace people can't see you. I'll stay here, in case someone shows up."

"Upstairs," Jon said. He led Alex to his bedroom.

"This is nice," Alex said, looking around the room Jon took for granted. "Someday Miranda and I will have a house like this."

"It's okay," Jon said. "The Goldmans' house is a lot nicer.

Most of my friends' houses are. Lisa has a good job, but she's not important."

"You don't have to apologize," Alex said. "Where will Miranda be sleeping?"

"Downstairs, I guess," Jon said. "There's a little bedroom by the kitchen. Val used to sleep there. Alex, what is this? How did Dr. Goldman get you here?"

"He asked for me to be his driver," Alex said. "So they sent me. We went to the hospital first, but they wouldn't let me in. He saw Miranda and says she was all right. Subdued, he said. Very sad. But physically all right. May I sit down?"

"Oh, I'm sorry," Jon said. "Sure. Take the chair." He sat on the bed.

"I went to the school and saw Laura," Alex said. "Lisa said you'd seen her, that there was no mistake, but I had to see it for myself. What did you tell Miranda? Not everything, I hope."

"Just that Mom was shot," Jon said. "Protecting her students."

"Thank you," Alex said. "I think that's what we should tell Matt, also. I'm sorry you had to see her like that, Jon. I'm sorry you heard the whole story."

Jon looked at Alex. He'd never really liked him. Alex had been Julie's overprotective brother, and then for reasons no one understood, Miranda had fallen in love with him, and Alex became family.

Dad and Lisa loved Alex, Jon reminded himself. But they'd loved Julie more. If it weren't for Miranda, Alex would have drifted away from them years ago.

"It's not easy to talk, is it?" Alex said. "We have history, but it's fragmented. We're family, but we're strangers. Acquaintances. If Julie had lived, it would have been different."

"Or if you'd stayed in Texas," Jon said.

"Yeah," Alex said. "That, too."

Jon wanted to confront him, force him to admit the truth about Miranda and Julie. But to his own surprise, he said, "Thursday, after I saw Mom, I met one of the guards who killed her." He hadn't told anyone that, hadn't intended to tell anyone. It was his shame, his nightmare. But now he was sharing it with Alex.

"That must have been very hard," Alex said.

"The thing was, I liked him," Jon said. "He was a ballplayer. We talked baseball. How can that be, Alex? How can someone that evil be . . . I don't know . . . normal? Likable? Is it me? Am I that bad?"

"You're not bad," Alex said. "There's nothing bad about you."

"You don't know the things I've done," Jon said.

"No," Alex said. "I don't. But we both know what Miranda did."

Jon stared at him.

"Carlos told me what you talked about," Alex said. "Carlos is pretty smart in his own way. He realized about ten seconds after you left that you hadn't known about Miranda and Julie. Knowing Carlos, he didn't make it pretty."

"He said Miranda drugged Julie with sleeping pills," Jon said. "Then she smothered her to death."

"That's what Miranda told me," Alex replied. "She wouldn't lie about it."

"She's been lying about it for years," Jon said. "I didn't know. I bet Mom didn't know, or Dad, or Matt. You didn't know at first, either, did you? Miranda told you right before we got to Sexton. That's why you went to Texas."

Alex nodded. "Miranda said she'd tell your folks if I wanted her to, but I said no. I told Carlos, and that was it until Carlos told you. I assume you haven't told Miranda that you know?"

Jon shook his head. "I hated her," he said. "For killing Julie and for not telling me. I've felt like Julie dying was all my fault, but it wasn't. It was Miranda's."

"It was all our faults," Alex said. "Certainly mine. Mine more than anyone else's. I'd told Miranda about the pills, how to use them. My sister Bri had died alone, as alone as a person could be. Julie and I found her. I couldn't protect either of them. But I swore Julie wouldn't die that way, that she would never suffer the way Bri had."

"Miranda didn't have to do it," Jon said.

"She was afraid I was dead," Alex said. "She did what she knew I would have done. Then I came back and she was afraid of how I'd react if I knew the truth. If I hadn't pressed her so hard to marry me, she would have kept it to herself. But she felt she couldn't marry me if I didn't know."

"And you left her," Jon said. "As soon as you heard."

"I was going to go to Texas anyway," Alex said. "I had to tell Carlos about Julie. I thought I'd go to Texas, tell Carlos, and kill myself."

"But you didn't," Jon said. "You told Carlos and came back and married Miranda."

Alex nodded. "I told Carlos what Miranda had done. He asked if I would have done it if I'd been there. I said I hoped I would've had the courage to. Carlos laughed. He said I never would've had the courage. It was amazing that Miranda wanted anything to do with me, and if I had half a brain, which he doubted, I'd go back and marry her and let her get me through life, since I obviously couldn't do it on my own. All of which was true. That night I realized I couldn't kill myself. I couldn't do it to Miranda. I felt an enormous guilt about Julie, but so did Miranda, and she'd had the courage to be with Julie to the very end so that Julie wouldn't die alone. If I killed myself, Miranda would feel she'd killed me by telling me the truth. And I loved Miranda. How could I do that to her when she had done so much for me?"

"So you went back and married her," Jon said. "Happy ending."

"You can hate her," Alex said. "You can hate me. Maybe you hate yourself, and you need to hate us, too. I don't know. What I do know is you don't have a lot, Jon. Yeah, you have a nice bedroom in a nice house, and you have a half brother and a stepmother, and they both love you. Sarah's nice and you have her until you screw it up and lose her. What else do you have, Jon? No parents. Julie's dead. You see Matt twice a year if you're lucky. You want to cut Miranda and me out of your life? Is that going to make you feel better?"

Jon sat absolutely still.

Alex glanced at the clock. "I have to get going," he said. "I wanted to tell you how sorry I am about Laura, how much she meant to me, but there's something else. Miranda and I will be leaving as soon as the baby's born. Don't tell anyone, especially not Lisa. I know she wants Miranda here, but it's not going to happen. Miranda and I made the decision after Carlos told us he'd lost the money. Laura told us to go, that she'd stay in White Birch as long as you were in Sexton. So this isn't because of her death, and it has nothing to do with you or how you feel about Miranda and me. It's what's best for us and the baby. We'll make it to Matt's somehow, and he'll get us to that town he told us about. You can come, too, anytime you want. You'll always have a home with us. We're family. Like it or not, you're stuck with us."

Jon stood up with him. To his surprise, Alex embraced him.

"You take care," Alex said. "You're my brother, Jon, and I love you."

Jon listened as Alex walked downstairs and apologized to Dr. Goldman for taking so long. He heard the door close and the car drive away.

Only then, only when he knew with absolute certainty that he was alone, did Jon begin to cry, four years of grief and anger and guilt flowing out of him. But even as he cried, he knew that when the tears stopped, the grief and anger and guilt would still remain. Like it or not, they were family.

Sunday, July 12

After church Jon was asked by most of the people he knew why he hadn't been to Zachary's or Tyler's funerals.

He told them the truth, that his mother had died. After four years of deaths no one asked how or when. They simply heard the answer, said they were sorry, and moved on.

Lisa had just come downstairs from putting Gabe to bed for his nap when the doorbell rang. Jon was surprised, but Lisa didn't seem to be. She opened the door and let a girl in.

"This is Ruby," she said to Jon. "Ruby, I understand you didn't know better, but from now on use the back door."

"Yes ma'am," Ruby said.

Jon stared at her. She was a kid: two, three years younger than him. Even if Lisa hadn't told her about the back door, Jon would have known she was a grub.

"Ruby, this is Mr. Jon," Lisa said. "My stepson. He lives here. My son, Gabe, is upstairs napping. You'll meet him later. He's only three, so you don't have to call him Mr. Gabe."

"Yes ma'am," Ruby said. She gave Jon a shy smile. He didn't smile back.

"Carrie is no longer working for us," Lisa declared. "She'll be going to a new family tomorrow. Ruby is our domestic now. She'll be doing all the work until Miranda comes, and then Miranda will help her."

"Lisa, I have to talk to you," Jon said. "Alone."

"All right," Lisa said. "Ruby, put your bag in your bedroom, the little room next to the kitchen. Yes, down the hallway. After you unpack, I'll show you around the house, tell you what you'll be doing. Tonight I'll help you cook supper, but after that you'll be expected to do it on your own."

"Yes ma'am," Ruby said. "Thank you, ma'am." She left the room, carrying her little bag with her.

"I don't understand," Jon whispered angrily. "Where's Carrie? What's going on?"

"Jon, please," Lisa said. "You think I like this? I was told another family, a more important one, needed a nursemaid, and it would set a good example if I let them have Carrie. I said that would leave me with no help until Miranda had her baby, that someone had to be here to take care of Gabe and clean the house."

"And this is what they sent you?" Jon asked. "How old is she?"

"I don't know," Lisa said. "Fifteen maybe. She's one of the high school kids from White Birch."

"The ones Mom died for?" Jon shouted.

"Quiet," Lisa said. "Yes, the ones she died for, if you want to put it that way. What was my alternative? Quit my job? Well, then we're out of Sexton and Ruby would be working for a family here regardless. I need you to help me on this, Jon. Ruby's had less than a week of training. I don't want you cleaning floors for her, but try to be nice. Spend as much time as you can with Gabe. This is going to be hardest on him, losing Val and Carrie both. All right? Make the best of a bad situation. That's all I'm asking."

"This makes me sick," Jon said.

"Fine," Lisa said. "Be sick. Things are bad, Jon. Just don't make them worse."

Monday, July 13

Jon hadn't looked forward to school, but it was better than staying home and trying to avoid Ruby. Gabe was used to Carrie being gone on Sundays, but Jon didn't relish being there when he found Ruby in her place.

He sat down for lunch with Sarah, and Luke and Ryan joined them. Jon wasn't sure how Sarah was going to react to Ryan's presence, but she was nice to him, letting him tease her a little bit and teasing him in return. Jon even found himself laughing. He hadn't known he still could.

The sound of laughter greeted him when he got home. The house was a mess, but Gabe and Ruby were having a fine time running around the house, playing tag. First Gabe ran up to Ruby, poked her with his finger, and yelled, "Tag!" Then he ran away, and Ruby made a big deal of trying to catch up to him. When she finally did, she poked him back, yelling "Tag!" even louder than Gabe.

"Play!" Gabe screamed at Jon.

"Do you know the rules, Mr. Jon?" Ruby asked.

"I think I can figure them out," Jon said. He promptly poked her with his finger, and yelled, "Tag!"

Then Gabe ran over to him, and the game progressed. Jon

° 186 °

didn't think Gabe would ever agree to stop, and Ruby didn't seem to care. But Lisa, Jon knew, wouldn't be happy with things the way they were.

"Ruby, you need to start cleaning," Jon said. "Have you done anything today?"

"I tried, Mr. Jon," Ruby said. "Honest, I did. But little Gaby here needed some fun."

"Ruby's my best friend," Gabe said. "We played all day. Tag, Ruby!"

"Did he have his nap?" Jon asked.

"Was he supposed to?" Ruby asked. "Seems to me he's doing just fine without one."

"He takes a nap every day at one o'clock," Jon said.

"I'll make sure of that tomorrow, Mr. Jon," Ruby said. "You want something to eat? Your kitchen kinda scares me, but Gaby here can help."

"Ruby let me cook my lunch," Gabe said. "I put the honey on my bread all by myself."

"Ruby, honey is only for special occasions," Jon said.

"Today was a special occasion, Mr. Jon," Ruby said. "I didn't even know they still made honey. Haven't seen any in so long. We sure did enjoy it, didn't we, Gaby?"

Jon knew he should have scolded Ruby for eating the honey. But if Lisa hadn't bothered to explain what food was for family and what food was for domestics, he wasn't about to.

Instead he looked at Gabe, who was glowing with happiness. "Let's play some more," Jon said. "Tag, Gabe! Bet you can't catch me!"

Jon was standing at his window, staring at the faint outline of the moon, when Ruby walked in.

"What are you doing here?" he asked, painfully aware that he had nothing but pajama bottoms on.

"I can't sleep in that room," Ruby said. She was wearing a cotton nightgown, flimsy enough that Jon could see the outline of her body. "It's so quiet. Can I sit down, Mr. Jon?"

Jon nodded, expecting her to sit on the chair. Instead she crawled into his bed, her knees propped up, her head resting against his pillow.

"I get so lonely down there," she said. "All alone and all you folks up here. I'd love to sleep with little Gaby, but Mrs. Evans says that's where the new grubber girl will stay. She says I should like it, having my own room, but I never was so alone. Always had lots of people to share my room with me."

"Are you from White Birch, Ruby?" Jon asked. "Did you always live there?"

"No, Mr. Jon, I did not," Ruby said. "We worked a chicken farm back in West Virginia, but they stopped bringing us food, so we ate all the chickens and had to get going. We tried for Oklahoma, since Momma has family there, but then Daddy heard there was work in Tennessee. He and Momma work in the greenhouses. Me and my sisters live with them and Mrs. Duncan's daughters. Mrs. Duncan's a domestic, same as me now, so she's only in the apartment on weekends. We're all in the room together, me and my sisters and the two Duncan girls."

"How many sisters?" Jon asked.

"There's four of us," Ruby said. "Me and my twin, Opal, and Jasmine and Cheyenne. I had two little brothers, but they're gone.

I had a teacher named Mrs. Evans. That's your name, isn't it, Mr. Jon? Like Gaby's momma?"

"Yes," Jon said.

"The guards killed her," Ruby said. "I never saw anyone killed like that. Then the guards made us walk all the way to the bus terminal. I was so scared they were going to kill us, too, but all they did was put us on buses and bring us here. I never saw Sexton before. It's so pretty. We stayed in a dormitory, and they tried to teach us girls how to cook food like clavers eat, and how to clean, and be polite. It wasn't so bad because Opal was with me, and I knew the other girls from school. Then Sunday, they took us to our houses. They said we had to stay in Sexton for a whole year and not go back to White Birch once. I don't even know if my family knows what happened to us."

"I'm sure they know," Jon said.

"Mrs. Evans, my teacher, she was real nice," Ruby said. "We all knew we was going to be grubs. We didn't have a chance to be nothing else, and there's nothing wrong with grubber work. But Mrs. Evans said we should be proud of the work we did. She said everybody's good at something. She said she was good at telling stories and raising her kids, but she wasn't any good at being married. That made me feel better about things, because my parents love each other so much. They're always hugging and kissing, and Momma says they never go to bed mad at each other. So maybe they're grubs, but they're still better than Mrs. Evans at being married. Aren't you tired, Mr. Jon? You could get in bed with me."

Jon thought about all the grubber girls he'd had. He'd known nothing about them. They might have heard his name, Tyler or one of his other friends calling out to him, but that was it. The girls' names hadn't been important. The girls hadn't been important. For all he knew, Ruby had been one of them.

"How old are you, Ruby?" he asked. Not a question he'd ever bothered to ask a grub before.

"Fifteen," she said. "Almost."

It would be so easy, Jon thought. Lisa wouldn't know, or if she did, she wouldn't care. She never asked him what he did in White Birch, but she was no fool. She had to know. She'd be angry if Ruby didn't do the cleaning, but that was it. She probably expected Ruby to end up in Jon's bed or, more likely, Jon to end up in Ruby's.

"Go to your room," Jon said. "That's where you should be sleeping, Ruby. You'll get used to the quiet soon enough."

"Don't you like me, Mr. Jon?" Ruby asked. "I like you."

"I do like you, Ruby," Jon said. "That's why I want you to go to your room and get a good night's sleep. Mrs. Evans expects you to work very hard. She'll be angry if you don't. Now get out of my bed and go where you belong."

Ruby got out of the bed. "If I do all the cleaning Mrs. Evans wants tomorrow, can I come in here again, like tonight?"

Jon shook his head. "I have a girlfriend, Ruby," he said. "She wouldn't like it if you came in here."

"You sure you're a claver boy?" she asked. "I never knew a claver boy to care about his girlfriend before."

Jon laughed. "I'm a slip," he said. "Go to bed, Ruby. I'll teach you how to make scrambled eggs in the morning."

Wednesday, July 15

"What do I do now, Mr. Jon?" Ruby asked.

"We put the vegetables in the pot," Jon replied. "Gabe, watch where you're going."

Ruby giggled. "Don't pay him no mind, Gaby," she said. "You drive your trucks wherever you want."

Gabe rammed his toy truck into Jon's leg and laughed in triumph.

Jon shook his head. "Ruby, you can't let him get away with things," he said.

"Why not?" Ruby asked. "You and his momma surely do. All right, the vegetables are in the pot. Never saw so many vegetables at once. And a whole chicken. All that for just the three of you. It's a marvel how you claver folk eat."

"We'll get a lot of meals out of this chicken," Jon said. "And it wouldn't surprise me if Mrs. Evans let you have some of it, if you do all your work."

"She's a good woman," Ruby said. "I hope Opal's with as nice a family. Though I do say you could be a little kinder to me, Mr. Jon. Especially late at night."

"Are you mean to Ruby?" Gabe yelled.

Jon ignored him. "Make sure there's enough water in the pot so it doesn't burn," he said to Ruby. "Now put the pot on the stove. That's right. Low flame. Keep an eye on it." He cut a carrot in half, gave part to Gabe and offered the other part to Ruby.

"You sure?" she asked.

Jon grinned. "I'm sure," he said. "You've worked hard all day, Ruby."

Ruby nibbled at the carrot. "I love being in such a clean house," she said. "Back in West Virginia, Momma and us girls cleaned whenever we could. But in White Birch, no matter how hard you clean, it stays dirty. I can't wait until I go home and tell them all about how clean things are in Sexton. Bet they won't believe me." She took another bite. "One year minus a week," she said. "I wonder if they'll even recognize me."

Jon laughed. "You're pretty memorable, Ruby," he said. "Nobody's going to forget you."

"I don't know," Ruby said. "Half the time my daddy can't remember which one's me and which one's Opal. Momma can always tell us apart, but we'd confuse Daddy something fierce. I think I miss Opal most of all."

"I have an older brother," Jon said. "I don't see him very often."

"I figured your daddy was dead," Ruby said. "Gaby, keep away from the stove. What with you living with Mrs. Evans and all. What about your momma? Is she dead, too?"

Jon nodded. It was better if Ruby didn't realize her teacher had been Jon's mother. By the standards of Sexton, Mom had been a dangerous revolutionary. The fewer people who made the connection between her and Jon the better.

"What did you do for fun back in West Virginia?" Jon asked. "Besides playing with Opal and your sisters."

"It's kinda hard to remember," Ruby said, turning away to wash the utensils. "I liked gym. We had races and we played kickball. School in White Birch didn't have any gym. Do you have a gym where you go to school, Mr. Jon?"

"Yeah," Jon said. "I'm on the soccer team, so I spend a lot of time there."

"Jon's the best," Gabe said. "I saw him play. He can kick the ball a hundred miles!"

"Fifty miles on a bad day," Jon said.

"I wish I could play soccer," Ruby said. "Sometimes I feel like I'm tied up, can't do anything. Not here, Mr. Jon. You and Mrs. Evans and little Gaby, I love doing for you. But it's like my teacher, that other Mrs. Evans, used to say. Sometimes you have to bust out. She didn't say it like that, but that was what she meant. Don't get me wrong. I'm happy I'm a grub, working in a nice house like this. But sometimes I wish I could run the way I used to back home. Run till my feet can't carry me no more and then keep on running."

Jon cut another carrot in two. He offered half of it to Ruby, who hesitated and then accepted it. "I do get hungry," she said.

"Then help yourself to some food," he said. "You're here to work, not starve."

"Thank you, Mr. Jon," Ruby said. "Maybe tonight you'll let me show you how grateful I am?"

"Not tonight, Ruby," he replied. He left her and Gabe and walked into the living room.

That afternoon he'd had his first afterschool since the riot. It had been pretty much as he'd expected. Coach screamed, cursing them for their cowardice, singing the praises of Tyler and Zachary, two boys who understood the importance of winning. He made a point of signaling out Jon, calling him every name in the book for not hitting the shot in White Birch when he was told to.

Jon knew if he stayed in Sexton, he'd be expected to play on the Sexton soccer team through college. That meant five more years of listening to Coach. Five years of humiliating people just to make sure they understood the superiority of clavers.

The only time, Jon thought, that he'd actually enjoyed playing soccer had been during the White Birch match, when the game had felt real and victory wasn't guaranteed. He didn't know where the grubs had learned the game, how they'd found time and strength to practice, but somehow they had, and for that reason alone, the game had felt real and exciting and worth winning.

White Birch was the biggest and best-run of all the area grubtowns. If they didn't have gym, none of the other towns did, either.

It struck Jon that what he wanted to do was teach grubber kids soccer, basketball, running, any kind of sport. Girls and boys. They should all have that chance to bust out.

It was a dangerous idea. The kids were being raised to be domestics, laborers, miners. The clavers knew the danger of letting them bust out.

But somehow he'd find a way. He'd get the Rubys and the Opals and all the other kids in all those towns running and playing and busting out.

He'd make Mom proud.

Friday, July 17

"I have something to tell you," Jon said to Sarah. He'd gone to her house after supper, and they sat on the porch. The southern breeze made things warmer and more humid, but the air was cleaner, and the evening sun was visible through the cloud cover.

"I have something to tell you, too," Sarah said. "You go first."

Jon no longer was sure telling Sarah was a good idea. "No," he said. "Ladies first."

"Guests first," Sarah said. "What is it, Jon? Is Miranda all right?"

"Lisa called the hospital today, and they said she was," Jon replied. "This isn't about Miranda. It's about me."

"I'm listening," she said.

"I woke up last night, and I was hungry," Jon said. "Before, I would have gone downstairs and told Val to make me something. I wouldn't have cared that she was sleeping. She was a grub and I was a claver. Only then I met you and I started thinking about things differently." He laughed. "I still would have woken her up, but I would have said please and thank you and maybe even apologized."

"Val isn't there anymore for you to wake up," Sarah said.

"No," Jon said. "Carrie isn't, either. We have a new girl. That's what she is, a girl. Her name's Ruby. She's fourteen."

"A high schooler," Sarah said. "Daddy was offered one, but he said no. We're managing with one domestic. I help out when I can."

"Lisa has to have someone to take care of Gabe," Jon said. "She didn't have a choice. And Ruby seems okay with it. Gabe's crazy about her. It's like Carrie never existed."

"Is she sleeping in the nursery?" Sarah asked.

Jon shook his head. "She's downstairs, by the kitchen. If I'd gone downstairs, I might have ended up in her bed. She's invited me to. But I didn't want to do that to us."

Sarah turned away from him. "There isn't going to be an us," she said. "That's what I have to tell you."

"What do you mean?" Jon asked. "Do you still want me to leave Sexton?"

"No," she said. "Oh no, Jon. I love you. I want to be with you. But Daddy says it's not safe here for me anymore. He's sending me to my uncle's in Virginia."

"But you're coming back," Jon said, panic sweeping over him. "It's just for August and then you'll come back."

She shook her head. "I begged Daddy to let me stay. But he and my uncle both think it's best for me to go. Daddy said I could let you know, but you can't tell anyone else. I'm leaving a week from Monday."

"How?" Jon asked. "It's hundreds of miles away."

"My uncle's getting me a travel pass," she replied. "Daddy was going to ask for Alex to drive me, but I told him not to because of the baby. Alex will want to spend as much time with Miranda and the baby as possible, and it's a long drive to Virginia."

"Alex can go," Jon said. "Miranda isn't going back to White Birch."

"Why not?" Sarah asked.

Jon thought of Alex's fantasies of getting out, but that's all they were. Fantasies. You needed money and passes to travel. Alex didn't have an uncle to provide them.

"Lisa arranged for Miranda to be our domestic," Jon said. "She's coming after the baby's born."

"Miranda's your sister," Sarah said. "Lisa's stepdaughter. She's going to be your grub?"

"It wasn't my idea," Jon said. "Lisa thought it would be better this way. You've seen Mom's apartment. That's no place for a baby."

"Laura never would have approved," Sarah said.

"She knew," Jon said angrily. "She approved. And you know something? You shouldn't call her Laura. You only call her that because she wasn't a claver."

Sarah looked stricken. "Oh, Jon," she said. "I never thought about that. But you're right. I'm sorry. I'm just as bad as everyone else. No, I'm worse, because I go around acting like I'm better."

"It's not your fault," Jon said, reaching out to take her hand. "It's just the way they've taught us."

"We could run away," Sarah said. "I could go with you to your brother's. We could be grubs together."

Jon kissed her. "You'd make a lousy grub," he said. "It's okay, Sarah. Go to Virginia. I'll know you're safe there. I'd like somebody I love to be safe."

"We won't lose each other," Sarah said. "We'll work something out."

Jon knew they wouldn't, they couldn't. But Sarah needed her fantasies, and Jon wasn't going to deprive her of them.

"We'll work something out," he said instead, and kissed her with a promise of a different world, a different life, where people in love could work things out.

Chapter 12

Ruby was on her hands and knees scrubbing the hallway floor with Gabe attempting to help when the phone rang. She shrieked at the unexpected sound.

"That thing scares the living daylights out of me," she said. "We had a phone back home in West Virginia, but I don't remember it ever ringing that loud."

"I'll get it," Jon said. He stepped around Ruby and picked up the phone. "Evans residence," he said, hoping Ruby might learn.

"Jon, it's Lisa," she said so softly Jon could hardly hear her. "I can't talk long. Call Dr. Goldman. Tell him to come over as soon as he can."

"He's probably at the clinic," Jon said.

"Call him there," Lisa said. "Just get him. Miranda had her baby. They're dropping her off at the house any minute now. I don't know what shape she's in."

"The baby?" Jon asked.

"Dead," Lisa said. "So deformed they wouldn't let her see it. They baptized the poor thing before it died. That should be some comfort to Alex at least."

"Shouldn't Miranda stay in the hospital another day or two?" Jon asked.

"She's a grub," Lisa said. "As far as they're concerned, they've done enough. Call Dr. Goldman. I'll be home as soon as I can."

"Something the matter?" Ruby asked as Jon hung up the phone.

"It's Miranda," Jon said.

"Oh, the other grubber girl," Ruby said. "She had her baby?"

"The baby died," Jon said. He went to the living room and searched Lisa's desk for her address book. He carried it back into the hallway and dialed the clinic's phone number.

Dr. Goldman got on the phone. Jon told him what he knew.

"I'll see what I can find out," Dr. Goldman said. "I'll ask for Alex to be my driver. We'll get there as soon as we can."

"Tell Alex the baby was baptized before it died," Jon said.

"I will," Dr. Goldman said. "If Miranda gets there before I do, put her in bed and keep her warm. Physically she's probably fine, but this could be very hard on her emotionally. Especially so soon after losing her mother."

"Thank you," Jon said, and hung up. Ruby looked at him.

"Stop scrubbing the floor," he said to her. "Get your things out of your bedroom and move them into the nursery. Take your sheets, blankets, everything, and put them on the bed in there. Then take the linens from the nursery and put them on your old bed. You understand all that?"

"Yes, Mr. Jon," Ruby said. "But I don't understand why you're making such a fuss over a grub."

"She's not just a grub," Jon said. "She's my sister."

Ruby stared at him. "I swear I'll never understand clavers," she said.

"Just do what I tell you," Jon said. "Now!"

"Don't yell at Ruby," Gabe said. He walked over to Jon and began kicking him.

Jon lifted Gabe off the floor and carried him upstairs. "You'll stay in the nursery until I say otherwise, you little brat," he said. He slammed the door on Gabe, who began shrieking.

"Ruby, don't let Gabe out of his room," Jon said, rushing back downstairs. "And don't play with him or be nice to him. We need to get your room ready right away."

"Yes, Mr. Jon," Ruby said. In a minute she was carrying the dirty sheets and blankets, along with her bag of clothes.

Jon carried the scrub brush and bucket into the kitchen and emptied out the water. There was a chance they'd bring Miranda in through the front door. It was better for the floor to be dirty and dry than clean and wet.

But they brought her to the back door. The ambulance motor kept running as an orderly dragged Miranda over to Jon and dropped her in his arms. Without saying a word he left.

Miranda looked half dead. Jon tried to shift her weight so he could carry her, but she didn't help him any. So he dragged her as the orderly had and got her onto the bed in what had been Ruby's room.

"Miranda," he said, but she didn't respond.

"Ruby, come here!" he shouted.

Ruby clattered down the stairs, Gabe running right behind.

"Don't blame me, Mr. Jon," Ruby said. "Gaby wouldn't stay put."

"Stay out of the way, Gabe," Jon said. "When I lift Miranda up, Ruby, pull the blankets off the bed."

Ruby did as Jon told her. Then they swung Miranda onto the bed and covered her with the blankets.

"Get another one from my room," Jon said. "I don't think she's warm enough."

"Is she dead?" Gabe asked, walking around so he could get a better look.

"No, she isn't," Jon said, but he wasn't sure how alive she was, either. Miranda's breaths were shallow and she was very pale.

Ruby ran into the room carrying the blanket. "You're gonna be awful cold tonight if you let her have all those," she said.

"I'll worry about that tonight," he said. "Have you made supper yet, Ruby?"

"No, Mr. Jon."

"Then why don't you go into the kitchen and make it," Jon said. "Take Gabe with you. And keep quiet."

"Yes, Mr. Jon," Ruby said. "Come here, Gaby. We're going to make you a nice supper."

Jon sat on the bed next to Miranda and held her hand. Did she understand about the baby? And if she did, how could she bear losing both Mom and the baby? He held on to his sister's hand and wished he could tell her how much he loved her, how much he'd hated hating her.

Lisa arrived before Dr. Goldman. She walked into Miranda's room and then went back to the kitchen. "Bring me in a chair," she said to Ruby, and in a moment the chair was there and Lisa was sitting in it.

"She'll be all right," she said to Jon. "I can't say I'm surprised. All those chemicals she was working with in the greenhouses. No wonder the baby was born so deformed."

"It doesn't matter why," Jon said.

"Of course it does," Lisa said. "I got Miranda when we thought we were getting a greenhouse. She's a greenhouse worker, Jon, not a domestic. She'll be back in the greenhouses by Wednesday."

Miranda moaned.

"It's all right, Miranda," Lisa said, stroking Miranda's forehead gently. "You're going to be fine. You just need to get your strength back."

Miranda murmured something.

"She wants Laura," Lisa said, and then her face crumpled. "Oh, Jon, how is she going to manage? This is all so unfair."

Jon stared at her.

"What?" Lisa said angrily. "You think I don't love her? She's Hal's daughter. I've watched her grow up. Of course I love her. I feel so helpless."

The doorbell rang. Ruby ran to answer it.

"Miranda!" Alex cried. "Where is she?"

"We're back here," Lisa said. "Ruby, show them in."

Alex raced past Ruby to Miranda's bedside. Dr. Goldman followed, and Sarah came as well, lingering in the doorway.

"Alex, give me a minute to examine her," Dr. Goldman said. "If you could all excuse us for a moment."

"Come, Alex," Lisa said, taking him by the hand. "Let's wait here in the kitchen. Ruby, why don't you take Gabe upstairs for a bit?"

"I have supper cooking," Ruby said. "Mr. Jon told me to make supper."

Jon realized Sarah was staring at Ruby. Ruby must have realized it also because she returned the look. "You Mr. Jon's girlfriend?" she asked.

"That's none of your concern, Ruby," Lisa said. "I told you to take Gabe upstairs and stay with him. I'll make sure supper isn't burned."

"All right, Mrs. Evans," Ruby said. "Come on, Gaby. We'll have a good time upstairs while all the grownups stand around worrying."

"I'll see you later, darling," Lisa said to Gabe. "When we grownups have stopped worrying."

Jon didn't think Alex ever would. He was almost as pale as Miranda, and he kept shaking.

Dr. Goldman came out a couple of minutes later. "She'll be fine," he said. "She was in labor for over twelve hours, and that left her weak. When they told her about the baby, she became hysterical, so they sedated her. It's wearing off now. Alex, go in and talk to her. Let her know everything is going to be all right."

Sarah walked over to Jon and hugged him. He didn't dare think about how soon she would be gone. There had been loss enough that day.

Dr. Goldman let Alex sit with Miranda for ten minutes before telling him they had to go. "I don't think there'll be any problems," he said. "But call me if there are."

"Thank you for coming," Lisa said. She embraced Alex. "It'll be all right," she said. "Miranda will be back to normal in a day or two."

They walked to the front door together and watched as Alex helped Sarah and Dr. Goldman into the car.

"Will he be okay?" Jon asked Lisa as they walked to the kitchen.

"If she is, he is," Lisa said. "She's the world to him. Ruby, it's time for supper. Bring Gabe downstairs."

"Yes, Mrs. Evans!" Ruby shouted.

"I'm not hungry," Jon said. "I think I'll sit with Miranda."

"All right," Lisa said. "Ruby can always heat you up some-thing later."

Jon went back in and sat on the bed. Miranda turned her head and faced him. "Jon?" she said.

"Yes, Miranda," he said. "I'm here."

"My baby," she said.

"Miranda, I'm so sorry," Jon said. "The baby died."

"No," Miranda said. "I heard it cry."

"It lived for a few minutes," Jon said. "Long enough for them to baptize it. I'm sorry, Miranda. I don't know if it was a boy or a girl."

Miranda closed her eyes, and Jon thought she was going back to sleep. "Girl," she said. "They said girl."

"Girl," Jon said. Liana. Named for Alex's sisters. Now just Baby Girl Morales, if they even bothered to make a record.

"She isn't dead," Miranda said, and she grabbed Jon's hand and held on to it tightly. "Jon, she's alive. I know it."

"Miranda, you don't want her to be alive," Jon said. "She was deformed. Her death was a blessing."

"No!" Miranda said. "She's alive. My baby's alive!" She began sobbing.

Lisa walked into the room. "Eat some supper, Jon," she said. "I'll sit with Miranda."

"They took my baby!" Miranda cried. "Lisa, they took my baby."

Lisa stroked Miranda's cheek. "No, sweetie, they didn't," she said. "God took your baby. She's in heaven now with your par-ents."

Miranda screamed. Lisa held on to her while Jon stood frozen.

Ruby walked in and touched him. "Come, Mr. Jon," she said.

"There's nothing you can do. Let that poor girl cry herself to sleep. In the morning it'll all be better."

Sunday, July 19

Lisa, Gabe, and Ruby went to church while Jon stayed home with Miranda. He helped her walk around the house and sat with her in the living room.

"What did they tell you?" she demanded. "About my baby."

"Lisa called me and then Dr. Goldman spoke to someone at the hospital," Jon replied. "Your baby was born alive but died a few minutes later. She was deformed. Everyone's told you that, Miranda."

"I don't believe it," she said. "I don't." She paused. "Jon, are you sure Mom's dead?"

"Yes," he said shortly. "I saw her body. Alex saw her, too. She's dead, Miranda, and so's your baby. You have to learn to accept it."

"Alex didn't tell me," she said. "I guess he didn't have the chance. Where is she, Jon? What did they do with her body?"

"A lot of people died that week," Jon said. "The clavers were brought back for funerals. The ones from White Birch are going to be cremated."

"Going to?" Miranda said. "What is this, July what?"

Jon thought about it. "The nineteenth, I guess," he said.

"And the people were killed on the Fourth?" she asked. "Two weeks ago and they haven't cremated them yet? Was Mom killed on the Fourth? When did you see her?"

"I saw her on the Fourth," Jon replied. "Miranda, somehow she knew she was going to die. She told me how much she loved you, loved all of us. She died a couple of days later."

"Where did you see her body?" Miranda asked. "Where did they leave her?"

"They left her in front of the school," Jon said. "But they say they're clearing out the bodies today. They'll take her to a body pit and cremate her with everyone else. Now, can we change the subject?"

"Where do you think they took my baby?" Miranda asked. "They wouldn't bury her with the clavers. Do you think they took her back to White Birch and put her with all those other bodies? Or maybe they just threw her out with the garbage?"

"Miranda, I'm sorry," Jon said. "But it's just a body. What difference does it make what they did with it? They won't let you see her, and even if you could, you can't bring her back to life. You can't make her whole."

"You tell me Mom's dead, and you say you saw her and Alex saw her," Miranda said. "So I have to believe you. But you didn't see my baby and Alex didn't see my baby, and I heard her cry the way newborns do. The next thing I know, they're plunging a needle into my arm and I wake up here. What if she isn't dead, Jon?"

"Maybe you're right," Jon said. "Maybe she is alive. But she's so deformed it's just a matter of time before she dies, and they didn't want you hanging around at the hospital, so they lied about it. I'm not saying clavers don't lie. They do. But if they did lie, it was to protect you."

Miranda looked away.

"Lisa says the baby was deformed because of the work you did in the greenhouse," Jon said. "The chemicals you handled. Miranda, if you and Alex leave, you'll be able to have a healthy baby. This one died. Mom died. People die all the time. You have to accept it and move on."

"Jon, I killed Julie," Miranda whispered. "This is my punishment."

"I know about Julie," Jon replied. "Carlos told me. That's why I was so angry with you. But I never thought you'd be punished. Not like this. Do you know what Mom would say if you told her that? She'd kill you!"

Miranda managed a slight smile.

"How are you feeling?" he asked. "Physically, I mean."

"A little weak," she said.

"I think we should do some more walking," he said. "You need to get your strength back before you go to White Birch."

"I feel so hollow," she said. "I feel like everything I love has been torn out from me."

"It hasn't," Jon said. "You have Alex and me and Matt. You even have Lisa and Gabe if you want them. Come on. Let's walk some more, and then I'll make you something to eat. I've become a pretty good cook, you know. Sarah made me."

Monday, July 20

Lisa came into the bedroom where Miranda and Jon were sitting. "Miranda, they're expecting you at the greenhouses on Wednesday," she said. "You're going to have to go home tomorrow."

"Good," Miranda said. "I miss my job. And if I'm busy, I won't think so much. But I don't know how I'm going to get home. How am I supposed to get to the bus terminal if I'm not allowed to walk in Sexton?"

"I'll call Sarah," Jon said. "She takes a car into White Birch in the afternoon. She could give you a lift to the clinic. You can walk home from there."

"I'd like that," Miranda said. "The school's just a few blocks from the clinic. It's like Mom's buried there. I know it's not the same, but I need to say good-bye to her, and that's as close as I can get."

"I think that's a good idea," Lisa said. "I still ache because I couldn't say good-bye to my parents. Jon, call Sarah and see if she can give Miranda a lift. Maybe she'll be lucky and Alex will be the driver."

"Alex," Miranda said, and for the first time in days she looked almost happy. "At least I'll be with Alex again."

Tuesday, July 21

"Ready for the match Sunday, Evans?" Ryan asked at lunch.

"As ready as you are," Jon said. "Not much."

"Me, either," Luke said. "It's not as much fun without Tyler and Zachary."

"Plus, it's a two-hour drive," Ryan said. "Two hours of Coach screaming at us on the way there and two hours of him screaming on the way back."

"Why don't you quit?" Sarah asked. "Find a different after-school to do."

"Like what?" Ryan asked. "Giving the grubs milk and cookies like you do, Goldman?"

"Milk and cookies," Luke said. "I haven't thought of them in years. Remember Halloween? Trick-or-treat? I'd eat all the candy right away. Boy, did I get sick."

Sarah didn't seem to care about Halloween. "We do real work at the clinic," she said. "Not that you know what real work is."

Ryan shuddered. "I hope I never find out," he said. "What's the point of being a claver if you have to work like a grub?"

Jon and Luke laughed. Sarah scowled.

"Someday, Goldman, I'd like to see you smile," Ryan said. "Does she smile for you, Evans?"

"Not very often," Jon said. Sarah reached across the table and swatted him. "It's true, Sarah. We fight more than we smile."

"He's a challenge," Sarah said to Ryan and Luke. "But I'll whip him into shape."

Jon wished that were true. But with Sarah leaving in a week, he knew she wouldn't have the chance.

"Are you going to spend August bandaging the grubs?" Ryan asked. "Or are you taking the month off like the rest of us?"

"I don't know yet," Sarah said. "I'd like to keep working, but my father has other ideas. I know you think the people in White Birch don't deserve anything, but they're human, Ryan. The same as you and me."

Luke shook his head. "They're not, Sarah. I used to think like you, but I've seen too much, heard too many stories. Like the one Dad told Mom and me Saturday night."

"I don't care what your father told you," Sarah said.

"I do," Ryan declared. "What happened, Luke?"

Luke looked like he didn't need much encouragement. "Dad said there was a grubber girl at the hospital here," he began. "She was pregnant and they decided to let her stay until she had the baby. She was treated as good as a claver. Even after the riots. Food, nurses, everything."

Sarah glanced at Jon, who shook his head almost imperceptibly.

"She has the baby," Luke continued. "They tell her it's a healthy baby girl, and she gets hysterical. She says if she doesn't bring home a son, her husband will beat her. She actually begged them to kill the baby. She got so hysterical they had to sedate her.

She never did see the baby. She left the hospital refusing to. I guess she went back to White Birch and told her husband it died."

"What happened to the baby?" Jon asked, trying to sound as though he didn't really care.

Luke smiled. "There's a happy ending," he said. "The baby's being adopted by a claver family. She'll never know where she came from."

"Is she still in the hospital?" Sarah asked. "The baby?"

"I don't think so," Luke said. "I think the family took the baby home that day. I can ask my dad if you want."

Sarah shook her head. "Don't bother," she said.

Ryan laughed. "Admit it, Goldman," he said. "No decent human being would act that way. Grubs are animals, just like I've been telling you."

"It takes one to know one," Sarah said, looking at her watch. "I've got to go. I don't want to keep the driver waiting."

"I'll walk you outside," Jon said. He'd been doing that since school had reopened, so he knew Ryan and Luke wouldn't think anything of it.

"See you tomorrow," Sarah said. "Maybe by then you'll have some manners."

"Don't count on it, Goldman," Ryan said.

"See you in the gym," Jon said. "Come on, Sarah."

They walked out of the lunchroom without speaking. Even when they were outside, Jon spoke so softly only Sarah could hear him.

"Miranda was right," he whispered. "Her baby's alive."

"They stole it," Sarah said. "Jon, we've got to get the baby back."

Jon nodded. "We have to be quiet about it," he told her.

"Don't say anything to Miranda. It's better if she thinks the baby's dead until we can figure out what to do."

"It'll be so hard," Sarah replied, "driving in to White Birch with her and not saying anything."

"Distract her," Jon said. "Distract yourself. Talk to her about me. Ask her what I was like as a kid. Ask her about Alex. She'll expect you to distract her anyway, to keep from thinking about everything that's happened. Just relax, as much as you can."

"I'll talk to Daddy," Sarah said. "We have to make sure no one else had a baby recently."

"Be careful," Jon said. "It's safer for him not to know."

Sarah stood on her tiptoes and kissed him. "Love you," she said. "I'll talk to you tonight."

"Love you, too," Jon said. He watched as she walked to the car. Alex wasn't driving. That was a relief. The drive to White Birch was going to be hard enough for Sarah. At least she was spared having Alex in the car.

For once Jon was grateful for four hours of workouts and practices. He focused on the work, not minding when Coach shouted at all of them for being fat, lazy bums. The more noise Coach made, the less Jon had to think.

When he got home, he played with Gabe. They stopped only when Sarah called to say Miranda had been the only grub at the hospital for the past week.

"You didn't tell your father why you asked?" Jon said.

"No, I was careful," Sarah said. "I told him we'd been talking at lunch about whether laborers could stay at the Sexton hospital. I said I thought they all could. Daddy set me straight. What are we going to do, Jon?"

"I don't know yet," he admitted.

"Mr. Jon, dinner's ready!" Ruby called.

"Go have your dinner, Mr. Jon," Sarah said. "I'll see you in the morning."

Jon played with Gabe after supper until Lisa got home and put him to bed. Jon peeked in and wished Gabe a good night. "I have to talk to you," he said to Lisa. "Privately."

"All right," Lisa said. They went downstairs and found Ruby in the kitchen washing the dishes. "Ruby, did you clean the living room today?"

"Yes ma'am," Ruby said. "Little Gaby helped me."

"Little Gaby could've done a better job than you did," Lisa said. "I want you to clean that entire room, Ruby. Finish the dishes and then dust everything in the living room and scrub that floor until it's spotless."

"Lisa," Jon said. "It's eight o'clock. Ruby's been working since six o'clock this morning."

"If she did the work right the first time, she could go to bed now," Lisa said. "And if you insist on talking to me about how I should treat my domestics, then do it in private."

"I do want to talk about it," Jon said.

"Fine," Lisa said. "We'll talk. What are you waiting for, Ruby? Didn't I give you a job to do?"

"Yes ma'am," Ruby said. "I'll do it right away."

"And we'll go upstairs and talk about the servant problem," Lisa said. "Come on, Jon. Let's get this over with."

They walked to Lisa's bedroom, but she shook her head. "We'll talk in yours," she said softly. "Mine's over the living room."

Jon nodded and followed Lisa to his bedroom, then closed the door.

"Did you have to do that to Ruby?" he asked.

"She didn't clean the living room," Lisa said. "Did you look at it, Jon? It was filthy. I know you think she's a sweet girl, and I assume you're sleeping with her, but she has to learn her job."

"I'm not sleeping with her," Jon said.

"Fine," Lisa said. "I apologize. I had a long day, Jon. What's so important that we have to talk about it privately?"

"It's Miranda," Jon said.

Lisa nodded. "I checked," she said. "All the corpses were removed on Sunday."

For a moment Jon didn't know what she was talking about. Then he remembered Mom. "Good," he said. "I'm glad. But that's not it."

"What is it, then?" she asked.

"Luke told us something at lunch today," Jon replied. "A grubber girl had a baby at the hospital on Saturday. A perfectly healthy baby girl. Only the grub said her husband would kill her if she brought home a girl. She got hysterical so they sedated her and sent her home. A claver family took the baby. They're going to adopt her."

"Tell me you're kidding, Jon," Lisa said. "Please tell me this is a joke."

"Miranda was the only grub in the hospital this week," Jon said. "Lisa, they stole Miranda's baby."

"Did you tell Miranda?" Lisa asked. "Did Sarah?"

Jon shook his head. "You and Sarah and I are the only ones who know," he said. "Lisa, we have to get the baby back."

Lisa sat absolutely still.

"Lisa," Jon said. "Remember when you thought you might lose Gabe? It's the same thing."

"No, it's not," Lisa said. "It's worse. At least with Gabe I would've had a choice. I can't believe they did that. No, actually I can. Women here are so desperate for babies, they'll even take a grubber one. We don't know what the hospital told them. Maybe they said Miranda died in childbirth."

"Or maybe they didn't care just as long as they got a baby," Jon said. "Lisa, that's why they kept Miranda in the hospital so long. So they could be sure her baby would be healthy before they gave it to clavers."

"Your righteous indignation isn't helping any," Lisa said. "And don't talk so loudly. We have enough problems without Ruby hearing."

"Sorry," Jon said. "But I can't keep from thinking about what Miranda's been through. Mom, and now this."

"We can't get Laura back," Lisa said. "But maybe we can find the baby. I should be able to figure out who got her. We know it's a claver family. They'd need a wet nurse and a nanny."

"Do you remember anyone asking?" Jon asked.

Lisa shook her head. "Things have been so crazy the past few weeks. My guess is it was a green-file request. My assistant handles those since they're automatically granted. I'll look through the paperwork tomorrow. It's got to be there somewhere."

"Maybe they'll give us the baby when we tell them the truth," Jon said.

"Maybe they'll throw us out of Sexton," Lisa said. "I'm not kidding, Jon. We'll get Miranda's baby. I promise you that. But no one can know. No one's going to care that the baby was stolen. They'll say we're kidnappers. Don't say a word about this, not even to Sarah. I'll see what I can find out, and we'll go from there."

"Miranda and Alex have to get their baby back," Jon said. "Lisa, they have to."

Lisa nodded. "We'll figure something out," she said. "For everybody's sake."

"Ruby, this kitchen is disgusting," Lisa said.

"But I scrubbed it this afternoon," Ruby said. "Honest I did."

"You don't have an honest bone in your body," Lisa said. "You think you can get away with this?" She ran her finger over the counter, and even Jon saw the grime.

"I didn't know I was supposed to clean the counters," Ruby said, sounding close to tears. "No one ever taught me that."

"I'm teaching you," Lisa said. "Ruby, Gabe adores you, and I appreciate all the time you give him. But you're the only domestic in this house, and it's your job to keep it clean. Jon, when Carrie was here, didn't she clean as well as look after Gabe?"

"It's a lot of work, Lisa," Jon said.

"I work, too, Jon," Lisa replied. "We all do. Scrub the countertops, Ruby. Then the floor. I don't care if you cleaned it already. You want to eat tomorrow, you clean tonight. Jon, don't give me that look. I'll talk to you upstairs."

"I know we have to have privacy," Jon whispered to Lisa when they got to her room. "But do you have to take it out on Ruby?"

"I'm not beating her, Jon," Lisa said. "And I can forbid her to eat to my heart's content and she'll still eat whatever she wants. She eats more than Val and Carrie put together."

"She's entitled," Jon said. "She's doing both their work."

"Do you want to fight about Ruby?" Lisa asked. "Or do you want to hear what I found out?"

"Ruby can wait," Jon said. "Do you know who has the baby?"

Lisa nodded. "Only one family requested a wet nurse and a nanny in the past month. Both of whom started working on Saturday."

"That's great," Jon said. "Who are they?"

"It's better if you don't know until we have a plan," Lisa replied. "You probably won't know them by name anyway. But they're very powerful."

"We knew they would be," Jon said.

"I didn't realize how powerful," Lisa said. "Powerful enough to have a private guard service twenty-four hours a day. We can't put a ladder to the nursery window and steal the baby."

"They're the ones who stole the baby," Jon said.

"That's not the point and you know it," Lisa said.

"All right," Jon said. "You have the name and we need a plan. Anything else?"

Lisa scowled. "My assistant saw me going through the green files," she said. "When we get the baby, they'll trace it back to me."

"Miranda and Alex are going to have to leave anyway," Jon said. "We'll go with them."

"How?" Lisa asked. "It's one thing to say we have to leave. It's a whole other thing to do it."

Jon grinned. "Sarah and I figured that part out," he said. "Alex is driving Sarah to Virginia on Monday. If anyone stops them, Miranda's there as her grub. Then Alex drops Miranda and the baby off at Matt's and takes Sarah to Virginia. They can figure out where to go after he gets back."

Lisa fell silent, thinking things over. Jon waited for her to speak.

"They can take Gabe with them," she said.

"Sure," Jon said. "You and Gabe and me. We're clavers. Sarah's travel pass will cover us."

"What time is she leaving?" Lisa asked.

"Early Monday," Jon replied. "That's all I know."

"The earlier the better," she said. "There's a two a.m. grubber bus to Sexton. Alex and Miranda will need special curfew passes. I'll tell Dr. Goldman to arrange it for them. We get in the car, grab the baby, and get out of Dodge."

"Where's Dodge?" Jon asked.

Lisa laughed. "It's an old expression," she said. "Jon, are you sure Sarah's agreed to all this? What we're doing is dangerous and illegal."

"She wants to help," Jon said. "But I'll explain the risks to her."

"We shouldn't tell her father," Lisa said. "Or Alex or Miranda, and certainly not Ruby. The only chance we have is if we keep things absolutely quiet."

"Sarah's coming over tomorrow evening," Jon said. "We'll go to the garage. No one can hear us there. We'll talk everything out. After we've been there a couple of hours, you'll come out to chase Sarah home. We'll tell you what we've decided then."

"I'd better go downstairs," Lisa said. "Ruby's probably suspicious already."

"It's going to work," Jon said. "It has to."

Lisa nodded. "It has to," she said. "We'll make it work."

Thursday, July 23

"Sarah, it's time for you to go home," Lisa said, knocking loudly on the closed garage door.

Jon opened the door for her.

"Jon's talked to you?" Lisa whispered as Jon closed the door.

"We have it all figured out," Sarah replied. "I'm a little worried about Daddy, but my uncle can get him out of Sexton if he has to."

"You can take Gabe?" Lisa asked.

"And you and Jon," Sarah said. "Nobody's going to care how many clavers are in the car."

"We can't risk Gabe waking up until we're out of Sexton," Jon said. "Sarah's going to get a sedative at the clinic and give Gabe a quarter of it if that's okay with you."

"I'll give Ruby the rest," Lisa said. "We don't want her waking up and asking questions."

"That's a good idea," Jon said. "I should have thought of it."

"Sarah, do you understand what you're doing?" Lisa asked. "The house is under armed guard. You won't be able to walk in and take the baby."

Sarah grinned. "That's exactly what we're going to do," she said. "Let me tell you the plan."

Sunday, July 26

The Sexton clavers beat the Winston grubs 13–2.

Jon scored five goals. He figured it was the last time he'd be playing for Coach. He might as well leave him happy.

Monday, July 27

"They're going to be here in a few minutes," Jon said early that morning. "Lisa, why aren't you ready?"

"I am ready," she said. "Gabe's sound asleep. When they come, you take him and go."

"You're going with us," Jon said.

Lisa shook her head. "Jon, I can't," she said. "What if they

· 218 ·

blame my assistant? She's a grub, Jon. You know what they could do to her?"

"They could put you in prison," Jon said. "They could kill you. Is your assistant's life that important?"

"It's not just her life," Lisa said. "They could go after Carrie if they think she was involved. They could go after Ruby. I have a responsibility to all of them, Jon. I have to protect them."

"I still think you should come with us," Jon said. "For Gabe's sake."

Lisa shook her head. "I've made enough mistakes," she said. "I'm not going to have innocent blood on my hands. Matt and Syl will look after Gabe. They promised your father and me they would if anything ever happened." She took Jon in her arms, holding him tightly. "I love you," she said. "Get Gabe. I want to kiss him good-bye."

Jon went upstairs and took Gabe out of his bed. "You have a wonderful mother," he whispered, carrying the sleeping boy downstairs. Lisa walked over to them and kissed her son.

"Keep him safe," she said.

"I promise," Jon replied. "I hear the car, Lisa. We've got to go."

Lisa went to the closet and pulled out a suitcase. "Gabe's trucks are in there," she said. "His clothes. Some of yours." She kissed Jon and Gabe. "Go," she said. "I love you both."

Jon cradled Gabe in his left arm while holding on to the suitcase. Alex had the car running but the lights off. Miranda sat by his side, Sarah in the back.

"Put the suitcase in the front with me," Alex said. "We can't slam the trunk."

Jon did as Alex said. Then he put Gabe in the back seat and sat down next to him. "Start driving, Alex. Make a left at the stop sign. Sarah'll give you the directions from there."

"I don't understand," Miranda said. "I thought we were stopping at Lisa's so you could say good-bye to Jon. What's Gabe doing here? Does Lisa know you've taken him?"

"Lisa knows," Jon said. "She's not coming."

"Why not?" Sarah asked. "Alex, at the next stop sign make a right."

"She'll get to Matt's on her own," Jon said, hoping that was true.

"What about Matt?" Miranda asked. "Alex, is this the way out of town?"

"Not that I know of," Alex replied. "You'd better tell me what's going on, Jon. If this is some kind of elopement, I'll put a stop to it right now."

"It's nothing like that," Jon said. "I have something to tell you, both of you, but you can't react. No screaming, no crying. We can't risk Gabe waking up."

"We promise, Jon," Miranda said. "Just tell us."

"Your baby didn't die," Jon said. "They stole her. We're stealing her back."

"What the hell do you mean?" Alex asked.

"I mean just what I said," Jon replied.

"Is she all right?" Miranda asked, so softly Jon almost didn't understand her.

"Yes," Sarah said. "We haven't seen her, but as far as we know she's fine."

"They lied about her being deformed," Jon said. "They lied about all of it."

Miranda began to cry. Alex clenched the steering wheel tightly.

"Who?" he said. "Who did this? I'm going to kill them."

"Listen to me," Sarah said, and they could all hear the claver in her voice. "You can kill whoever you want, but then you won't get your baby back. It's your choice. Do you want revenge or do you want your daughter?"

Miranda was sobbing. Jon reached over and put his hand on her shoulder. "We'll get her back," he said.

"Make the next right," Sarah said. "Alex, we have a plan. It's risky, but I think we can pull it off. If something goes wrong, remember that Charles and Amy Stockton have your baby. Go three more blocks and make a left. Charles and Amy Stockton."

"We'll need to get out of Sexton as fast as possible," Jon said. "No one will be looking for us at Matt's, so you can leave us there and take Sarah on to Virginia."

"If we don't come out with the baby, go," Sarah said. "Hide out in White Birch until you can figure out another plan."

"I can't let you do this," Alex said. "It's my baby." He touched Miranda gently. "Our baby."

"We have a plan, Alex, and you're not part of it," Sarah said. "Except as the driver. Go one more block. Okay, see that white house on the corner? Park directly in front of it, but turn your lights off. Keep the motor running, though, and have the back doors open."

Miranda turned around and looked straight at Jon. "You can do this?" she asked. "You can bring my baby to me?"

Or die trying, Jon thought. Instead he reached over and kissed his sister on her cheek. "Do you have everything?" he asked Sarah.

"Take the sign," she said. "And the tape. Let's put the surgical masks on now. The gowns can wait until we're out of the car."

"I'll never be able to thank you," Alex said.

"You don't have to," Jon said. "We're family. Come on, Sarah."

"Surgical masks, surgical caps, surgical gowns," Sarah said as they got out of the car. "The only thing they'll see are our eyes.

Remember, Jon, let me do the talking. You go upstairs and get the baby and her things. Do you have the suitcase?"

"Can't you see it?" Jon asked.

"I'm nervous, all right?" Sarah said. "Okay. Let's do this. Put the sign on the door and start knocking."

They walked to the front of the house — a mansion, really. Lisa had told them they had six domestics but only the guard and the wet nurse should be there. The rest would be in White Birch until the morning.

Jon attached the sign to the front door. "Ring the bell?" he asked.

Sarah nodded. "Three times," she said. "Then start knocking and shouting."

Jon pressed hard against the doorbell. He could hear it ringing in the house but no other sounds. He began to pound on the door. "Medical emergency!" he yelled. "Open the door!"

The guard opened the door. He had his gun already pulled out and pointed it at Jon's head. "Who the hell are you?" he growled. "And what the hell do you think you're doing?"

"We're here to see Charles Stockton," Sarah said.

The guard stared at her and pulled the safety.

"If you kill us, you're signing your own death warrant," Sarah said. "Now either get Charles Stockton here now or be prepared to die."

A man and a woman came to the top of the stairs. "What's going on here?" the man asked.

"Mr. Stockton?" Sarah asked.

"You want me to kill them?" the guard asked.

"Mr. Stockton, your baby is highly contagious," Sarah said. "You have to listen to me. Your life, all your lives are in danger."

"My baby?" Mrs. Stockton said. "What about my baby?"

"Mrs. Stockton, I'm very sorry," Sarah said. "Shortly after the baby was born, its mother died. We performed an autopsy, and the blood workup came in tonight. The grub died of osteomyelitis. If she had it, the baby has it. It's invariably fatal."

"Are you saying our baby is going to die?" Mrs. Stockton cried.

"I'm saying you're all going to die," Sarah said. "Unless we get the baby out of here and you clean every single thing in this house. We'll take the baby back to the hospital and isolate her until she dies. Tell your guard to put his gun down, and let this grub go upstairs. He'll take the baby and all her things. It's the only chance you have, Mr. Stockton."

"Let him go," Mr. Stockton said to the guard.

Jon began walking upstairs.

"You're taking my baby?" Mrs. Stockton said. "Charles, tell them they can't."

"I'm sorry, Mrs. Stockton," Sarah said. "We have no choice. The incubation period is a week to ten days. If you keep the baby a moment longer, not only are you at risk, but everyone else you have contact with. The house is quarantined. You can let your domestics in to do the cleaning, but none of you can leave until someone from the hospital authorizes it."

"You can't do this to us," Mr. Stockton shouted. "My father's on the town board."

"Do you want to die?" Sarah asked. "Do you want your wife to die? If you see your father before you've completely disinfected your home and yourselves, you risk killing everyone you see, including your father and the entire damn town board. The baby's going to be dead by tomorrow night anyway. Is it worth the risk?"

"We've had the baby for over a week now," Mrs. Stockton said. Jon could see the tears flowing from her eyes. For the briefest moment he felt sorry for her. "Wouldn't we have seen something?"

"There's a two-week period between infection and symptoms," Sarah said. "Arthur, what are you waiting for?"

"Sorry, ma'am," Jon said. "Excuse me, please. Can you tell me where the nursery is?"

Mrs. Stockton pointed to a door. "Charles, what are we going to do?"

"Demand our money back for starters," Mr. Stockton said. "Take the baby. Wake up the wet nurse and tell her to start cleaning the house. I knew this grubber baby was a bad idea. Maybe next time you'll listen to me."

"It was the only way." His wife sobbed. "I wanted a baby so much."

Jon told himself not to feel sorry for her. He walked into the nursery and saw a baby sleeping in her crib. The wet nurse was standing next to her.

"Who are you?" she asked. "What are you doing here?"

"Stay where you are," Jon said. "The hospital sent me to take the baby."

"Is she sick?" the wet nurse asked.

Jon nodded. He longed to look at Liana, to see what she looked like, but there wasn't time. Instead he opened the chest of drawers and threw things into the suitcase. "Diapers," he said.

"In here," the wet nurse answered, pulling them out and handing them to Jon.

Jon pulled out a laundry bag from the suitcase. "Put the dirty diapers in here," he said. "All of them." He knew from traveling half the country with Gabe how important diapers could be.

The wet nurse emptied a hamper into the laundry bag.

Jon threw all the rest of the baby clothes into the suitcase then handed it to the wet nurse. "Take these downstairs," he said. "I'll take the baby. It's dangerous for you to be holding her."

"I've been holding her for a week now," the wet nurse said.

"Well, you won't be anymore," Jon said. "Now move it!"

Mr. and Mrs. Stockton stared at them as they walked down the stairs. Mrs. Stockton was crying uncontrollably, but her husband was doing nothing to comfort her.

"Give me the baby," Sarah said. "You carry the bags." She stared directly at the guard. "What are you waiting for?" she asked. "Open the door."

"Do it," Mr. Stockton said. "Get that damn grub baby out of here."

The guard let them out. Sarah and Jon walked briskly to the car. Alex stood by the door, waiting for them.

Sarah handed him the baby. "Give her to Miranda," she whispered. "We have to get out of here fast."

Alex held his daughter for the briefest of moments before handing her to Miranda. He hopped into the car. "Let's go," he said, and began driving away.

Sarah and Jon pulled off their surgical gear. "He'll call his father first," Sarah said. "But even if his father calls the hospital, they won't know what to tell him. They'll say to wait to talk to someone in charge in the morning. I think we have two or three hours."

"Left turn here?" Alex asked.

"Yeah," Sarah said. "Then another left and drive straight to the town gate. Do you have the travel pass?"

"Right here," Alex said.

"Alex, she's so beautiful," Miranda said. "Look, she's awake. Do you think she knows who we are?"

"She knows," Alex said. "She knows we love her and she's safe."

Part Three

Chapter 13

"This should do," Alex said a couple of hours later. He pulled the car over to the side of a country road.

"Should we be stopping so soon?" Miranda asked. The baby was sleeping contentedly in her arms.

"This'll only take a minute," Alex said. "See that brook? We'll use the water to baptize the baby."

"They baptized her in the hospital," Jon said.

"That's what they said," Alex replied. "They also said the baby was deformed and dead. I'm not taking any chances. Come on everyone. Let's do this."

"Gabe's still sleeping," Sarah said. "I'll stay in the car with him."

"Gabe will be fine," Miranda said. "Sarah, you have to join us. You're Liana's godmother."

"Oh no, I can't be," Sarah said. "I'm Jewish. I can't be your baby's godmother."

Miranda laughed. "I wouldn't be holding my baby if it wasn't for you," she said. "You and Jon. You're the godparents, like it or not. Right, Alex?"

"Right," Alex said. "Everybody out. Except Gabe."

They left the car and, holding on to each other's hand, walked down the slope to the brook.

"Are the godparents here?" Alex asked.

Jon squeezed Sarah's hand. "We are," he said.

"Alex, do you know what you're doing?" Miranda asked.

Alex grinned. "I'm winging it," he said. "But I don't think God will mind." He bent over, wet his fingers with the water from the stream then made the sign of the cross on the baby's forehead. "I baptize thee . . ."

"Liana Hope," Miranda said. "Liana Hope Morales."

"Oh, I like that," Sarah said. "Oops. I'm sorry."

"I like it, too," Alex said. "I baptize thee Liana Hope Morales in the name of the Father and the Son and the Holy Spirit. Amen."

"Amen," they all said.

"Can I hold her?" Jon asked. "Just for a moment?"

"Of course you can," Miranda said. "You're her uncle. Make sure to support her head. Yes, that's right."

Jon stared at his niece. Dawn was breaking, and hazy sunlight made it possible for him to see what she looked like. Her hair was dark like Alex's, but her eyes were Miranda's. "Liana Hope," he said. He held his pinkie out, and the baby grabbed it. "Look at that," he said. "That's amazing."

"I think all babies do that," Sarah said. "But Liana Hope is the most beautiful one ever."

Jon kissed his niece on her forehead and then handed her back to Miranda. "The most beautiful one ever," he said.

"We've got to get going," Alex said. "We can't take any more chances."

Jon nodded. "You go on," he said. "I'm going back to Sexton."

"Jon, what are you talking about?" Miranda asked.

"I can't let Lisa face this alone," Jon said." You keep going. I won't say anything about where you are. You can trust me."

"It's not a question of trust," Alex said. "Jon, do you have any idea of what you're risking?"

"You might never see us again," Miranda said.

"I know," he said. "But I can't ask Lisa to take the blame for something I did."

"I did it, too," Sarah said. "I'll go back with you."

"Sarah, go to Virginia," Jon said. "I want you to be safe, remember?"

"Matt will know where we are," Miranda said. "Take care of Lisa, Jon. And thank her for everything she did."

"You'll have to walk back to the highway," Alex said. "You should be able to hitch a ride with a trucker. Tell them you were going to visit family, but the car broke down, and your driver vanished, so you need a lift back. Give us until tomorrow. Lie low today. All right?"

"All right," Jon said.

"Will you see my father?" Sarah asked.

"I'd better not," Jon said. "We don't know how this is going to play out. Maybe no one will care, and Lisa and I will get away, no problem. But if there is trouble, I've got to do what I can to protect her."

Alex nodded. "Take care, Jon. Do what you can for Lisa."

"I love you," Jon said, hoping that each of them, even the sleeping children, knew he meant it. "I'll find my way back to you, somehow. I promise."

Sarah embraced him, but she broke away and walked with Alex and Miranda to the car. Jon stood by the stream and watched as they drove off. He thought he heard Sarah crying, but Alex pulled away so rapidly, he couldn't be sure.

It didn't matter. They were all about to start new lives, better lives. Jon was starting his own new life. Just not a better one.

Tuesday, July 28

He'd gotten a lift with a trucker who was hauling a couple dozen grubs to work in the greenhouses. From the sounds in the back, the grubs weren't too happy about it, but the trucker said he was earning a lot of overtime hauling grubs from all over to replace the ones who'd died during the riots.

Jon thought about the truck Alex had wanted so badly, but he couldn't imagine him hauling grubs. Carlos would have, though, and Alex would have taken his share of the money. He wouldn't have told Miranda where the money came from. Bad times made for big secrets.

The trucker let Jon off at the greenhouses. From there Jon had to walk to the nearest claver bus stop, about four miles. It was dark by the time he got home, but he didn't mind. He felt safe being in Sexton. It wasn't safe, but for a little while at least Jon was a claver, and clavers were safe.

Still, he felt uneasy when he saw the house was dark. He called for Lisa, then Ruby, but there was no answer.

Most likely Lisa was at work, he told himself. Ruby might have taken off when she saw Gabe was missing. Or Lisa might have sent her back to White Birch or to some clavers who needed another grub. Jon couldn't picture Lisa scrubbing floors, but maybe without Gabe around, Lisa didn't care if the floors were clean.

It was also possible the police had tracked Lisa down and she and Ruby were being held. Even if Lisa claimed full responsibility, the cops might keep Ruby. If they let Ruby go, there'd be no reason for her to come back. She'd be sent to a different family, to crawl into a different man's bed.

Jon sat in the living room, thinking about his options. He couldn't go to the police, not unless he knew Lisa was being held. If she was, he could take full blame, and the police might release her. But if the police hadn't made the connection yet between Lisa and the baby, it would be a disaster for Jon to show up.

He could call her office, to see if Lisa was there, but that would only be to make himself feel better. If she wasn't there, it could make things worse. Maybe Lisa had changed her mind and left Sexton. She could have called into work that morning, said she was sick and not coming in, and grabbed a ride out of town with a trucker, just as Jon had grabbed a ride in with one. For all he knew, Lisa could be at Matt's already. She could have brought Ruby with her.

Maybe Lisa had figured out a way to let the authorities know she was to blame and no one else was. Or maybe she didn't care anymore if someone else was held responsible just as long as she could be with Gabe.

Or maybe she was working late and would come home any minute, and she and Jon could discuss what to do next.

Jon went into the kitchen and took some chicken out of the refrigerator, but after a bite or two he put it back. He was tired, dirty, and hungry, but more than anything, he was scared. How many years had it been since he was alone in a house? Even back in Pennsylvania it seemed like there had always been someone around. And back in Pennsylvania there had been no reason to feel this engulfing terror.

He walked upstairs. He couldn't be sure what tomorrow would bring, but he'd be better off getting a good night's sleep. It could well be the last one he'd have in this house, in any house.

Lisa's bedroom door was closed. Jon opened it and turned on a light. She was sitting in her desk chair, her head down on the desk. Almost immediately Jon noticed the gun lying on the floor by her side.

Jon had been with his father when he died. He had seen his mother's corpse hanging from a tree. Death had been as much of a part of his life as hunger and fear.

He walked to Lisa. She'd shot herself in her heart. There was no way of knowing if the shot had killed her or if she'd died a slower death, her blood flowing out of her. It didn't matter, really. Dead was dead.

She'd left a note.

I take full responsibility for the kidnapping of the Stockton baby.

The only other people involved were the baby's biological parents.

I knew the baby's father for a number of years and arranged for his wife to be my domestic. When I realized their baby had been taken from them without their consent, I came up with a plan to return the baby to them. I told them what to say to the Stocktons, and I arranged for them to have a car to leave Sexton with their baby.

No one else knew of the plan.

Lisa Evans

Jon put the note back on the desk and left the room. He'd decide what to do about Lisa some other time. He had to make sure Ruby was gone. He didn't think Lisa would've killed her, but he needed to be certain. There was a chance Ruby was hiding in the house somewhere.

Besides, looking for Ruby distracted him. And he needed the distraction.

He went through the entire house, opening closets and cupboards and small spaces Ruby couldn't possibly have crawled into. He checked the garage, went back and searched the house all over again. Then he gritted his teeth and returned to Lisa's bedroom. Ruby wasn't under the bed or in the closet or anywhere else. She'd probably heard the shot, saw Lisa's body, and run.

But wherever she ran to, it wasn't to the authorities. Lisa had been undisturbed since her death Tuesday morning. Maybe even Monday. There were ways to test how long a person had been dead, but he was no expert. Dead was dead.

He went to his bedroom and sat on the bed. He could leave, he thought, walk to the greenhouses in the morning and grab a lift with a trucker. He could make his way to Matt's, slowly, cautiously. Someone would have to tell Gabe his mother was dead. Jon had told Miranda about Mom, after all. By now he was a pro.

The problem was Ruby. If Jon could be sure she'd truly gotten out, then he could leave, too. But how could Ruby have managed that? Even if she'd gone back to White Birch, to her family, she'd be picked up by a guard and punished for running away. And if she were still in Sexton, the same thing would happen.

She couldn't have been caught yet because she would have told the police about Lisa. But she would be caught. It was inevitable. And once she was, the police might decide she was responsible for everything. Notes could be destroyed. Suicides could be called murders. Why would a claver have helped a pair of no-good grubs? Ruby must have been in on it, helped grab the baby, then killed Lisa and run away.

She was Jon's responsibility. In some ways, she was Jon's friend.

He would have to tell someone about Lisa. He would have to stick around, hoping no one suspected him, until Ruby was found. And once she was, he'd have to protect her. If he survived all that, and he wasn't sure he would, he could leave Sexton.

But he couldn't protect Ruby unless he protected himself first.

He walked back to Lisa's room and stared at her. She was trying to protect everybody. If Ruby had stayed in the house and called the authorities, she might have been fine. If he hadn't come home, he'd be fine. Everybody would be fine. But he'd come home and Ruby had run, and decisions had to be made.

He went downstairs and found the address book. It was nine thirty. Too late to call people, but he didn't have a choice.

The first call Jon made was to Dr. Goldman. It was nice to pretend he could be kept out of things, but that option no longer existed.

"I apologize for calling so late," Jon said, "but there's something I have to tell you."

"Is it Sarah?" Dr. Goldman asked. "Have you heard something from Alex? Is Sarah all right?"

"She's fine," Jon said. "It's Lisa. She killed herself."

"Are you sure?" Dr. Goldman asked.

"Yes sir," Jon said. "She shot herself. I came home and found her."

"Oh, Jon," Dr. Goldman said. "I'm so sorry. Does Gabe know?"

"He's not here," Jon said. "He's with Miranda." He paused, trying to decide what he had to tell Sarah's father, what he could avoid telling him.

"Dr. Goldman, Sarah's fine," he began. "But she's with Alex and Miranda and Gabe and the baby. Miranda's baby was alive, and we found her and got her back to them."

"Sarah did that?" Dr. Goldman asked.

"We all did," Jon said. "Lisa, too. Lisa left a note saying she was completely responsible, her and Alex and Miranda. She says she knew Alex, but she didn't say anything about Miranda being family."

"You're going to have to call the authorities," Dr. Goldman said. "I would do it for you, but I think it would be better if you make the call."

"Yes sir," Jon said. "I'll make that call right now."

"I'll be there in fifteen minutes," Dr. Goldman said.

"No," Jon said. "Thank you, but I'm better off if you stay away. Sarah's better off, too. If I need you, I'll call."

"I don't like leaving you alone," Dr. Goldman said.

"I don't like being alone," Jon replied. "But it's better if I am. I'll tell them I called you. Don't lie about that. Just about Miranda."

"I'm here if you need me," Dr. Goldman said. "And, Jon? Your mother would have been proud of your helping Alex and Miranda. Very proud. Don't ever forget that."

"I won't," Jon said. "Thank you."

Alex had told him he had special obligations. Mom would expect him to protect the people who hadn't been given the same chances he had. Miranda, Alex, Ruby.

Well, he was a claver and a soccer star, and that used to count for something. Jon made his next phone call.

"I'd like to speak to Mr. Hughes," he told the domestic who answered the phone. "This is Jon Evans. I was a friend of Tyler's."

Jon waited nervously until Mr. Hughes came to the phone.

"Yes, Jon," he said. "What is it?"

"I'm sorry to call so late, sir," Jon said. "And I'm sorry I never had a chance to tell you how bad I felt about Tyler."

"You weren't at his funeral," Mr. Hughes said. "A lot of people noticed that."

"My mother died," Jon said. "In the riots. I'm really sorry, Mr. Hughes, but I couldn't handle it. Tyler, I mean. Tyler's funeral."

"I didn't know," Mr. Hughes said. "I'm sorry, Jon. These are terrible times."

"Yes sir," Jon said. "Mr. Hughes, my stepmother killed herself. I'm here, at our home, and I just found her. I called Sarah's father, Dr. Goldman, and he told me to call the authorities. I'm sorry, sir. I thought you'd know who to call."

"Are you sure it's suicide?" Mr. Hughes asked. "Where are your grubs?"

"We only have one," Jon said. "I don't know where she is. But Lisa, my stepmother, left a note. It's something about this other grub we had. I don't know what it means."

"Give me your address," Mr. Hughes said. "I'll call the police and tell them to come. I'll come, too. You were one of Tyler's closest friends, Jon. If you're in trouble, he'd want me to help."

"Thank you, sir," Jon said. "That means a lot."

"Keep calm," Mr. Hughes said. "This is a terrible tragedy, but you're a strong young man, and I know you'll get through it."

Jon thanked him again and hung up. He didn't feel like a strong young man. He felt like a weakling, a liar. But then again, he'd been a weakling and a liar for years now. He knew how to be a weakling and a liar, and he knew how to survive.

For the moment that would have to be enough.

Thursday, July 30

He told the same story to everyone—Mr. Hughes, the police, Luke, Luke's father, Ryan, Reverend Minter, the people Lisa worked with, the people at her funeral. Each time he told it, he knew he was lying, but with each time it sounded more and more like the truth, even to him. He grew comfortable with the lies, more comfortable than he'd ever felt lying about Julie.

He told them he'd come home from the soccer match too keyed up to stay at home. He wanted to celebrate, and the best place to do that was White Birch. He caught the last grub bus in Sunday night, and after that, he admitted with chagrin, he wasn't too sure what had happened except that it involved a lot of potka and any grubber girl he could find.

Mr. Hughes, the police, Luke, Luke's father, Ryan, Reverend Minter, the people Lisa worked with, and even the people at Lisa's funeral laughed at that. Getting drunk and enjoying yourself with grubber girls was what claver boys were supposed to do in White Birch. No one was expected to remember all the details.

School was out until September. So Jon stayed in White Birch an extra night, an extra day. The potka didn't run out, and neither did the girls.

But by Tuesday evening he'd run out of money for the potka and the girls. Besides, Lisa might be worried. So he took a claver bus to Sexton and made his way home.

As soon as he got there, he passed out. If he had given it any thought, and he wasn't sure he had, he must have figured that their grub had taken Gabe to the market. Lisa would have been at work.

When he came to, it was night and he found he was alone. He searched for the grub, for Lisa, for Gabe, and found only Lisa, dead in her bedroom. He'd called Dr. Goldman first, because he lived nearby. Then he called Mr. Hughes.

Yes, he'd seen the note, but no, he didn't know what it meant, or where Gabe was. Maybe the grub had run off with him after she found Lisa's body. Maybe Lisa had sent him away with the grubs she'd mentioned in her suicide note.

No, he didn't know the grubs. All he knew about them was that when Lisa had gotten her promotion, she'd been told she could have a private greenhouse and another domestic. Lisa had told him she found the perfect girl, someone who could work in the greenhouse and help with the housework as well. Lisa seemed very interested in the grub, to the point that she had Jon visit her in the hospital a couple of times. So at some point, he must have learned her name was Miranda and she was expecting a baby.

Miranda was dropped off at their home after she'd had the baby, which had died. Deformed, Jon remembered. Deformed and dead. This was after the riots, and Lisa's greenhouse had been delayed, so they sent Miranda back to White Birch, leaving them with just one domestic, Ruby.

He didn't remember Lisa seeming upset about anything, except training Ruby. And he didn't remember Lisa mentioning that she knew Miranda's husband. Now that he thought about it, he knew Miranda had a husband, because Lisa had mentioned that Miranda would go back to him. He didn't remember the husband's last name. Why should he? Who bothered remembering their grubs' last names?

He'd known Lisa since he was a little boy, and he'd lived with her for three years. It never occurred to him that she would violate the laws, do anything that might put him and especially Gabe at risk. He didn't know anything about the Stockton baby or who the Stocktons were. He'd been in White Birch getting drunk and having as many girls as he could.

Jon made it through the funeral, listening to everyone saying how brave he was and how difficult they found it to believe that Lisa would do something like that. Not the suicide, he knew, although that was included in their shocked remarks. It was that she had turned against the clavers, helping out grubs based on some long-ago relationship. Everyone knew what animals grubs were. Everyone knew that baby would have been much better off with clavers. Now that baby was lost and so, presumably, was Gabe, kidnapped by the grubs, lost to Sexton forever.

Jon nodded and agreed with them and said how shocked he was, too, how sad at Gabe's disappearance, and how guilty he felt because he hadn't been home, hadn't talked Lisa out of that crazy plot. And all of them, even the police, told Jon it wasn't his fault, that Lisa had been keeping many secrets from him, that if a claver boy couldn't go into White Birch and have a good time, what was the point of this whole crazy world?

Jon said he didn't know, but he would always feel terrible about what had happened, and all of them said that proved what a good boy he was, how brave and honest.

Luke skipped the funeral. "He feels responsible somehow," Ryan told Jon. "If he hadn't told you about the grubber baby, none of this would have happened."

"He shouldn't blame himself," Jon said. "I'm the one who told Lisa. If anyone's to blame, it's me."

Ryan shook his head. "It's not your fault, either," he said. "Those grubs probably had something on her. It wouldn't surprise me if they murdered her and forged that note."

"It doesn't matter," Jon said. "Nothing matters. Dead's dead."

Chapter 14

The days leading up to the funeral had been punctuated with phone calls. But now the house was quiet, and the ringing of the phone startled him.

"Jon Evans?"

"Yes."

"This is Sergeant Hawkins at the police station. We found your missing grub."

"I'll be right there," Jon said, hanging up the phone.

He raced to the bus stop, but when he didn't see any buses coming, he began running to the station. It wasn't until he was almost there that he realized he could be running into a trap. Sarah's father wasn't the only one who knew Miranda was Jon's sister. Ruby knew, also. And if she'd told the police, they could be waiting for him.

I'm a claver, Jon thought, rehearsing his arguments for the police. She's a grub. There's no proof Miranda and I are related. Ruby was lying. All grubs lie. Or maybe, to be charitable, she misunderstood something Lisa had said. Or maybe she was making it all up because she hated Lisa, hated Jon.

The important thing was what had she done to Gabe. That was what the police should be concentrating on. Where was Gabe?

When Jon walked into the police station, he saw the police had been trying to find that out without his prodding. He winced at the fresh bruises on Ruby's face.

"What's she told you?" Jon asked. "I'm Jon Evans. It's my half brother who's missing."

"I'm Sergeant Hawkins," the police officer said. "I called you a few minutes ago, Mr. Evans. You sure this is your grub?"

Jon nodded. "Her name's Ruby," he said. "She used to look prettier."

The sergeant laughed. "This is Officer Summers," he said. "He's been having a little talk with the grub about everything she knows."

"Mr. Jon," Ruby said, "I don't know where Gaby is. I swear I don't. I woke up with a terrible headache, and the gun went off and Gaby was gone. Honest. I looked all over for him and I couldn't find him. I went outside to look, and I kept looking and looking, and I never could find him. You believe me, don't you, Mr. Jon? You know how much I love that little boy."

Jon could see the terror in her eyes. He only hoped no one could see the fear in his.

"Why don't I take her home?" he said. "I might do better getting the truth out of her there."

"Sorry, Mr. Evans," Sergeant Hawkins said. "No can do. This little grub's a runaway."

"I understand that," Jon said, the way a friend of Tyler Hughes's would. "She ran away from my home, and that's where I'll take her back to."

The sergeant shook his head. "Grubs don't contract to people," he said. "They contract to the enclave. She didn't run away from you. She ran away from the enclave. Grubs that do that get punished. That's the law."

"What'll become of her?" Jon asked, trying not to look at Ruby, at the bruises and the tears and the terror.

"Jail, until we got a truckful to send to the mines," Sergeant Hawkins replied. "Once she gets there, well, a pretty girl like this one will keep busy enough." He and the officer laughed.

"How long will that be?" Jon asked. "Before there's a truckful?"

Officer Summers shrugged. "I'd say we're about halfway there," he said. "Enough potka, enough Sundays off, a couple of weeks maybe."

"Please, Mr. Jon," Ruby said. "I'm begging you. Save me."

Officer Summers slapped her. "Keep your mouth shut, grub," he said. "This is none of your concern."

Jon didn't want Ruby to be sent to the mines. None of what had happened was her fault. But even more than that, he didn't want Ruby stuck in a jail cell telling whoever would listen that Miranda was Mr. Jon's sister, Mrs. Evans's stepdaughter. By now Sarah was probably safe in Virginia and Alex was on his way to the town Matt had told them about. They were all right. But Jon wouldn't be.

"What if I marry her?" Jon asked, almost as startled by the words as the policemen seemed to be.

"Marry her?" Sergeant Hawkins said. "Marry this grub?"

"Yes," Jon said. "Right now."

"I never heard of that," Officer Summers said. "A claver marrying a grub. Can he do that?"

"I don't see why not," Sergeant Hawkins replied. "No law against it that I know of."

"Fine," Jon said. "Good. Give her to me, and we'll get married. Then I'll take her home and find out what she did to Gabe."

"Wait a second," Ruby said. "Maybe I don't want to marry you."

"So what?" Jon said. "We're getting married. Let her go, Sergeant Hawkins. The church is only a couple of blocks away. Reverend Minter can perform the ceremony."

"Not so fast," Sergeant Hawkins said. "Yeah, you can marry the grub. No law against that. But you can't take her home and act like nothing's changed. You marry a grub, you can't be a claver. It's that simple."

Jon wasn't going to be a claver much longer if Ruby started talking. "Fine," he said. "We'll go the church, get married, go home, get my things, and leave Sexton."

"You'd do that for her?" Officer Summers asked. "Give up being a claver for some little grub?"

"It'd be worth it to me to find out where my brother is," Jon said. "Besides, she looks better in bed. Can we go now?"

"You can't go back to the house," Sergeant Hawkins said. "That's the rule. You marry a grub, you can't go back. Understand? I'll go to the church with you, and we'll find the reverend and he'll marry you. Then you give me your claver ID badge and get the hell out of here."

Jon knew the sergeant was making up the rules as he went along, but he also knew he had to get Ruby as far away from Sexton as possible. He needed to protect them both.

"Look, the kid is probably dead," Sergeant Hawkins said. "The grub killed him, or maybe his mama did. You still want to get married? You can change your mind, and we'll put the grub in jail, where she belongs. There are plenty of other grubber girls, and they look pretty much the same in bed."

"I'll marry her," Jon said.

"Don't say you weren't warned," the sergeant said. He grabbed

Ruby's arm and pulled her off the chair. "It's your wedding day, grub girl," he said. "Congratulations."

"Here are the cuffs," Officer Summers said, tossing a pair to the sergeant. "Don't want the bride making a break for it."

Jon watched as the sergeant cuffed Ruby's wrists. He told himself it didn't matter, none of this mattered. He loved Sarah, but she was in Virginia, lost to him forever.

If he wanted to stay alive and out of the mines, this was the only thing to do. The marriage was meaningless. Somehow he'd shake Ruby off and find Miranda and Alex.

The sergeant half dragged Ruby the few blocks to the church. "She sure isn't crazy about marrying you," he said.

"Yeah," Jon said. "I'm the only one who's crazy."

The sergeant laughed. He laughed pretty much all the way to the church.

Lisa's funeral had been there the day before, Jon thought. Reverend Minter had said the eulogy. Now he was being approached by the sergeant and asked to perform a quick but legal marriage ceremony.

"You sure about this, Jon?" Reverend Minter asked. "I don't want you rushing into something if you're not one hundred percent certain."

"I'm certain," Jon said. "Look, Reverend, I've known Ruby for a while. I have very strong feelings about her."

The sergeant laughed even harder.

Jon ignored him and Ruby, who looked like she wanted to kill all of them. "Just perform the service," Jon said. "Then we'll leave Sexton and get out of your hair."

"Keep it short," Sergeant Hawkins said. "This one is real impatient." He held up Ruby's cuffed arms.

"Do you have a ring?" Reverend Minter asked.

Jon shook his head.

"Well, it doesn't matter," the reverend said. "All right. What are your full names?"

"Jon Evans," Jon said. "Jonathan."

"Ruby," she whispered angrily.

"Come on, girl," Reverend Minter said. "What's your last name?"

"Tell him to let go of my hands," Ruby said.

"Sergeant, please," the reverend said.

Sergeant Hawkins let Ruby's arms drop.

"Maybe you could remove her cuffs?" Reverend Minter asked.

"She stays cuffed until she's out of Sexton," the sergeant replied. "Think of them as her wedding ring."

Jon nodded. "Ruby, tell them your name," he said. "Let's get this over with."

"Grub," Ruby said. "Ruby Grub."

Sergeant Hawkins struck her hard against her cheek.

"No!" she cried. "That is my real name. Ruby Grubb. G-R-U-B-B."

The three men burst out laughing. When one of them stopped, one of the others would make a joke about really marrying a grub, and they'd laugh all over again.

Reverend Minter was still snorting when he began the ceremony. "Do you, Jonathan Evans, take this woman to be your lawfully wedded wife? Do you promise to honor and cherish her, for better or worse, in sickness and in health, forsaking all others, to be faithful only unto her?"

"I do," Jon said.

"And do you, Ruby Grubb"—and here the reverend cracked up again—"do you take this man to be your lawfully wedded husband? Do you promise to honor and obey him, for better or worse, in sickness and in health, forsaking all others, to be faithful only unto him?"

Ruby nodded. The sergeant kicked her.

"I do," she mumbled.

"Take her wrist," the minister said. "Now repeat after me. With this ring, I thee wed."

"With this ring, I thee wed," Jon said, holding on to the handcuff.

"Look, Reverend, could you speed this up?" Sergeant Hawkins asked.

"I now pronounce you man and wife," the reverend said.

Sergeant Hawkins tossed the handcuff key to Jon. "You may now uncuff the bride," he said. "Give me your ID badge, Evans, and get going."

Jon uncuffed Ruby and then removed his badge. He hoped the sergeant didn't see him shaking. It was one thing to participate in this sham of a wedding. It was another to give up the badge that had protected him for so long.

Sergeant Hawkins grabbed the ID badge and then cuffed Jon to Ruby. "All right," he said. "Sooner the two of you are out of Sexton the better."

"Good luck, Jon," Reverend Minter exclaimed as the sergeant pushed Jon and Ruby onto the street.

"Keep walking," Sergeant Hawkins said. "Don't make me hurt you on your wedding day."

Jon kept his head down, hoping no one he knew could see him. He knew it didn't matter, that he'd never be back to Sexton, never see the people he'd shared his life with, but still he felt overwhelmed with shame. He was no longer a claver. As far as Sergeant Hawkins was concerned, he was no better than a grub trespassing on Sexton property.

At least Ruby was keeping quiet. Jon understood she'd never thank him for saving her from the mines, but he knew what he was giving up for her. And because of her.

The sergeant walked behind them and alternated prodding Jon and Ruby with his gun butt. When he had to, Jon pulled Ruby along, making her walk even faster.

They got to the gate. The sergeant showed his identification to the guard. "I'm uncuffing them now," he said. "Then they're out of here."

"You can let them loose," the guard said. "I got them in my sites."

Sergeant Hawkins uncuffed Jon first, then Ruby. He pushed them out of the gate, out of Sexton.

"Get the hell out of here," he said. "Don't either of you show your faces in Sexton again."

For a moment Ruby stood still. Then Jon grabbed her arm and pulled her away from the gate.

"Come on," he said. "The highway's this way."

"What makes you think I'm going with you?" Ruby asked.

"You want to live, don't you?" Jon said. "Come on." He grabbed her hand and held it tightly as they began walking away.

"Hold it, mister," Ruby said. "I can see the sun. Which way you taking me?"

"East," Jon said.

"White Birch's west of here," she said. "Why ain't we going west?"

"Because we're not going to White Birch," Jon said. "Now, come on, Ruby. The guard can still shoot us. We've got to get moving."

Ruby stood still. "I'm going home to White Birch," she declared.

Jon wanted nothing more than to be rid of her. But Ruby in White Birch was almost as dangerous as Ruby in Sexton. She could still talk. She could still be overheard. Jon could still be found.

"You're coming with me," he said. "You married me, Ruby."

"I didn't want to!" she cried. "You all made me."

"Nobody made you," Jon said. "Nobody can make a person get married. Not if they really don't want to. A minister married us, Ruby. A man of God. And you vowed you would obey me for the rest of your life. That was a vow you made to God, and if you break that sacred vow, you'll be damned in hell for all eternity. I say we're going east. We're going east."

"What're you going to do to me?" she asked.

Jon shook his head. "I'm not going to do anything to you," he said. "I never did, and I'm not about to. But we have to get moving. It's for your sake, Ruby. If you go back to your parents, the police will find you. They'll blame you for Lisa's death, for Gabe's kidnapping. I'm taking you someplace where you won't get hurt. Once we're there, we'll decide what to do next. All right? You know you can trust me. I've never hurt you."

"You'll be sorry," she said, but she began walking in Jon's direction.

"I'm sorry now," Jon said. "Come on. It'll be dark soon. Let's get some distance between us and Sexton while we can."

Ruby scowled. "Don't come anywhere near me tonight," she said. "I don't care what God thinks. I ain't gonna obey you that way."

"Fair enough," Jon said. "Let's go."

Chapter 15

"We gotta stop," Ruby said. "I can't walk another step more."

"All right," Jon said. He estimated they'd walked about ten miles the day before, and today they'd been walking since dawn. Each step was getting harder. He hadn't eaten in close to a day, and he had no idea how long it had been since Ruby had.

They sat on the ground by the side of the highway. Jon saw the fifth truck of the day.

A few days ago he'd waved his ID badge and a trucker had pulled over immediately. Now they whizzed by with no intention of helping.

Well, they'd help Ruby. But Jon wasn't letting her out of his sight.

"How much longer do we gotta go?" Ruby asked, rubbing her feet.

"I don't know," Jon admitted. "A few more days, I guess."

"We ain't gonna make it without food or water," Ruby said.

"We had water a few hours ago," Jon said. "We'll get food somehow."

"Water probably poisoned," Ruby said. "Biggest mistake I ever made in my life, letting you marry me." She wiggled her toes. "Think we really are married?"

"I know we are," Jon said. "The minister doesn't do fake weddings." He shuddered to think what Ruby might do if she decided they weren't really married. It was the only hold he had on her, and they were still too close to Sexton for him to take any chances.

"Can I ask a question?" he said, following her example and rubbing his feet.

"You're gonna anyway," Ruby said. "Gotta obey you, I guess."

"I don't think you'll burn for all eternity if you don't answer," Jon said. "What I want to know . . . Well, when we were at Lisa's, you were all over me. I had to push you away. But since we got married, you won't let me anywhere near you. Why not?"

Ruby shrugged. "You was a claver before," she said. "Now you're just a grub. That's why not."

"I'm not a grub," Jon said.

"Well, you ain't no claver," she said. "If you ain't a claver, you must be a grub."

"That's not true," Jon said. "The world isn't just clavers and grubs. Take those cops yesterday. They weren't grubs. And teachers. They're not grubs. They're just not clavers. They're something in between."

"All I know is clavers and grubs," Ruby said. "And I ain't letting no grub have me. Not even if he says he's my husband."

"I married you to protect you," Jon said. "You know what would've happened to you in the mines? You want to guess how long you would've lasted?"

"We ain't gonna last too long unless we get some food," Ruby said. "Ain't that an exit sign up ahead? Maybe there's a town there."

Jon squinted. "It's for Bellingham," he said. The Sexton team had played them back in October. "It's a grubtown. They won't have any food for us."

"We ain't gonna get any anyplace else," Ruby said.

Jon felt sick at the thought of begging from grubs. "No," he said.

Ruby stared at him. "I know I promised for better or poorer until death," she said. "And I guess God'll strike me down if I don't obey you, whether I want to or not. But there's no food on this highway, and we don't know when we'll see water next. I say we go to Bellingham, to the church there, and do some work. Ministers are kind. They gotta be. It's their job when they ain't marrying people, even those who don't want to."

It would be different if they worked for food, Jon told himself. It would be different if they got the food from a minister. Besides, even if he could go a few more miles before stopping, that didn't mean Ruby could. He'd made the same vows, for better or worse. Like it or not, he owed her.

"Okay," he said. "We'll go to the church in Bellingham and see if we can work for food. But then we start back on the road. The farther we get from Sexton the better."

Ruby put her shoes back on and rose. "You sure do hate that enclave of yours," she said.

"They're not crazy about me, either," Jon replied. "Let's hope the minister in Bellingham is as nice as you say."

Ruby began walking toward the exit ramp. "Grub work," she said. "Grub food. You'll get used to it, Mr. Jon. One of these days you'll know you're a grub, just the same as me."

Monday, August 3

"I have to admit it," Jon said as he sprawled on the ground next to Ruby. "You were right."

"Right about what, Mr. Jon?" Ruby asked.

"About working for our food, Mrs. Ruby," Jon replied.

"I told you not to call me that," Ruby said. "'Mrs. Ruby' sounds stupid."

"Well, so does 'Mr. Jon,'" Jon said. "But I can't get you to stop. Even though you're supposed to obey me."

"Well, I don't see you doing much honoring or cherishing, neither," Ruby said.

Jon laughed. "Fair enough," he said. "Good night, Mrs. Ruby."

"Good night, Mr. Jon," Ruby mumbled.

Ruby fell asleep quickly, Jon had learned over the past few days. But no matter how much labor Jon had done or how hungry he was, sleep didn't come easily.

He'd thought spending so much time with Ruby would have tempted him, but when he thought about her as his wife, the image of Sarah flooded over him. Sarah's lips against his, her heart pounding as he held her tightly.

Jon understood that as the world now was, he would never see Sarah again. But what he'd come to understand was how quickly worlds could change. Four months ago he hadn't met Sarah. One month ago he hadn't met Ruby.

One month ago his mother was still alive. A week ago Lisa was.

He willed himself to fall asleep. They'd leave at dawn and get as much walking in as they could before finding a town and looking for work. Maybe someone would feed them before they began their scrubbing. Then, with the money they made today and the money they'd make tomorrow, they could buy enough food to last them until Sunday if they were careful.

Things will be different, he thought, as he drifted off to sleep. Different. Better. In a week things will be better.

The job Ruby had found for them that day was cleaning a grubber school. Claver schools had grubs to do their cleaning, but no one bothered cleaning a grubber school. For the promise of a dollar and a breakfast of potatoes and cabbage, Jon and Ruby had swept and scrubbed the floors. Now they were outside washing the windows, Jon on the ladder doing the second story while Ruby stayed on the ground.

"When you think they washed these windows last, Mr. Jon?" Ruby asked.

"Not since the world came to an end," Jon said as he tried to remove four years' worth of filth. "Ruby, if I'm not a claver anymore, why don't you call me Jon?"

"I only call my friends by their rightful names," Ruby replied. "You ain't my friend, Mr. Jon."

At first Jon thought he was laughing so hard he made the ladder rattle. Then he realized it was the familiar rumble of an earthquake. Not what he wanted to feel on top of a ladder.

"Hold on tight!" Ruby shouted. She raced over to the ladder and held on to it as it shook wildly.

Jon grasped the side of the building. He was only one flight up, he told himself. Even if he fell, it wouldn't be so bad.

But if he fell the wrong way, he could end up with a concussion or a broken ankle, or any of another dozen things that in this world could prove fatal.

The tremor passed, but Jon continued to shake as he scrambled down the ladder. "Thank you, Ruby," he said.

"Nothing to thank me for, Mr. Jon," she replied. "You take over these downstairs windows. They're too tough for me."

"No, Ruby," Jon said. "I'll be okay."

"I don't doubt that," she said. "But I don't feel like scraping you up off the ground." She climbed up the ladder and began washing the windows, the pale glow of moonlight illuminating her work.

Eventually they finished and went in to get some sleep in what had been the nurse's office. Ruby lay down on the floor.

Jon took her hand and gently raised her up. "You take the cot," he said. "I'll sleep on the floor."

"You sure?" she asked. "Don't seem right somehow."

"It's right," he said. "Good night, Ruby. Thank you."

"Don't know what you're thanking me for," she mumbled before sinking into sleep.

Jon stretched out on the floor. Good thing he'd washed it, he thought. Clavers should never sleep on unwashed floors.

Wednesday, August 5

They'd spent the afternoon cleaning a clinic run by a grub who'd flunked out of med school twenty years ago. He promised them some money, but when they finished, he said he didn't have any on him. If they came back tomorrow, he'd see what he could do.

Money would have meant food at the local market, but hunger was an old friend, and Jon knew how to live with it. Besides, he'd swiped an old road map, hiding it until he and Ruby were back on the road.

As soon as they took a break, Jon pulled the map out and traced their path. When he figured out where they were, he located Coolidge, where Matt and Syl lived. It was north and east. Working for food slowed them down, but if they found work tomorrow and rationed their food for the rest of the week, they had a chance of getting there before nightfall Monday.

Maybe they could beg for food at a church on Sunday. That would make the rest of the journey easier.

Begging for food from grubs. Jon shook his head. If Luke could see him now. Or Coach. But he'd earned the food they'd gotten until now.

Jon grinned as he remembered how he'd tried to help Carrie with the housework. How he'd claimed training for soccer was work. How he hadn't known how to make breakfast.

Mom would be proud of him now, he thought. Sarah would be, too.

They were both lost to him. But it hurt a little less to know they'd both be proud.

Thursday, August 6

"Well, that's what Daddy always said."

"What, Sarah?"

Ruby laughed. "You sleepwalking or something? Look around, Mr. Jon. You won't see no claver girls here."

Jon shook his head. He hadn't been sleepwalking, but he had been trying to remember the details of the dream he'd had just before waking. Sarah was in it. They were in the garage, only it wasn't the garage. It looked more like a cottage, with furniture and a fireplace giving off warmth and light. He could remember the sensation of Sarah's skin next to his.

"Sorry, Ruby," Jon said. "I had something else on my mind."

"Someone else," she said. "This Sarah of yours. She someone special?"

"You met her," Jon said. "What did she seem like to you?"

"I can't answer that," Ruby replied. "Claver boys, well, they ain't different from grubber boys. Boys all want the same thing. That's just your nature. I never really known a claver girl though. The few I've known mostly looked right through me, so I never much bothered to look back. Why ain't you with this Sarah, if you think about her so much?"

"She's in Virginia," Jon said, hoping that would explain it all.

"That where we're going?" Ruby asked. "That's a long haul from Tennessee, Mr. Jon. Me and my family walked it from West Virginia, and that's got to be closer than Virginia proper."

"We won't be going that far," Jon told her. "I don't expect to see Sarah again."

"What do you expect?" Ruby asked.

"Nothing from you," Jon said. "Except companionship."

Ruby snorted. "Don't know how much longer you should expect that from me, neither," she said. "One of these days I'm going to leave you be and go off, do something good with my life. Don't need to waste all my energy on a lost soul like yours."

"I wish you could have known Sarah," Jon said. "She wouldn't put up with too much from me, either."

"Well, I guess claver girls is smarter than I thought," Ruby said.

"Could be," he said. "Grubber girls are certainly smarter than I thought."

"That's 'cause you claver boys never did learn to think," Ruby said. "Come on, Mr. Jon. I think I see a stream up ahead. Water ain't food, but it's better than nothing."

"How long we been walking?" Ruby asked.

Jon looked at his watch. "About six hours," he said.

"Not today," she said. "How many days we been walking?"

"A week," Jon said. "Today's our one-week anniversary."

"Don't you think it's time to honor me by saying where we're going?" Ruby asked. "Or don't you know?"

Jon took his time before answering. Ruby was tough — stronger and smarter than he would have guessed. But they'd put in over a hundred miles and not in a straight line. There was no way she could walk back to White Birch on her own, and she wasn't foolish enough to take a lift from a trucker.

"We're going to my brother's," Jon said. "If we're lucky, we should get there Monday night."

"I didn't know you had a brother," Ruby said.

"Gabe's my brother," Jon pointed out.

"That's not the same," Ruby said. "This brother of yours, he's older than you?"

Jon nodded. "Five years," he said. "He and his wife live in Coolidge."

"Do they know we're coming?" she asked. "You call them to let them know?"

"They're not clavers," Jon said. "They don't have a phone."

"If they ain't clavers, what are they?" Ruby asked. "Grubs like us, Mr. Jon?"

"I'm not a grub," Jon said. "As you perfectly well know, Mrs. Ruby."

"Pardon me," she said. "Is this brother of yours a grub?"

"No," Jon said. "He's a courier. That's like the cops and the teachers. Not clavers but not grubs either. Like me."

"His wife a courier?" Ruby asked.

"She's a domestic," Jon said reluctantly.

Ruby burst out laughing. "She's a grub," she said. "Marry a grub, you're a grub, too. Right, Mr. Jon?"

"They were married before they got here," Jon said. "Besides, what's the difference?"

"Plenty," she said. "What happens when we get there?"

"I've been thinking about it," Jon said. "Gabe's staying with them. I guess with Lisa dead, they're his parents now."

Ruby stood still. "Wait a second," she said. "All that time the cops were beating me, you knew where Gaby was?"

"They hit you a grand total of twice while I was there," Jon said. "And once was at our wedding. It had nothing to do with Gabe."

"They hit me plenty before you got there," Ruby said. "I still got bruises. They kept asking me what I did to that little boy, and every time I told them I didn't know nothing about it, they hit me again."

"I'm sorry," Jon said. "Come on, Ruby. Let's keep walking."

"No," Ruby said. "Not till you admit it was your fault I kept getting hit."

"What difference does it make?" Jon asked. "It happened. It's over and done with."

"My life ain't over and done with," Ruby said. "I got family back in White Birch. My parents don't know what's become of me, whether I'm alive or dead. All because you lied about where little Gaby was."

"All because you ran away," Jon said. "Everything happened because you ran away, Ruby."

"Mrs. Evans didn't shoot herself because I ran away," Ruby

cried. "Gaby didn't end up with your brother because I ran away. I don't know what's going on, Mr. Jon, but I know it ain't my fault."

"All right," Jon said. "Things happened because of Miranda, and I guess you were a victim. At least partly. And yes, I knew where Gabe was and I didn't tell the police, and they hit you and you didn't deserve it. And I didn't do anything to protect you except marry you, which is pretty big, and I don't remember hearing you thank me, but all right. We'll let that pass. We're going to my brother's, and he and my sister-in-law have Gabe. That's what I was thinking about. Gabe was crazy about you, Ruby. You could stay with Matt and Syl and take care of Gabe for them. You'd be safe there. You could make a whole new life for yourself."

Ruby started walking again. Jon gave her a moment then caught up with her.

"You'll really like them," he said. "Matt . . . well, Matt's great. And Syl's been through a lot, but you'll like her, too. Think how happy it would make Gabe if you were there."

"You're crazy, you know that?" Ruby said. "Grubs can't have domestics."

"Why not?" Jon said. "There's no law against it."

Ruby laughed humorlessly. "Don't need to be no law," she said. "This — whatshername, Silly."

"Syl," Jon said. "S-Y-L."

"Syl," Ruby said. "Syl the grub. She earns enough for her own food most likely and that brother of yours earns enough for his food, and maybe if they eat a little less, there's enough for Gaby. I work for them, no food for me. There don't need to be no law, Mr. Jon. Grubs got to eat, too. Thought you'd figured that out by now."

"It was just an idea," Jon said. "Anyway, that's where I'm

going. You don't want to go, fine. Go your own way. Just don't tell anyone where I am. A lot of people could get hurt if you do. Gabe could get hurt."

"Sounds like you're the only one in trouble," Ruby said. "How could they hurt a little claver boy?"

"He's not a little claver boy anymore," Jon said. "Not with Lisa killing herself. If Gabe's lucky, they'll give him to decent people to raise. That's if he's lucky. You want that on your conscience?"

"I didn't ask for none of this," Ruby said. "Rich people's problems."

"You want to hear something funny?" Jon said. "I didn't ask for it, either."

"You really marry me just to save me?" Ruby asked.

"Not just to save you," Jon said. "To save me, too. Look, I don't know what's going to become of you. I really thought your living with Matt and Syl and Gabe was the answer, but you're right. You wouldn't be earning any money, and food costs money." He wished they'd stop talking about food. It reminded him how hungry he was, how much more walking they had in store before they could begin to think about getting any.

"They really nice people?" Ruby asked.

Jon nodded.

"Well, I guess that's as good a place as any to go," she said. "You know anything about their enclave? What kind of work they have for grubs?"

"No," Jon said. "Just that Syl's a domestic."

"I love that word," Ruby said. "Can't call her a grub, can you? You never had a problem calling me that, but not that sister-in-law of yours. Not family."

"Miranda was a grub," Jon said. "You know that."

"Was?" Ruby asked. "What's she now?"

"I don't know," Jon said, which was pretty much the truth. "We'll get all the answers when we get there and decide what's best for you. I promise you that, Ruby. You promise you won't ever tell anyone where I am, and I promise we'll do right by you."

"Nice of you to make that offer a hundred miles from home," Ruby said. "You're a real gentleman, Mr. Jon."

Jon grabbed her by her shoulders. "Listen to me," he said. "I'm not happy about any of this, either, all right? My mother was slaughtered. My stepmother killed herself. I lost both of them in a month. Everything I had was taken from me. I'll never see the girl I love again. I'll never see my home, my friends. I'm as tired and as dirty and as hungry as you are. I'm probably more scared than you are because I can only hope my family is all right, that Sarah is all right. You know where your parents are, where you sisters are. Hell, you have parents. That puts you two steps ahead of me right there."

"Take your hands off me!" Ruby said. "You touch me again like that, and the whole world is gonna know where you are."

Jon let go of her. "All right," he said. "Fine. I'm going to my brother's. You go wherever you want." He began walking away.

"You can't do that!" Ruby shouted. "You're my husband. You come right back here, Jon Evans. You know what could happen to me walking on this highway all by myself? You want my dead body on your conscience, too?"

Jon stared at Ruby. But all he saw was Julie.

"No," he said. "No, I don't want that. Look, Ruby, my life is in danger. My family's lives are, too. Sarah, her father, we're all in jeopardy. But you're right. You didn't ask for it, and it's not fair what's happened to you. If you want, we'll turn around and go back to White Birch. I'll leave you, I don't know, five miles from there. A safe distance. Then I'll start back. If I do that for you, would you promise not to turn me in? Is it a deal? If that's what you want, we'll turn around right now."

Ruby rolled her eyes. "My momma warned us about clavers," she said. "All they do is take. They see a little grubber girl, they take what they want from her, no please, no thank you."

"Your mother was right," Jon said. "That's just what I did."

"But you ain't no claver anymore," Ruby said. "You ain't no decent, hard-working grub, neither. But you're getting there, and I don't see much point to hurting you. We'll go to that brother of yours, that fancy domestic Sylly. I wasn't counting on seeing little Gaby, but I guess I can handle that if I have to. What's the name of that town they're in?"

"Coolidge," Jon said.

"Maybe I'll find myself a nice man in Coolidge," Ruby said. "Settle down. Raise my own family. Live a decent, hard-working life, like my folks. You can go off, do whatever you want. Find that girlfriend of yours before she settles down with some decent, hard-working claver. Assuming there is any, which, according to my momma, there ain't."

"Thank you," Jon said. "You're better to me than I deserve."

Ruby snorted. "You just figure that out?" she said. "You clavers ain't just mean. You're dumb and mean. Come on. Let's get to that precious brother of yours while you still got the strength to walk."

Saturday, August 8

But it was Ruby who lost the strength, Ruby who collapsed, crying she couldn't walk one step farther.

There had been no work for them Thursday or Friday, no food in almost three days.

"I'll walk to the next town," Jon said. "I think there's one in a couple of miles. I'll get you some food. But we need to get you off the side of the highway, back where the truckers can't see you. I don't think I can carry you, Ruby. Can you stand up? I'll help you walk if you can."

"I'm sorry I'm such a baby," she said, trying to stand. "Mr. Jon, I am so sorry. My knees won't lift me."

"You're not going to die out here," Jon said, bending to help her. "Put your arms around me. Right, like that. On the count of three I'm going to help you up. Use whatever strength you have, Ruby. Okay? One. Two. Three."

It took more strength than Jon knew he had in him, but he managed, with Ruby's help, to get her upright.

"Keep holding on," he said. "We don't have to walk far. Let's get you behind those trees. That should give you enough cover."

Even the twenty feet was a struggle, but Jon managed to drag Ruby over and position her where no one could see her.

"I don't know how long this is going to take," Jon said. "But I'll come back with food. I promise you, Ruby. Sit tight and don't give up hope. All right?"

"All right, Mr. Jon," Ruby said.

Jon bent over and kissed her on the forehead. "See you soon, Mrs. Ruby," he said, and went back to the highway to look for the nearest town.

He walked for almost an hour before seeing the exit sign. There was no guarantee there'd be a town there, and even less that someone would give him food, but he had no choice. He walked along the exit ramp, then kept going. A mile or so later he saw an old farmhouse with the glow of kerosene lamps in the windows.

He walked over and knocked on the door. "Please help me," he cried. "My wife is starving. Please give me some food for her."

The door opened. A man, wiry with muscles, pointed his rifle at Jon. "It won't hurt me none to kill you, boy," he said. "You might want to do your begging someplace else."

"Stop that, Virgil," a woman said. She walked to the door and stared at Jon. "Your wife, you say?"

Jon nodded. "I left her a few miles down the road," he said. "We haven't gotten work for a few days now. We haven't eaten since Wednesday."

"Still say it'd be easier to shoot him, Katie," Virgil said. "Feed him to the hogs."

"Hush up," Katie said. "Don't mind him, boy. He's got no company manners. Didn't before, and nothing the past few years improved him any. I must say, you look way too young to be married."

"What day is it?" Jon asked. "What date?"

"August eighth, I think," Katie replied. "We got a perpetual calendar, and I think that's what it said."

"I'm seventeen," Jon said. "I'll be eighteen in ten days. My wife's younger. Please, I'm begging you. Just a little food for her."

"Come on, Virgil," the woman said. "We can spare some of that potato bread I baked yesterday. Remember, you said it wasn't fit for the hogs? We can let the boy have that."

"I'm not giving no stranger my food," Virgil declared. "Tell me your name, boy, and where you're from, and why I shouldn't shoot you on the spot and feed you to the hogs."

"You shouldn't shoot me because it would make your wife

mad," Jon said. "And you'd have to butcher me before you feed me to the hogs, and there's not a lot of meat on me."

"He's got a point, Virgil," Katie said. "It'd put me in a terrible bad mood if you kill this nice young man."

Virgil lowered his rifle and pulled Jon to him, yanking his hair until Jon thought his neck might break. "I'm still waiting to hear your name, boy, and where you're from."

"Jon Evans," Jon gasped. "Sexton."

Virgil pushed him away. "Sexton," he said. "Ain't that one of them enclaves?"

Jon nodded.

"Clavers," Virgil said to his wife. "That's what they call them. Fancy boys with cars and money."

"No cars," Jon said. "No money, not anymore. Just a wife who's starving to death three miles down the road."

"Even clavers got to eat," his wife said. "And their little wives. You treat this boy nice, Virgil, while I go to the kitchen and get him some food. You hear me? You hurt a hair on his head, and I'll be madder than two hornets' nests."

"All right," Virgil said. "Give them that bread. It'd poison the hogs anyway."

"That bread and more," his wife said. "How far are you going, boy?"

"Thirty miles maybe," Jon said. "I've got family there."

"That'll be till Monday," she said. "Well, I can't give you enough for then. But you go back to the highway, and there's an exit about ten miles east. Braxton. They got a real nice church there. You get there tomorrow, they'll find a way to feed you and that little wife of yours."

"Thank you," Jon said. "I can't tell you how much this means to me."

"Well, Virgil here don't like to admit it, but we was young once, and poor as church mice," she said. "We had our share of helping hands. Now, you stand still, both of you, and I'll be right back."

"She's a good woman," Jon said. "You're a lucky man."

"She has her good days," Virgil said. "But she can't bake potato bread worth a lick."

Jon smiled. "We won't care," he said. "Right now we'd be honored to eat as good as your hogs."

When Katie returned, she'd packed all the bread, two potatoes, and a bunch of carrots. "Take it all," she said. "And Godspeed to you."

"Thank you," Jon said. "Ruby, my wife, she thanks you, too."

"Just get out," Virgil said. "And don't show your face here again."

"Never," Jon said. "I promise."

It was hard walking back to Ruby without eating any of the food, but he wanted to show her how much they had, to let her have the first bites before he allowed himself any.

He thought about how brave she was, how much her strength had helped him. It was funny. He was with her day and night, but he'd lost any interest he had in her as a woman, if he'd ever had any. Someday, maybe, he'd be over Sarah, but by then Ruby would have found that hard-working man she'd make a life with.

"Ruby!" he called as he saw her resting against a tree trunk. "I got us some food!"

"Real food?" she cried. "Really, Mr. Jon?"

"Well, the hogs won't eat it," Jon said. "But it's good enough for us."

Chapter 16

"Do you know their address?" Ruby asked. "Or are we gonna wander around Coolidge the rest of our lives looking for that brother of yours?"

"Forty-four fifty-two Route Thirty-seven East," Jon said.

"I don't suppose you know where that is," Ruby said.

"No, I don't," Jon said. "But the streets are full of people. Let's ask one and see if we can find out."

"Full of grubs," Ruby said. "You know that's what you want to call them. 'People.' You don't think of them as people. They're just dirty grubs like me."

The closer they'd gotten to Coolidge, the crabbier Ruby had become. Jon figured she was nervous about meeting his family. Nervous and hungry and exhausted.

"People or grubs," Jon said. "Let's ask one."

Coolidge looked like a rural version of White Birch. The people who lived there had the same worn-out look to them. But it was close to 7 p.m., and they were getting home from their jobs.

At that, the grubs looked better than he and Ruby did. They'd found a stream a few miles back and had washed themselves, but they'd been wearing the same clothes now for ten days and had only rinsed them out a couple of times during their journey.

"You ask," Ruby grumbled. "Use that claver charm of yours."

Jon found a man who looked a little less dead than the others. "Excuse me," he said. "I'm looking for Route Thirty-seven East."

The man spat in the vicinity of Jon's feet. "What for?" he asked.

"I've got family there," Jon said. "Can you tell me where it is?"

"Yeah," the man said. "But I don't reckon I want to." He walked away.

"Okay," Jon said to Ruby. "You go next."

Ruby scowled, but she walked over to a woman. "Thirty-seven East?" she said.

"Walk to the corner and make a left," the woman replied. "Go about a mile. You'll see the sign for it there."

"Well, thank you, ma'am, very much," Ruby said.

"Any time," the woman said, cracking what seemed to be a smile in Ruby's direction.

"How did you do that?" Jon asked as they began walking down the street.

"Like knows like," Ruby replied. "You still smell of claver."

Jon was pretty sure claver wasn't what the grubs were smelling, but he kept his thoughts to himself.

"How far down you think it'll be?" Ruby asked. "That big number."

"We've made it this far, we can make it a little farther," Jon said. "Come on, Ruby. Think how excited Gabe will be when he sees you."

"I don't know, Mr. Jon," Ruby said. "Maybe it's not that good an idea, him seeing me."

"Ruby, please," Jon said. "We've got to get there, and it's going to be dark pretty soon. Matt will feed us, and we can clean up and get some sleep. All right?"

"Don't matter what I think," she grumbled, but she began walking again.

She's shy, Jon thought. She's scared of meeting people she thinks of as clavers. She lost everything — her home, her family — and now she's meeting her new family; naturally she's reluctant.

But it still irritated him that she walked so slowly.

Route Thirty-seven East was to the right. Jon started looking at house numbers, but they were only in the 2000s.

"It's miles from here," Ruby said. "We're never gonna get there."

"You know how many miles we've walked to get here?" Jon asked. "Close to two hundred. More probably, with all the detours we made to get food. So what if it's another mile or two? Keep walking."

"And what if I don't?" she said.

"Fine," Jon said. "Don't. Stand here for the rest of your life. I don't care. I'm finding forty-four fifty-two with or without you."

"You'd do that?" Ruby cried. "Leave me here, standing all alone, not knowing a soul? That ain't honoring me."

Jon stared at her. The past few days they'd gotten along so well. Jon knew the rules and he obeyed them. Ruby lowered her guard in return. They'd talked about growing up, what their lives had been like before.

But now she was the Ruby he'd forced out of Sexton. The Ruby who'd made it clear that she hated him. The Ruby he'd had to threaten with eternal damnation to make her listen to him.

"Cut it out," he said. "Go or stay. It's your choice. But I'm not standing here one minute longer." He turned away from her and began walking.

He got a three-minute head start on her, but then she caught up with him. She was panting from exertion, and he stopped to let her catch her breath.

"It's not that much farther," he said. "Look, there's thirty-two hundred."

"I'm coming," Ruby said. "But I ain't talking."

"Fair enough," Jon said.

It took another twenty minutes before they reached the 4000s. By the time they got to the 4200s, they were in nearly deserted country. It took another ten minutes to reach the 4300s. By then the only houses were decrepit-looking trailers.

"I like White Birch better," Ruby said. "Kind of scary out here."

"You're right," Jon said. "Okay. Forty-four thirty-eight. Matt's should be one or two houses down."

"What kind of people live like this?" Ruby asked. "All alone, no neighbors?"

Jon thought about Ruby's family's apartment: six kids and three adults sharing four rooms. He understood that Matt and Syl got to live in their own home because Matt was a courier — not quite a grub, if not a claver.

"That's it," Jon said, pointing to Matt's home. "Come on, Ruby. We're here."

Ruby held back. "Maybe you should go in first," she said. "Give you folks a chance to say hello."

"You're my folks, too," Jon said, certain that if he left Ruby alone, she'd run away. "Let's go."

He could see lights in the house, so he knew someone was home. His hand shook from exhaustion and nerves as he knocked on the door.

"Who is it?" Syl yelled from inside.

It had been three years since he'd heard her voice. For a moment he was fourteen again, and Syl was the girl who'd stolen his brother from him.

He took a deep breath. "Syl, it's Jon," he said. "Let me in."

Syl opened the door. She pointed a gun at him until she realized it really was Jon. Then she put the gun down and raced into his arms.

"Jon!" she cried. "Come in. I don't believe it. How did you get here? Is everything all right?"

"Everything's fine," he said. "Syl, this is Ruby. We got married a couple of weeks ago."

"Married?" Syl asked. "Well, I guess Miranda was your age when she got married. Oh, what difference does it make? Come in. Hi, Ruby. It's a pleasure to meet you. Wait. I've got to put the gun away." She carried it out of the hallway and then escorted them to the living room. The furniture was shabby, and the house had a faint formaldehyde smell. But Jon saw one of Gabe's trucks in the corner of the sofa, and he knew he was home.

As though to prove it, Gabe walked slowly into the living room. "Syl, people are talking," he said as he rubbed the sleep out of his eyes.

"Gabe, it's me," Jon said. "And Ruby."

It took a second, but then Gabe raced over to Jon. Jon picked him up and swung him around. "Oh, Gabe," he said. "Gabe." He kissed Gabe on his head and his cheeks and swung him around again.

Gabe clawed his way down. "Who's that?" he asked, pointing at Ruby.

"You remember Ruby," Jon said. "She was your . . ." He

stopped before he said "grub." "Your friend," he said. "Remember? You played tag with her and she made your meals?"

Gabe stared at her. "She's not Ruby," he said.

"Don't be silly," Jon said. "Of course she is."

"No, Mr. Jon, actually I'm not," Ruby said. "This little one never saw me before in his life. My name is Opal Grubb. Ruby's my sister."

"Her twin," Jon said, thinking back on the conversations he and Ruby had had. "The one your father couldn't tell apart sometimes."

"I have no idea who you are or what's going on," Syl said, "but I think we'd all be better off having this conversation sitting down."

Jon held on to Gabe, who seemed more than happy to sit on his lap. Ruby — No, Opal took the chair opposite them. Syl sat with Jon.

"Where's Mommy?" Gabe asked. "Mommy said she'd come take care of me."

Jon had dreaded this moment for weeks. But he knew he had no choice. He held his little brother tightly, hoping Gabe could feel his love.

"Gabe, do you remember how Val used to be in the house every single day?" he said gently. "And then one day she wasn't there anymore? Do you remember what your mommy said when you asked her where Val was?"

Gabe nodded. "She said Val was gone. Maybe she was dead. She'd never come back."

"That's what dead means," Jon said. "It means someone will never come back. Gabe, your mommy is dead."

"No," Syl murmured. Jon nodded almost imperceptibly.

"She wanted to come, Gabe," Jon said. "Your mommy

loved you so much. But sometimes things happen that can't be helped."

"NO!" Gabe screamed. "I want my mommy!"

"Gabe, I'm sorry," Jon said, tears streaming down his cheeks. "I'm so sorry."

Syl slid over and took Gabe from Jon. "Gabe, listen to me," she said. "Do you know how long a week is?"

Gabe shook his head.

"A week is seven days," Syl told him. "Remember yesterday when we were counting? Why don't you count to seven, Gabe? Show Jon how smart you are. Use your fingers, and count to seven."

"One," Gabe said, holding up a single finger. "Two. Three. Four. Six. Seven."

"Almost," Syl said, lifting Gabe's middle finger. "Five, then six, then seven. Seven's a pretty big number, isn't it?"

Gabe nodded.

"Two weeks is fourteen days," Syl said. "See, I'm counting to seven, too." She held up seven fingers. "Your seven fingers and my seven fingers, that's how long you've been here, Gabe. Two weeks. Fourteen days." She lifted Gabe's hand to her mouth and kissed it, then let him relax his fingers.

"They've been the hardest fourteen days of your life," she said to Gabe. "And today is the worst day you've ever had, maybe the worst day you'll ever have. Your mommy is gone, Gabe, and you must feel so sad and angry and scared."

Gabe began to cry.

Syl held on to him tightly. "You should feel sad," she said. "You won't see your mommy again. And you should feel mad. Jon said that was Ruby and he was wrong. And maybe you're a little mad at Mommy for not being here. But I don't ever want you to feel scared. Matt and I love you so much, Gabe. You'll always have a home with us. Jon loves you and Miranda and Alex love you. Jon?"

"I love you, Gabe," he said. "You're my brother. I'll always love you."

Syl stood up, still holding on to Gabe. "I think you should go back to bed, sweetie," she said. "You can keep crying as long as you want, just as long as you remember how many people love you. All right?"

Gabe nodded.

Syl kissed him. "Who's the best boy in the whole wide world?"

"Me," Gabe mumbled.

"That's right," Syl said. "You're the best boy in the whole wide world, and don't you ever forget it." She carried Gabe down the hall, and Jon could hear her singing a lullaby very softly.

"You all right, Mr. Jon?" Opal asked.

Jon wiped the tears off his cheeks. "We need to talk," he said.

"Talk," she said. "I'm listening."

"Is Ruby all right?" he asked. "Where is she? Why the substitution?"

"Ruby took my place, that's all," Opal replied.

"And nobody there noticed?" Jon asked.

"All I did for those folks was scrub their floors," Opal said. "The only parts of me they ever saw was the top of my head and the top of my rear. Ruby and I tried it out the day before the cops found me. No one knew the difference."

"But you could have been sent to the mines," Jon said. "You did that for Ruby?"

"I'm the older," she said. "And a whole lot tougher. Ruby couldn't handle none of that. Guess if you really knowed her, you'd know that. Course if you really knowed her, you'd have knowed I ain't her."

"She'll be okay?" Jon asked.

Opal nodded. "They're nice folks," she said. "Never hit me once. Course I know how to clean a lot better than Ruby. But she'll learn. She'll be okay."

"I'm glad," Jon said. "I liked Ruby."

"You got something else to be glad about," Opal said. "Can't see how we's married, given you thinking you was marrying Ruby."

Jon laughed. "You're right," he said. "I guess we're not."

"Not what?" Syl asked, joining them.

"Married," Jon said. "Turns out we're not."

"How's the little one?" Opal asked.

"He's sleeping," Syl replied. "It'll hit him again tomorrow, but he's all right for now."

"You were great with him," Jon said.

"He's a great kid," Syl said. "Spoiled rotten but really very sweet. Matt and I've tried so hard to have children. We feel like Gabe's a blessing that fell into our laps." She paused. "Matt wasn't optimistic about Lisa's chances, but we never thought she'd die. What happened, Jon?"

"I'm sorry to interrupt, Miss Syl," Opal said. "But could I have some water to drink?"

"Oh, I'm sorry," Syl said. "Come into the kitchen. I'll find you something to eat."

"That's real kind of you, ma'am," Opal said.

"Call me Syl," she said. "Now sit down and let me get you something. How about some potato bread? Things are a little tight around here since I can't work anymore and we have Gabe to feed, but there's still more than enough. Here, some carrots. Jon, the glasses are over there. We have running water, thank goodness." She sniffed. "You stink," she said. "Your clothes are in your suitcase. Opal, you should fit in mine. If you don't mind cold water, you can shower before you go to bed, and I'll wash your clothes in the morning."

"Thank you, Syl," Jon said, handing Opal one of the glasses and sipping some water from the other. "Where's Matt?"

"Working," Syl said, putting the bread and vegetables on a plate, which she handed to Opal. "He left yesterday. He'll be gone for a couple of weeks."

"I'm sorry I missed him," Jon said.

"Why don't you stay?" Syl asked. "Opal can sleep in my room, and you can share Gabe's."

Jon swallowed a bite of carrot. "It's not a good idea," he said. "A couple of days ago I told some people my name and where I was from. I didn't say I was going to Coolidge, but they might figure it out. It's too dangerous for all of us if I stay."

"Start from the beginning," Syl said. "What happened to Lisa?"

"She killed herself," Jon said. "She left a note taking full responsibility for stealing Miranda's baby from the Stocktons. It probably would have worked except I came home. And Ruby ran away."

"The cops picked me up, thinking I was Ruby," Opal said. "And Mr. Jon here decided to rescue me."

"We got married," Jon said. "Well, I thought we got married."

"We said our 'I do's,'" Opal said. "But we never did no consummating."

Syl shook her head. "I liked Lisa," she said. "She was easier for me than Laura. Oh, Jon, I haven't said how sorry I am about Laura. You've really had a rough time of it. How are you doing?"

"I don't know," Jon said. "So much has happened. I don't think I really understand it yet, that she's gone."

"She was my teacher," Opal said. "She was a good woman."

"I didn't know you knew," Jon said. "I never told Ruby."

"I can figure things out faster than her," Opal replied. "Miss Syl, I swear these are the best carrots I ever had."

"Will you please stop calling me that," Syl said. "Sister-in-law or not, you're family."

"I thank you kindly," Opal said. "I think I'll take that shower now. I don't know that I ever felt this dirty before."

"Follow me," Syl said. "I'll get you some clean clothes and a towel and soap. Jon, you wait here. We still have things to talk about."

Jon looked at the carrots but refrained from eating another. He'd forgotten how beautiful Syl was, but she'd aged in the last three years, gotten even thinner. Matt earned decent money, but with Gabe in the house, Syl was probably eating less than she should.

Syl came back a few minutes later. "Keep eating," she said. "You look starved."

"I'm fine," he said.

"All right," she said, and began putting the carrots away. "It's hard for Gabe. He's used to a lot of foods we don't have. But he won't go hungry."

"Will you?" Jon asked.

"Lisa put some money in Gabe's suitcase," she replied. "She must have known what she was going to do. Your friend Sarah wanted to go into town and wave her claver ID around at the market, but Alex wouldn't let her. Sarah's a nice girl, Jon. Very smart. Matt likes her a lot."

"I like her, too," Jon said. "I took Ruby with me — well, I thought she was Ruby — because she knew Miranda was my sister. The only way I could get her away from the cops was by marrying her. Only when I did, I had to turn in my claver ID."

"Strange times," Syl said. "They make us do strange things. Do you have plans, Jon?"

"I thought we'd go to that town Matt told us about," Jon said. "The one Alex and Miranda went to. If they'll let us in."

"I think they will," Syl replied. "Matt says they don't care about people's pasts. Everyone starts out equally. At least that's the plan. They call it New Harmony. It's in Kentucky, about seventy-five miles from here."

"Seventy-five miles," Jon said. "A couple of hours by car. Do you think Miranda and Alex will be safe there?"

"As safe as anyplace," Syl said. "Matt and I will move there when he gets back. Alex took Miranda and the baby there, dropped Sarah off with her folks, and went back to New Harmony. When Matt finishes his last run, Alex will come back here and drive us. We were hoping you and Lisa would show up by then. Does Opal know about it?"

"Not yet," Jon replied. "I'll talk to her about it in the morning. Do you know how to get to New Harmony, Syl? Can you draw me a map?"

Syl burst out laughing. "Matt's a courier," she said. "The whole house is filled with maps. I'll show you the route tomorrow. You can take the map. Matt won't be using them anymore, thank goodness."

"Night, Miss Syl," Opal called. "See you in the morning."

"I'm coming in," Syl replied. "Jon and I are through here."

"Thank you," Jon said. "Thanks for everything, Syl. Thanks for loving Gabe."

"You're my brother," Syl said. "And now Gabe's my son. It's easy to love both of you."

Tuesday, August 11

Gabe was still sleeping when Jon walked into the kitchen early the next morning. He was surprised to find Syl there. "You're up early," he said.

"So are you," she said. "Opal's still asleep."

"She's exhausted," Jon replied. "The trip was hard for her. I knew where we were going and why, but she came along because no one gave her a choice."

"She has choices now," Syl replied. "Not a lot, but more than she probably had in White Birch."

"How many bikes do you have?" Jon asked. "I counted three in Gabe's room."

Syl smiled. "It was the bike room before Gabe moved in. Matt likes having spares around. He keeps an extra three in there."

"And Alex is going to drive you to New Harmony?" Jon asked.

"That's the plan," Syl said. "Matt figured New Harmony will be thrilled to have a car. And Alex can't return it to Sexton."

"It's a pretty big car," Jon said. "It should fit all of you and a lot of your things, too."

"We don't have a lot of things," Syl said. "Gabe's trucks don't take up much room. Jon, are you asking if you can take two of the bikes for you and Opal?"

He nodded. "I'd like to get there as fast as possible," he said. "The bikes would make a big difference."

"They'd make a big difference for us, also," Syl said. "If you and Opal take them, they'll be waiting for us when we get to New Harmony. It's a great idea."

"Do you have the map?" Jon asked. "I'd like to check the route out."

"Here," Syl said. "This is the route Matt showed Alex."

Jon looked at the map. "It looks pretty straightforward," he said. "Do you know if there's a lot of trucking around there? The fewer people who see us the better."

"Matt said no when Alex asked," Syl replied. "But there's always a chance. Sexton's been sending more and more food to this part of the state. I don't know what we'd do without their greenhouses."

"New Harmony isn't importing food, is it?" Jon asked.

Syl shrugged. "Probably," she replied. "This is an imperfect world, Jon. The people at New Harmony are trying a different approach, but that doesn't mean they're saintly. Don't go in with illusions. They'll just break your heart."

"I saw Mom's body riddled with bullets," Jon said. "Any illusions I had died with her."

"I'm sorry," Syl said. "I keep thinking of you the way you were in Pennsylvania. We've both grown up since then."

"I've done a lot of bad things," Jon said. "I'm glad they're not saints in New Harmony. I'd never fit in if they were."

"I know," Syl said, and rolled her eyes. "Saint Alex."

Jon laughed. "He's lost a lot of his saintliness over the years," he said. "He called clavers 'fat asses.' I heard him."

"That's a start," she said. "If we're all going to be in New Harmony, I'd better learn to love him."

"We'll be a family again," Jon said.

Syl nodded. "That's been Matt's dream for so long now," she said. "We'll make it work."

"Make what work?" Opal asked, coming into the kitchen.

"Life," Jon said. "Opal, would you like to go to New Harmony with me?"

"What's New Harmony?" she asked.

"It's a town about seventy-five miles from here," Syl replied. "No grubs, no clavers. Just people working together."

"If you don't want to, we'll figure out a way of getting you back to White Birch," Jon said.

"I can't go back," she said. "You know that, Mr. Jon. Ruby's taken my place and I've taken hers."

"Matt and I are going to move to New Harmony, Opal," Syl said. "But not for a couple of weeks. If you want, you can stay here until then, and we'll see about getting you work in Dickerson. They always need girls to do cleaning."

"So I could be a grub here," Opal said. "Same as White Birch? Or I could go to this place and take my chances?"

"We'll all be taking our chances," Jon said. "I can't go back, either, Opal. It's not even safe for me to stay here."

"You'd make a better grub than I ever thought you would," Opal said. "All that walking made a real man of you, Mr. Jon. But I guess I'll see what not being a grub'll feel like."

"You weren't always a grub," Jon said. "When you were growing up, you weren't."

"Oh, Mr. Jon," Opal said. "Back on the farm the only ones who didn't think we was grubs was the chickens. You don't need the name to be a grub."

"Then this is your chance not to be," Jon said. "We're friends, Opal. I could use some friends in my life."

"Seventy-five more miles," Opal said. "That's a whole lot of walking to get to some strange place."

"Syl's letting us borrow two bikes," Jon told her. "We can

leave after Gabe wakes up and get to New Harmony by tomorrow afternoon."

"I don't know," Opal said. "I ain't rode a bike since I was real little. What if I fall?"

"It's been a long time for me, too," Jon said. "I'll be falling, too. We'll fall together."

"That's fair enough," she said. "When do we start?"

Wednesday, August 12

"You sure this is New Harmony?" Opal asked as they rode their bikes down Main Street.

"I'm pretty sure," Jon said. "Syl said the town was originally named Westfield, and that's the exit we took."

"We took that exit miles ago," Opal said. "We passed lots of little towns, with no one in them. Maybe one of them was New Harmony."

"Look," Jon said, gesturing toward a storefront with a sign: NEW HARMONY MEETING ROOM.

"Looks empty," Opal said. "Maybe no one's around to meet us."

"It's the middle of the afternoon," Jon said. "Everyone's working. Relax, Opal. We'll find out where Miranda and Alex are, and everything will fall into place."

"Don't say that word 'fall,'" Opal said. "It's no comfort to me that you fell, too."

Jon grinned. He'd picked up a couple of bruises. But he and Opal had gotten the hang of it and made great time.

"Let's say this is New Harmony," Opal said. "How are we gonna find that sister of yours? You don't even know their address.

And my recollection is people don't warm up to you much when you go asking."

"You want to do the asking?" Jon asked.

"They ain't my family," Opal said. "You do the finding this time."

"All right," Jon said. "I'll ask in there."

"It says 'Health Clinic,'" Opal said. "What makes you think they're sick?"

"I don't," Jon replied. "But I bet Miranda took the baby in first thing. You stay outside with the bikes. I'll go in and see what I can find."

"You'll find trouble," Opal said, but Jon ignored her. She was scared, and that was how she acted when fear got the best of her. Not that he blamed her. It was one thing to find New Harmony. It was another to know what to do there.

He was relieved the door was unlocked. "Hello?" he called. "Anyone here."

"Just a second," a girl called out.

It was Sarah. Jon knew that voice as well as he knew any. Sarah's voice.

He told himself not to be an idiot. Sarah was in Virginia. That was where he wanted her to be, safe with her powerful uncle. Protected.

But it was Sarah's voice. And in a matter of seconds it was Sarah Jon was holding. Sarah, lost to him and now found. Sarah, whose tears and laughter he was now sharing.

"Oh, Jon," she said. "I was so afraid for you. I thought I'd never see you again."

"What are you doing here?" he asked. "Why aren't you in Virginia?"

"We never got there," Sarah replied. "We had to wait until Matt got home, and that took almost a week. Alex drove us to New Harmony, and when I got here, I found a phone and called Daddy. He said you'd disappeared, and Lisa . . . Oh, Jon, I'm so sorry about Lisa."

Jon nodded. "What else did he say?" he asked.

"To stay where I was," she said. "It was the safest place for me to be. He'll come here when he can get a replacement for the clinic. Did you see Gabe? Is he all right?"

"I told him about Lisa," Jon replied. "But he doesn't understand yet. He asked me before we left when Lisa would come. But Syl's great with him, and when they get here, Gabe will have all his family with him."

"He'll love it here," Sarah said. "I do. The only thing that was missing was you."

"I'm here now," he said, and kissed her to prove it. "Miranda and Alex are all right?"

"They're fine," Sarah said. "I've been staying with them. Now you will be, too. Oh, Jon. I don't think I've ever been so happy."

Jon didn't want their next kiss to end. But as it did, he remembered Opal, standing outside, guarding the bikes, waiting for him.

"Come with me," he said to Sarah. "There's someone I want you to meet." He held her hand as they walked out the door.

"Ruby?" Sarah said, breaking away from Jon. "You brought Ruby here?"

"This is Opal," Jon said. "Ruby's twin. Opal, I want you to meet Sarah Goldman. Sarah, this is my friend Opal Grubb. That's G-R-U-B-B."

"That your Sarah?" Opal asked. "The one you're always pining for?"

"The same," Jon said. "She's living here now."

"Well, ain't that something," Opal said. "It's a pleasure to meet you . . . Sarah. Jon talked my ear off about you from Sexton right here."

Sarah extended her hand to shake Opal's. For a moment Opal didn't know what to do, but then she reached out and shook Sarah's hand.

"I want you to know nothing happened between Jon and me," Opal said. "I told him he'd better not try anything funny with me, and he was a perfect gentleman."

"I think he's perfect, too," Sarah said. "And I'm glad he has such a good friend."

"Opal, would you like to freshen up?" Jon asked. "Sarah, does the clinic have a bathroom?"

Sarah smiled. "With running water," she said. "There's a small kitchen, too, Opal, if you'd like to have a drink of water or some food."

"Wouldn't mind neither," Opal said. "And I can see the two of you wouldn't mind if I left you alone."

"We'll be in in a minute," Jon said.

"Two minutes," Sarah said.

"Take your time," Opal said. "You'll know where to find me."

Sarah waited until Opal had closed the clinic door behind her. "What happened?" she asked. "How did the two of you end up together?"

"She's my friend," Jon replied. "Nothing more. I tricked her into coming with me, and she tricked me into thinking she was Ruby."

"Trickery and deceit," Sarah said. "That's quite a basis for friendship."

Jon laughed. "I love you," he said. "And I can't believe you're here. Could we put off fighting until tomorrow?"

Sarah's kiss was all the answer he needed.

Nothing was going to come easy. Jon knew that. Nothing had for four years.

But the sun was visible behind the ash clouds, and with its light, Jon could see a future worth fighting for.

We'll make it work, he told himself. Together, we can make it work.

Author's Discussion Topics

How would things have been different for Jon if Dad had survived the trip to Sexton?

Would Jon have felt differently about the enclave rules if he hadn't met Sarah?

In each of the books with Mom featured, she finds a reason to throw a party. Why do you think socializing was so important to her, even in such dire situations?

Jon and Miranda both carry a great deal of guilt over Julie's death. Miranda talks only to Alex about it, while Jon has told no one. How would things have been different if Jon and Miranda had shared their particular truths immediately following Julie's death?

The "clavers," people who live in the Sexton enclave, feel a strong sense of entitlement because the work they do is regarded as essential for human survival. On the other hand, Ruby says she was a "grub," in effect a manual laborer, long before the cataclysmic events that led to the enclaves being established. Jon, as a "slip," falls somewhere between the two. Do these sorts of class distinctions exist today, in the real world, in your world? Do you think it's possible today for grubs to become clavers, or would they, at best, feel like slips?

Author's Note

Sometimes a writer sees a story as a whole, planning on taking a character from Point A to Point Z, in one volume, or two, or three or more.

Sometimes things just happen.

All four of my "moon" books just happened. It's lucky for me that they did, but there's no way I can claim I knew from the very first moment just how things would evolve.

That very first moment was a Saturday afternoon when I had nothing better to do than watch TV. I found an old sci-fi movie called *Meteor,* and I watched it all the way through, even though I'd seen it before and had a reasonably good idea who would live and who would die by movie's end.

Eventually the movie did end, and I turned off the TV. That was when I had the idea that literally changed my life. I said to myself, "What would it be like to be a teenager living through a worldwide catastrophe?"

My mind began racing. By evening's end I knew who the teenager was (a girl named Miranda, living in a small town in Pennsylvania with her mother, her big brother, Matt, and her little brother, Jonny) and what the catastrophe would be (knocking the moon closer to earth, thus strengthening its gravitational pull).

I spent three weeks doing the prewriting. Then I sat down at the computer and began what was the happiest writing experience of my life, creating the book that became *Life As We Knew It.*

I had decided that first evening that the book would be Miranda's diary, since I wanted to get the readers as close to the action as possible. And writing a fictional character's diary is a lot of fun. The story just spills out; it's almost like taking dictation.

I worked all day long, stopping only when I became so tired I knew it would be a mistake to keep writing. Thanks to the prewriting, I knew where the story was going, but I hadn't solved every single problem, so there was enough uncertainty that I could change things around and surprise myself on occasion.

It was more fun than work should ever be.

It was my job to write the book and my agent's job to sell it. She found it a wonderful home with Harcourt (now Houghton Mifflin Harcourt). Kathy Dawson was the first of two excellent editors I've worked with there. She helped me tighten the book, and guided it through the publication process.

There was only one problem. I wanted to write a sequel. Even while I was writing *Life As We Knew It,* I wanted to know what happened next. But Kathy said Harcourt had no interest in a sequel.

There are moments in my life when I'm really smart, and this was one of them. Instead of taking no for an answer, I said, "How about if I write a book about the exact same situation only with a completely different set of characters?"

"Fine," Kathy said. "Because that's not a sequel."

What I didn't tell Kathy was my intention to write that second book and then a third one, where Miranda from *Life As We Knew It* would meet the characters from what became *The Dead & The Gone*. Because I knew someday the people at Harcourt would come to their senses and say, "Of course we want a sequel, only now we want one for both books."

The Dead & The Gone was more challenging to write.

Miranda isn't exactly like me (for one thing she swims, a skill I've never quite developed), but Alex is nothing at all like me. I loved him and his sisters and his friends, and I loved ending the world all over again, but it wasn't the joyous experience *Life As We Knew It* had been. On the other hand, I took more pride in it, because it was that much harder to write, so it all balanced out.

The Dead & The Gone was published and I began hectoring Kathy about writing a third book. Mostly she said no, but sometimes she said maybe. I wrote a third book on my own that had very little to do with the first two, but I realized before showing it to her that it was a mistake. So I kept asking and waiting, and eventually Kathy said yes, and we had a long phone conversation where we decided on a plot that had absolutely nothing to do with Miranda and Alex.

Only then she called me back and said, "What we really want is a sequel."

So I finally got to introduce Alex to Miranda. I wrote *This World We Live In,* bringing together the characters from the first two books. It was back to Miranda's diary, and I got the answers to some of the questions I'd been asked by readers. And when Kathy left Harcourt and I began working with Karen Grove, I found my book in the hands of another excellent editor.

I was a happy writer. I'd written a trilogy, a very high-class thing to do. Life was good.

But people kept writing to ask me if there was going to be a fourth book. And then I took my cat in for his annual checkup, and my vet asked if there was going to be a fourth book.

So I contacted Karen and said, "My vet wants to know if there's going to be a fourth book. What should I tell him?"

And Karen said, "Do it."

So I did. I wrote an entire fourth book and sent it off to Karen. She read it. Everyone at Houghton Mifflin Harcourt read it. And although they never actually said so, they hated it.

That should have stopped me. But I loved my characters and I loved the world I'd created and I wanted to make my vet happy. I tried again, and ended up writing the book you're holding in some format or another at this very moment, *The Shade of the Moon.*

My vet has since retired, so he probably won't be asking me if there's going to be a fifth book. And since I'm writing this before *The Shade of the Moon* is published, I don't know if anyone is going to ask me that. Frankly, I don't even know what I'd want the answer to be, should I ever be asked.

But I do know that watching an old movie on a Saturday afternoon changed my life in a thousand different wonderful ways.

life as we knew it

When Miranda first hears the warnings that a meteor is headed on a collision path with the moon, they just sound like an excuse for extra homework assignments. But her disbelief turns to fear in a split second as the entire world witnesses a lunar impact that catastrophically alters the earth's climate—and results in mass devastation.

Told in Miranda's diary entries, this is a heart-pounding account of her struggle to hold on to the most important resource of all—hope—in an increasingly desperate and unfamiliar time.

★ "Each page is filled with events both wearying and terrifying and infused with honest emotions." —*Booklist*, starred review

the dead & the gone

Alex Morales was working behind the counter at Joey's Pizza when life as he knew it changed forever. He was worried about getting elected as senior class president and making the grades to land him in a good college. He never expected an asteroid would hit the moon. He never expected to be fighting just to stay alive.

★ "The powerful images and wrenching tragedies will haunt readers." —*Publishers Weekly*, starred review

this world we live in

It's been a year since a meteor collided with the moon. For Miranda Evans, life as she knew it no longer exists. Her friends and neighbors are dead, the landscape is frozen, and food is increasingly scarce.

The struggle to survive intensifies when Miranda's father and stepmother arrive with a baby and three strangers in tow. One of the newcomers is Alex Morales, and as Miranda's complicated feelings for him turn to love, his plans for the future thwart their relationship. Then a devastating tornado hits the town of Howell, and Miranda makes a decision that will change their lives forever.

★ "Readers will be moved by displays of compassion, strength, and faith as characters endure grim realities and face an uncertain future." —*Publishers Weekly,* starred review

8/16/13

DATE DUE

SEP 05 2014			

GAYLORD   PRINTED IN U.S.A.